The Anger of God

Paul Doherty was born in Middlesbrough in 1946. He was admitted to Liverpool University where he gained a First Class Honours Degree in History and won a state scholarship to Exeter College, Oxford. While there he met his wife, Carla.

Paul worked in Ascot, Newark and Crawley, before being appointed as Headmaster to Trinity Catholic High School, Essex, in 1981. The school has been described as one of the leading comprehensives in the U.K. and has been awarded 'Outstanding' in four consecutive OFSTED inspections. All seven of Paul and Carla's children have been educated at Trinity.

Paul has written over 100 books and has published a series of outstanding historical mysteries set in the Middle Ages, Classical Greece, Ancient Egypt and elsewhere. His books have been translated into more than twenty languages.

D1081513

Also by Paul Doherty

The Brother Athelstan Mysteries

PAUL DOHERTY

The Anger of God

CANELO

First published in Great Britain in 1993 by Headline Book Publishing, a
division of Hodder Headline PLC

This edition published in the United Kingdom in 2021 by

Canelo
31 Helen Road
Oxford OX2 0DF
United Kingdom

A CIP catalogue record for this book is available from the British Library.

Print ISBN 978 1 80032 568 5
Ebook ISBN 978 1 78863 891 3

First published in 1993 under the pseudonym of Paul Harding.

Look for more great books at www.canelo.co

Printed and bound in Great Britain by Clays Ltd, Elcograf S.p.A.

To my daughter Alexandra

Prologue

The man waiting in the corner of the derelict cemetery between Poor Jewry and Sybethe Lane jumped as an owl in the old yew tree above him hooted and spread ghostly wings to go soaring like a dark angel over the tumbled grass and briars. The watcher saw the bird plunge on its shrieking victim then rise effortlessly as a puff of smoke up against the starlit sky. The man shivered and cursed. He remembered stories from his childhood of the Shape-Shifters, those witches, crones of the darkness, who could change their appearance and haunt such deserted, lonely places. The night was warm, yet the man felt cold. These were troubled times. During the day he laughed at the gossip, the stories about an anchor and rope which hung down from a cloud and lay fixed in an earthen mound near Tilbury. Or how the king of the pygmies, large-headed and fiery-faced, had been seen riding a goat through the forests north of the city. Whilst devils, small as dormice, laughed and leapt like fish in a net in the grass around the gallows at Tyburn. Such stories merely mirrored the times and echoed the words of the prophet: 'Woe to the kingdom where the king is a child!'

A prophecy now coming to fruition in England: golden Richard was only a youth and the affairs of state rested in the grasping hands of his uncle, the Regent, John of Gaunt, Duke of Lancaster, who seemed unable to pour balm on the kingdom's wounds. French galleys were raiding and sacking towns along the Channel coast. In the north, the Scots spilled over the border in an orgy of burning and looting, whilst in the shires round London, the peasants, taxed to the hilt and tied to the soil, bitterly protested against the lords of the earth and plotted bloody rebellion.

Gaunt, however, was as slippery as a fish: unable to raise taxes from a rebellious Commons, he had now performed the miracle of uniting the warring Guilds of London to obtain money from the wealthy burgesses and merchants. This had to be stopped. The watcher in the shadows just wished there was an easier way to do it. He bit his lip. Gaunt had to be destroyed; it was necessary. When the revolt came, a new order would be established in the kingdom and the Great Community, the name the peasant leaders had given themselves, would decide who would live and who would die, who would wield power and who would exercise trade. The prudent ones in the government of the city were already preparing to make such men their friends.

'I am here.'

The man jumped. Was he hearing things?

'I am here,' the voice repeated, low and throaty.

'Where are you?'

'We are all around you. Don't move. Don't run. Just listen to what I have to say.'

'What is your name?' the man asked, trying to control the quick beating of his heart and the panic curdling his innards.

'I am Ira Dei,' the voice replied from the darkness of the cemetery. 'I am the Anger of God. And God's wrath will spill out against those who reap where they have not sown, who gather profits where they have no right, and who oppress the poor men of the soil as if they were worms and no more.'

'What do you want?'

'To make all things new. To take this kingdom into an age of innocence for: "When Adam delved and Eve span, Who was then the gentleman?"'

The man nodded. He had heard this doggerel verse chanted like a constant hymn by the peasants who wished to march on London, reduce the city to red-hot ash, seize the King's uncle, strike off his head and march in procession with that same head on a pike.

'Are you for us?' the voice asked.

'Of course!' the man spluttered.

'And do the Regent's plans move apace?'

'The banquet is tomorrow night.'

'Then you must act. Do what we want and we shall consider you our friend.'

'I have a scheme,' the man replied. 'Listen…'

'Silence!' the voice rasped. 'If you wish to be one of us, then thwart Gaunt's ambitions. How you do it need not concern us, but we shall watch. Adieu.'

The man strained his eyes against the darkness. He heard a twig snap, an owl hoot but, when he called out, his words rang hollow in the silence.

A mile to the south, on the black, stinking waters of the Thames, another hooded, cowled figure moved his small skiff between the starlings of London Bridge. He tied the rope carefully through a rusting ring and began to climb up the wooden beams, on to the blood-soaked trellis towards the decapitated heads gazing sightlessly from their poles across the river. The man cursed then grinned.

'What a night to choose,' he whispered to himself. The river stank like a privy because the dung barges, full of dirt and human refuse, had been busy all eventide unloading their mounds of muck into the water; the stink would last for days. Nevertheless, the thief had to move quickly: the French pirate had been executed the previous afternoon and his head would still be fresh, the skin clean and the eyes not yet pecked out by crows. Nonetheless, he had to be careful: rumours were already rife of how the civic authorities, particularly that fat giant Sir John Cranston, King's Coroner of the city, were becoming suspicious about the number of amputated limbs and severed heads being moved from London Bridge.

The thief, garbed all in black, with heavy boots to give him a firmer grip on the slippery rails, reached the balcony just under the blood-soaked poles. He crouched in the darkness, straining his ears to distinguish the differing sounds: a barge full of revellers, drunk as lords, making their way from the stews in Southwark back to Botolph's Wharf; the slop and murmur of the river, faint cries from its banks; the noise of ships being prepared for the morning tide; and, above all, the heavy footfalls of sentries as they walked backwards and forwards near the entrance to the bridge.

The thief waited for a while, breathing carefully, and at last, it seemed, the sentries grew tired and went back to warm themselves over their small brazier. He eased himself on to the top of the bridge and padded soft as a cat to where the long poles jutted out against the sky, each bearing its grisly burden. He stared up into the darkness. He had to be careful. So many executions, so many severed heads. He did not want to choose the wrong one. He had been there the previous evening when the head had been displayed but it could have been moved since. Then he saw the small pool of blood at the end of one pole. He smiled, carefully eased it out of its socket, plucked the severed head from the end, put it into his bag and climbed back over the rails down to his waiting skiff.

On the Southwark side of the Thames, in its maze of dingy, squalid streets, the taverns still blazed with light as the thief-masters and their gangs of rogues went about their nefarious business: the foists, naps, pickpockets and thugs all intent on seeing what profit the night would bring. Others, too, worked: the cat-hunters looking for cheap pelts and meat they could sell; the collectors of dog turds who would sell their smelly bags of refuse for the tanners to use; and the casual labourers, moving from ale-house to ale-house, seeking employment before the day even began. The streets hummed with noise but in a great, half-timbered, three-storeyed house which had definitely seen better days… all was darkness and silence.

The householder and his wife stood in petrified silence at the door to his daughter's room. They could see her by the light of a single candle, sitting up against the bolsters, the curtains of the bed pulled well back. As they waited for the terror to begin, the man looked beseechingly at the girl.

'Elizabeth, will it come again?' he pleaded.

His white-faced daughter just stared back, her eyes glassy and unseeing.

'Oh, Elizabeth,' the man breathed. 'Why are you doing this to us?'

'You know why!' the girl suddenly shrieked, leaning forward. 'You killed my mother to marry that bitch!' Her hand was flung out, finger pointing at her father's golden-haired, pretty-faced second wife.

'That is not true,' he replied. 'Elizabeth, your mother sickened and died. There was nothing I could do.'

'Lies!' the girl shrieked.

The man and his wife stared in horrified silence at this young girl who, when darkness fell, became another person. A veritable virago, a hag of the night, who claimed that the ghost of her own mother visited her to denounce both of them as murderers, assassins, poisoners.

'Listen!' she hissed. 'Mother comes again!'

The man let his arm fall from his wife's shoulders as a shiver ran up his spine, the hairs on the nape of his neck curling in terror. Sure enough, throughout the house the tapping and knocking began. First downstairs, then further up as if something was crawling between the wall and the wainscoting, slowly, cautiously, like a creature spat out by Hell, making its loathsome way towards this bed chamber. The knocking grew louder and began to fill the entire room. The man clapped his hands to his ears.

'Stop!' he yelled. He plucked the crucifix from his belt and held it towards his white-faced daughter. 'In the name of Jesus Christ, I command you to stop!'

But the knocking continued – a rattling clatter which threatened to beat him out of his wits.

'I can take no more,' the woman beside him hissed. 'Walter, I can take no more.'

And she ran down the stairs, leaving her husband trans-fixed in terror. Suddenly, the knocking ceased. The girl leaned forward, the skin of her face not only white but so taut it gave her a skull-like appearance, heightened by the raven-black hair tied tightly in a knot behind her head. The man took a step forward and looked into his daughter's face, so pale, so chilling: her eyes were lifeless, two spots of black obsidian, glaring hatefully towards him, the red, soft lips curled in a bitter sneer.

He was about to take another step forward when the rattling began again, a quick juddering noise, then fell silent. The man caught that dreadful, well-remembered stench. His courage draining from him, he fell to his knees, staring pitifully at his daughter.

'Elizabeth!' he pleaded. 'In the name of God!'

'In the name of God, Walter Hobden, you are a murderer!'

The man lifted his head. His white-faced daughter was staring at him, lips moving, but the voice was that of his dead wife. Her precise intonation, the way she would emphasize the 'R' in his first name.

'Walter Hobden, a curse on you for the wine you gave me and the red arsenic it contained – a deadly potion which rotted my stomach and cut short my life to leave you free to indulge your filthy lusts and hidden desires. I was your wife. I *am* your wife. And I come from Purgatory to warn you! I shall haunt you for as long as your soul is stained with my blood. Believe me, I have seen the place

8

in Hell prepared for you. You must confess! I must have justice, and only then will you receive absolution!'

Walter Hobden crouched, shivering in terror.

'No! No! No!' he murmured. 'This is not true! This is a lie!'

'No lie!' the voice shrieked.

Hobden could take no more. He turned and crawled like a beaten dog from the room, running down the wooden stairs as his daughter shivered, closed her eyes and fell back against the bolsters.

Hobden closed his own chamber door behind him, leaning against it, sucking in air as he stared, wild-eyed, at the fear-filled face of his second wife. She thrust a cup of claret towards him.

'Husband, drink.'

He staggered across, snatched the cup from her hand and gulped the rich, cloying wine.

'What shall I do?' he asked hoarsely. 'Why does Elizabeth do this to me?'

He came and sat beside her on the edge of the bed. She grasped his hand as he gulped the wine; his fingers felt like slivers of ice.

'Eleanor?' He stared over the wine cup. 'What can be done? Is she possessed? Has some demon taken over her soul?'

Eleanor's sharp eyes flickered in contempt. 'She's a liar and a mummer!' she jibed. 'She has taken to her bed with the vapours.' She wiped the sweat from her husband's brow. 'Walter, she is tricking you, playing some evil game.'

'How can she be?' he replied. 'You hear the knocking. I watch her hands. They are above the blankets. How could she arrange that, eh? Or the terrible smell or that voice? I have searched her room when she has been asleep and I can find nothing.'

'In which case,' Eleanor replied sharply, 'she is possessed and should be removed, together with that aged beldame her nurse, to some other place. A hospital, a house for madcaps. Or...'

'Or what?' he asked hopefully.

'If this is true, if her mother's ghost returns, then it must be a demon in disguise to spit out such lies. And both she and the room must be exorcized and blessed.'

'But who can do that?'

Eleanor prised the wine cup from his fingers. 'Priests are two a penny.' She put her arms round his neck and kissed him gently on his cheek. 'Forget these ghosts. Your daughter is a trickster,' she whispered. 'And I'll show her up for the liar she is!'

Chapter 1

Sir John Cranston sat in the window seat of a bed chamber in a house in Milk Street just off West Cheap. He stared through the mullioned glass window which gave a good view of the church of St Mary Magdalen, watching a prosperous-looking relic-seller lay out his stall and shout for custom. Cranston smiled mirthlessly as the fellow crowed, his words carrying faintly from the street below.

'Look, I have Jesus's tooth which he lost at the age of twelve! A finger of St Sylvester! A piece of the saddle on which Christ sat when he entered Jerusalem. And in this casket, specially embossed, the arm of St Polycarp – the only thing left after the lions tore him to pieces in the arena at Rome! Gentle folk, all these relics, blessed by the Holy Father, can and will perform miracles!'

Cranston watched the crowd of easily gulled spectators cluster around. A rogue, he thought. He looked across at the corpse laid out on the four-poster bed, the winding sheet, carefully wrapped round it, exposing only the face which now lay back, jaw gaping, eyes half-open.

'I am sorry, Oliver,' Cranston muttered to the silent room. He got up, crossed to the four-poster bed and stared down at the grey, sunken face of his former comrade.

'I am sorry,' he repeated. 'I, Sir John Cranston, King's Coroner in London, a man who sups with princes, the husband of Lady Maude of Tweng in Somerset, father of the two poppets, my beloved sons Francis and Stephen – I am sorry I could not help you. You, my comrade-in-arms, my right hand in our battles against the French. Now you lie murdered and I can't even prove it.'

Cranston gazed round the bed chamber, noting the rich possessions: the silver cups, the finely carved lavarium, cupboards and chairs quilted with taffeta, the silken cushions, testers, the gold filigree candelabra.

'What does it profit a man,' Cranston muttered, 'if he gains the whole world – only to be murdered by his wife?'

He fished in his wallet, brought out two pennies, fixed them on the dead man's eyes then covered the face with the sheet. He sighed, walked to the foot of the bed, and jumped at a sudden scurrying sound behind him.

'Bloody rats!' he muttered as he glimpsed the sleek, long-tailed, fat rodent slide under a cupboard and scrabble at the wooden panelling. Another darted from beneath the lavarium and easily dodged the candlestick an infuriated Cranston flung in its direction.

'Bloody rats!' he repeated. 'The city's infested with them. The heat's brought them out.'

He stared at the lonely, sheeted corpse of his friend. He had arrived to find Sir Oliver Ingham not only dead for hours, but with two rats gnawing at his hand. Cranston had roared abuse at Ingham's pretty young wife, but she had smiled slyly and said she had done her best to protect her husband's body since it had been found by a servant earlier in the day.

'He had a weak heart, Sir John,' she lisped, one soft, white hand on the arm of her 'good kinsman' Albric Totnes.

'Some kinsman!' Cranston muttered to himself. 'I bet the two were dancing between the sheets even as Oliver died. Bloody murderers!'

He dug into his wallet and fished out a short letter Oliver Ingham had sent him only the previous day. Cranston sat down and read it again as his large, protuberant eyes filled with tears.

> *I am dying, old friend. I committed the worst folly of an old man: I married someone two score years younger than me. A veritable May and December marriage, but I thought she would love me. I found she did not. Yet her smile and touch were enough. Now I find she has betrayed me and could possibly plot my death. If I die suddenly, old friend, if I die alone, then it will be murder. My soul will cry to*

God for vengeance and to you for justice. Do not forget me.

Oliver

Cranston neatly folded the piece of parchment and put it away. He had shown it to no one yet he believed his friend was right. Something in Cranston's blood whispered 'Murder', but how could he prove it? Sir Oliver had been found dead in his bed at mid-morning by a servant and Cranston, as both his friend and Coroner, had been sent for. He had arrived to find Ingham's young wife, Rosamund, supping with her 'kinsman' in the solar below, whilst the family physician, a balding, ferret-faced man in smelly robes, had simply declared that Sir Oliver's weak heart had given out and his soul was gone to God.

Cranston got up and walked to the side of the bed where the jug, knocked from its table by Oliver in his final apoplexy, still lay. At his insistence the doctor had sniffed the jug and then the cup, Oliver's favourite, and solemnly pronounced:

'No, Sir John, nothing in it except claret and perhaps a little of the foxglove I prescribed to keep Sir Oliver's heart strong.'

'Could more have been put in?' Cranston asked.

'Of course not!' the physician snapped. 'What are you implying, Sir John? A strong infusion of foxglove would leave the cup and jug reeking.'

Sir John had demurred and sent for Theobald de Troyes, his own physician, a man skilled in his art and patronized by many of the court. Theobald had given corpse, cup and jug a most thorough scrutiny.

'The physician was correct,' he announced. 'You see, Sir John, if Sir Oliver was given too much foxglove, his corpse would bear some trace. I can find nothing except the effects of a sudden seizure, whilst the cup only carries traces of claret and a little foxglove, but no more than a good doctor would prescribe. The jug smells only of foxglove.'

'Any mark of violence?' Cranston asked.

'None whatsoever, Sir John.' Theobald lowered his eyes. 'Except the rat bites on the fingers of the right hand. Sir John,' the physician had pleaded, 'Sir Oliver retired to bed last night, feeling ill. His servants heard him declare he felt weak and dizzy with pains in his chest. He locked his chamber door and left the key in the lock. The windows were similarly padlocked. No one could enter to do him mischief.'

Sir John had grunted, bade him farewell and sat in this chamber for the last two hours, wondering how murder could have been committed.

'I wish Athelstan was here,' he moaned to himself. 'Perhaps he would see something wrong. Bloody monk! And I wish he would bring that sodding cat with him!'

Cranston thought of Athelstan's fierce-looking tom cat, Bonaventure, whom his secretary and friend proclaimed was the best rat-catcher in Southwark. Cranston sighed, crossed himself, lowered his eyes and said the prayer for the dead.

'Grant eternal rest to Oliver, my friend,' he muttered as his mind drifted back down the passage of the years: Oliver, tall and strong, standing at his shoulder as the French knights broke through the English ranks at Poitiers. The roar of battle, the neighing of war steeds, the clash of swords, the silent purr of the arrow, the stabbing and hacking as they and a few others bore the brunt of the last desperate French attack. The ground underfoot had become slippery with blood. Cranston had stood, legs apart, whirling his sword like a great scythe against the French knights as they closed in for the kill.

A monstrous giant had rushed against him, his helmet in the shape of a devil's head with wide, sweeping horns, its yellow plume tossing in the evening breeze. Cranston, glimpsing steel-encased arms swinging back a huge battle axe, had moved to one side, slipped and gone down in the mud. He had expected to receive his death blow, but Oliver had stepped over him, taken the brunt of the blow with his own shield and, closing with the enemy, shoved his small misericorde dagger between cuirass and helm.

'I owe you my life,' Cranston confessed afterwards.

'One day you can repay the debt!' Oliver laughed as they both sat on the battlefield toasting each other in cup after cup of the claret they'd filched from the French camp. 'One day you *will* repay the debt.'

Cranston opened tear-filled eyes. He raised his right hand and stared at the corpse. 'By the sod, I will!' he muttered. He looked once more at the pathetic corpse under its winding sheet.

'In our golden days,' he whispered, 'we were grey-hounds racing for the hunt! Young hawks swooping for the kill! Ah, the days!'

Cranston tapped his broad girth, pulled the bed curtains close and stamped out of the chamber, pausing only to glance once more at the damaged lock.

He tramped like a Colossus down the stairs and marched into the solar where Lady Rosamund and 'kinsman' Albric were playing cat's-cradle in the window seat. Rosamund looked all the more beautiful in a gown of black damask and a carefully arranged veil of the same colour, her narrow face twisted into an approximation of grief. Cranston just glared at her, and even more contemptuously at her smooth-faced, sack-lipped, weak-eyed young lover.

'You are finished, Sir John?' Rosamund rose as the balding, red-faced giant marched towards her. She at least expected him to kiss her hand but Cranston seized her and Albric by the wrist and pulled both to their feet, squeezing hard as he pulled them close.

'You, madam, are a murdering bitch! No, don't widen your eyes and scream for help! And you, sir—' Albric's eyes fell away. 'Look at me, man!' Cranston squeezed harder. 'Look at me, you whoreson bastard!'

Albric's eyes came up.

'You are party to this. If you had the courage, I would challenge you to a duel and take the head from your shoulders. Don't forget, the offer's always there!'

'Sir John, this is…'

'Shut up!' Cranston growled. 'Upstairs lies the truest comrade a man could ask for. A good soldier, a shrewd merchant and the best of friends. Oliver's heart may have become weak but he had the courage of a lion and the generosity of a saint. He adored you, you whey-faced mare, and you broke his heart! You betrayed him. I know you killed him. God knows how but I will discover it!' Cranston shoved them both back into the window seat. 'Believe me, I'll see you both dance at Smithfield on the end of a rope!'

He spun on his heel and walked to the door.

'Cranston!' Rosamund yelled.

'Yes, bitch!' he replied over his shoulder.

'I am innocent of my husband's death.'

The Coroner made a rude sound with his lips.

'In ten days' time my husband's will shall be read out. All his property and his wealth will be mine. I shall use that wealth to prosecute you in the courts for slander and contumacious speech.'

'In ten days' time,' he retorted, 'I'll see you in Newgate! You may remove the corpse but nothing else. I have an inventory of what's there!'

Cranston walked into the passageway, trying to curb his anger at the derisive laughter behind him. Ingham's old retainer Robert stood near the front door, white-faced.

'Sir John,' he whispered. 'How can you prove what you say?'

Cranston stopped, one hand on the latch, and stared at the servant's lined, tired face.

'I can and I will,' he growled. 'But tell me once more what happened yesterday.'

'My master had been ill for days: fatigued, complaining of a lightness in his head and pains in his chest. He left supper last night with his wine cup. I saw him go to the buttery and fill the jug with a small infusion of foxglove to mix later with his wine as the physician had prescribed. Then he went to bed. He locked his chamber door and, because I was concerned, I stood guard.' The man's voice quavered. 'I thought I would let him rest but when the bells of St Mary Magdalen began to chime for mid-morning prayer, I tried to rouse him. I summoned the servants, we forced the door. The rest you know.'

'Couldn't someone have saved him from the rats?' Cranston retorted.

'Sir John, the house is infested with them. The Lady Rosamund hates cats or any animals.'

Sir John patted him on the shoulder. 'Your master will have justice. I will see to that. Now, pray for his soul and take care of his corpse. One of my bailiffs is coming to seal the room.'

Sir John walked out into Milk Street. He entered the church of St Mary Magdalen and lit five candles before the smiling figure of the Virgin and Child.

'One for Maude, two for the poppets,' he whispered, thinking of his fine, sturdy sons, now six months old. 'One for Athelstan,' he murmured, 'and one for Sir Oliver, God rest him.'

Sir John knelt, closed his eyes, and recited three Aves before realizing how thirsty he was.

He lumbered out of the church, down Milk Street and into a deserted Cheapside. The stall owners had now packed up for the day, removing their possessions back to the front rooms of their shops, taking down their booths and leaving the broad thoroughfare to the bone and rag collectors, a lazy-eyed whore looking for custom, snapping mongrels and sleek, fat alley cats who couldn't believe their luck at the myriad of rats which now plundered the mounds of rubbish and human refuse. A few tinkers and pedlars still touted for business; these shouted friendly abuse at Sir John, who gave as good as he got as he passed, swift as an arrow, into his favourite tavern, The Holy Lamb of God.

Sir John brightened at the cloying, sweet warmth of the taproom. A beadle was sitting in Cranston's favourite, high-backed chair before the open window which looked out on to a pleasant garden. Sir John coughed and the fellow scuttled away like a frightened rabbit. Sir John sat down, tapping the table and staring appreciatively at the dark polished timbers and white plaster of this most revered of drinking places. He smacked his lips and pushed further open the diamond-shaped, latticed window so he could catch the fragrance of the herb banks. Some people avoided The Holy Lamb. They claimed it was built over an old charnel house and was reputedly haunted by ghosts and sprites but Cranston saw it as a second home, being revered almost as a saint by the landlord's wife.

Years earlier she had been conned by a trickster who claimed he could draw both wine and sack from the same barrel. She had stupidly agreed to see him try. The man had bored a hole in one side of the barrel and told her to stop it with her finger, whilst he bored another hole from which he said the sack could come. The hapless lady had been left, forced to plug both holes in the barrel, whilst the rogue helped himself to certain monies. She had stood there, terrified, for if she had taken her fingers away, she would have wasted an entire barrel of beer, turned the taproom ankle-deep in ale and proclaimed herself a laughingstock.

Luckily, Sir John had appeared. He had rapped the rogue across the head, helped plug the barrel and, when the rogue had regained his senses, Cranston had made him stand outside the tavern with his breeches down and a placard round his neck proclaiming him to be a fraudulent trickster.

The same taverner's wife now came bustling towards him, a large cup of claret in one hand and a bowl of onion soup in the other. Sir John absent-mindedly smiled his thanks, sipped the claret and wondered how he could bring another trickster, the murderous Rosamund, to justice. He couldn't stop thinking of Oliver's lonely corpse in that desolate chamber, the sniggering wife and her sycophantic 'kinsman' below.

Cranston heard voices and raised his head as the relic-seller, whom he had seen in Milk Street, came sliding into the tavern.

'A rogue steeped in sin,' he muttered to himself.

The relic-seller was old, walking with a slight limp, but with a shrewd, cold, narrow face, gimlet-eyed, and a mouth as thin and tight as a vice. He was well-dressed in a costly velvet tunic and soft red leather boots, and the purse which swung from the embroidered belt chinked heavily with coins. He grinned and waved across to the Coroner, who just glared back and lowered his face over his cup. He really should go home and prepare for the evening, but his house was empty as the Lady Maude had taken the two poppets to see her kinspeople in the West Country.

'Oh, do come, Sir John,' she had begged. 'The rest will do you good. And you know brother Ralph will be delighted to see you.'

Cranston had shaken his head mournfully and wrapped his bear-like arms round his petite wife.

'I cannot come, Lady,' he declared gruffly. 'The Council and the Regent are most insistent that I stay in London.'

Lady Maude had pulled free and looked at him archly. 'Is that the truth, Sir John?'

'By God's tooth!'

'Don't swear,' she had insisted. 'Just tell me.'

Sir John had sworn upon his honour that he spoke the truth, yet it had been tinged by a lie. He couldn't stand brother Ralph, as unlike his sister as chalk from cheese. To put it bluntly, Ralph was the most boring man Cranston had ever met. His one passion was farming and, as Sir John had wryly remarked to Athelstan: 'Once you have listened to Ralph's two-hour lectures on how to grow onions, that's your lot for eternity!'

Nevertheless, Cranston felt guilty. Ralph was good-hearted and Sir John missed both his wife and the two poppets; large, plump and sturdy-legged, they would stagger up to their father, hand in hand, so he could rub their bald little heads. He wondered why Athelstan kept laughing every time he saw them, but the friar would always pull his dark face straight, chew his lip, shake his head and declare, 'Nothing, Sir John, nothing. They are just so like you.'

'Sir John! Sir John! How are you?'

Cranston started and looked up. Athelstan was standing over him, his olive face sweat-stained, his black and white gown with its black cord round the waist covered in dust.

'By the devil's tits!' Cranston breathed. 'What are you doing here, monk?'

'Friar, Sir John.' Athelstan grinned as he pulled up a stool and sat down. 'I walked across London Bridge to visit Father Prior at Blackfriars. He's letting me transcribe certain parts of Roger Bacon's work on astronomy. I called at your house and the maid said you were absent. Oh, by the way, Leif the beggar is eating your dinner.'

Cranston stared at the friar. You are lying, he thought. I wager you came over here looking for me. I know the Lady Maude left you secret instructions. Nevertheless, he was warmed by Athelstan's concern.

'I suppose you want me to buy a drink?'

The taverner's wife came bustling up.

'I have already bought them,' Athelstan replied. 'Claret for My Lord Coroner and a blackjack of the coolest ale for me.' Athelstan sipped at the froth and smiled. 'You are right, Sir John. There'll have to be taverns in Heaven.'

'How are those rogues in your parish?' Cranston asked.

'Sinners like all of us, Sir John,' he replied. 'Bonaventure's catching rats by the dozen. Benedicta is organizing a harvest festival. I offered to bake some bread before I remembered what a hopeless cook I am. Watkin the dung-collector is still at odds with Pike the ditcher.' Athelstan grinned. 'Watkin's wife shoved Pike over in the porch. She claims he was drunk and tripped. What they don't know is that one of Watkin's daughters wants to marry Pike's eldest son.'

'Do their families know?'

'Not yet. But when they do, you will be able to hear the screams in Cheapside. Cecily the courtesan has a new beau and consequently a new dress every day. Huddle is now painting the new sanctuary.' Athelstan put down his tankard, his face becoming serious. 'There are two other matters,' he added softly, but then fell infuriatingly silent.

Oh, no, Cranston thought, you're not leaving that rat hole of a parish you love so much? You haven't been relieved of your duties as my clerk?

Cranston stared at the dreamy-eyed friar. Athelstan had been appointed parish priest of St Erconwald's in Southwark and Cranston's secretarius because of past follies. As a novice, Athelstan had left Blackfriars and run off with his hero-worshipping brother to the wars in France. The boy had been killed and Athelstan had returned home to witness the grief of his parents and bear the furious reprimands of his monastic superiors.

'Well, what is it?' Cranston asked testily.

'Do you believe in Satan, Sir John?'

'Yes, I do, and the bugger's sitting over there.' Cranston nodded across at the relic-seller deep in conversation with another rogue in a corner of the tavern. Athelstan smiled and shook his head.

'No, Sir John, I mean the real Satan.' His words came in a rush. 'Do you believe he can possess someone?'

Sir John sat up straight. 'Yes, Father, I do. I believe there's a spirit world where beings rage against Christ and his saints. However, I also believe the average demon sits upon his rock in Hell and weeps at the wickedness he sees man get up to. Why do you ask?'

Athelstan toyed with his tankard. 'Satan may have come to Southwark. A woman approached me after Mass this morning and claimed her stepdaughter is possessed. Every night she raises the devil to accuse her father of murdering his first wife, her mother.' Athelstan blinked and looked at his tankard. 'The woman has asked me to perform an exorcism.'

Sir John looked at him strangely. 'But, Athelstan, you deal with such matters every day.'

'Oh, I know,' the friar replied, and grinned. 'Pernell the Fleming says there are demons no bigger than her thumb who lurk in the shadowy corners of her house to giggle and talk about her. Two years ago, Watkin the dung-collector and his wife suddenly thought the world was coming to an end: they sat on the roof of their house, the whole family with them, each holding a cross against the demon. The only thing to occur was that the roof fell in. Watkin hurt his ankle and injured his pride.' Athelstan wiped his mouth on the back of his hand. 'No Sir John, this is different. Just looking at this woman, I sensed something evil is happening in that family.'

'And will you do the exorcism?'

'Canon law says that every diocese has an officially appointed exorcist, but he can only act on behalf of the bishop and deals with very serious and public matters. It can take months to secure his services.' Athelstan sipped from his tankard. 'I did ask Father Prior's advice: he reminded me it was my duty to offer what comfort I can.' The friar pulled a face. 'Sir John, I suppose I'm frightened. As that woman talked, I had a bone-chilling feeling of evil.'

Cranston patted him with a bear-like paw. 'I'm sure all will be well,' he muttered. 'And don't forget, Brother, there's very little that will frighten old Jack Cranston. Bollocks!' he suddenly roared and, grasping Athelstan's half-filled tankard, slung it across the room at the large-tailed, heavy-bellied rat which had slipped out from beneath a cask. The tankard missed and the rat scurried away.

'Sir John, I was enjoying that.'

Cranston mumbled an apology and shouted for another tankard.

'I am sorry, Brother, but the city's infested with bloody vermin. I'd like to have words with one of your parishioners.'

'Ranulf the rat-catcher?'

Athelstan smiled and turned to thank the taverner's wife as she brought another tankard; Sir John mumbled his apologies to her.

'You have your choice of ratters,' Athelstan continued. 'Ranulf is forming a Guild of Rat-Catchers. They have asked for St Erconwald's to be their Guild church. In a few days' time they will all meet there for Mass and fraternal celebrations. You are right,' he added. 'The hot weather has brought your furry friends out in a teeming, voracious horde.' He drank and lowered his tankard. 'But why the temper, Sir John? It's rare to see you throw good drink away on a rat.'

Cranston drained his wine cup, roared for another, leaned forward and began to tell Athelstan about the mysterious death of his comrade, Oliver Ingham. Athelstan studied the Coroner closely. He could see the usually genial man was deeply hurt and aggrieved by his comrade's death. At first Sir John spoke haltingly, but grew furiously eloquent as he described what he had witnessed at Ingham's house. Finishing, he breathed noisily through his nose, drumming his stubby fingers on his broad girth.

'You are sure it's murder, Sir John?'

'As sure as I have an arse!'

Athelstan chewed his lip and stared round the now crowded tavern. 'If I can help?' he offered.

'Just think,' Sir John said. 'I know you, Athelstan. You'll wander off, sit and look at the bloody stars, and some idea will occur to you. When it does, come back and tell me.' Cranston slurped noisily from his goblet and smacked his lips. 'You said there was a second matter, Brother?'

Athelstan pulled his stool closer. 'Sir John, you must have heard the news about the growing unrest in the countryside around London? How the peasant leaders are forming themselves into a Great Community and swear to march on London. They say they will burn the city to the ground, kill all bishops and lords, and put Gaunt's head on a pole.'

Cranston leaned closer for what they were talking about was treason.

'I know, Brother,' he muttered. 'Taxes are heavy, the harvest not yet in, the gaols are full and the gallows laden. Every week news pours into the city of unrest in the villages, and attacks on royal officials increase. One tax collector in Hertford was beaten to death and hung on a gallows alongside a dead cat dressed like a bishop with its head shorn.' He sniffed. 'But why should this concern you, Brother?'

'Oh, for God's sake, Sir John! Walk the streets of Southwark and you'll see an army waiting for a sign: the oppressed, the villains, the cutthroats and thieves. The slightest provocation and they'll come pouring across London Bridge and the city will burn for weeks.' Athelstan lowered his voice even further as he played with a splinter of wood on the table. 'Some of my parishioners are involved. Pike the ditcher, Tab the tinker… they spend most of their time creeping like stoats out into the countryside for this meeting or that.'

'If they are caught,' Cranston muttered, 'they will hang.'

'I know, I know, and that's what worries me. There will be a revolt, there'll be death, murder and cruel repression.' Athelstan paused. 'Sir John, have you heard of a man who calls himself Ira Dei, the Anger of God?'

Cranston nodded. 'Everyone has,' he whispered. 'John of Gaunt has sworn a terrible oath that he'll see the man hung, drawn and quartered. You see, Athelstan, the peasants are justified in their grievances and, God knows, some relief must be sought for them. Their leaders are wild men – Jack Straw, the priest John Ball – but behind them all lurks the leader of the secret council of the Great Community, this shadowy figure who calls himself Ira Dei. His arm is long and very strong. Have you heard what happened in Aldersgate?'

Athelstan shook his head.

'In a shabby house there a sepulchral voice was heard issuing from the walls. A mob of hundreds of citizens crowded to hear what they thought was the voice of an angel. When they shouted, "God save our Regent, Duke John," there was no answer from the entombed supernatural being. When another shouted, "God save our young King Richard!" the voice answered, "So be it." When asked: "What is Duke John's future?" the voice mockingly replied, "Death and destruction". The Serjeants were sent to investigate and found a young woman within the walls pretending to be the angel. She had to sit in the pillory for days with her head shaved. But,' Cranston tapped his finger on the table, 'Gaunt believes Ira Dei was behind it. It shows his power and influence, my good friar.'

'And what will My Lord of Gaunt do?'

Cranston cocked his head as the bells of nearby St Mary Le Bow began to toll for evening prayer. 'Oh, Gaunt is worried. He cannot call a parliament for the Commons are hostile. But tonight, he holds a great banquet at the Guildhall and I am to be there.' Cranston took a deep breath. 'Gaunt hopes to bring peace to the warring factions amongst the Guilds. He has become the friend of the merchant princes of London and their leaders: Thomas Fitzroy, Philip Sudbury, Alexander Bremmer, Hugo Marshall, Christopher Goodman and James Denny. They will celebrate their newfound amity in an orgy of food, wine and false goodwill.'

He cleared his throat. 'You see, my good friar, one of Gaunt's most able lieutenants, the Lord Adam Clifford, has acted for his master in these matters. Each of the Guildmasters has placed a large ingot of gold in a chest kept in the Guildhall chapel as surety for their goodwill and support of the Regent.' Cranston drained his tankard and got up. 'And I, my dear Brother, have to be there to witness this farce!'

Athelstan looked up anxiously. 'So there'll be peace, Sir John?'

'Peace!' Cranston bent over him. 'My good friar,' he whispered hoarsely, 'tell your parishioners to be careful. Gaunt intends to raise troops and, believe me, the streets of London will soon run with blood as thick, deep and as scarlet as wine from the grape presses!'

Athelstan put down his own tankard and stood up. 'You really think so, Sir John?'

'I know so! At this very moment, as I have said, Gaunt is meeting our merchant princes at the Guildhall. The young King, together with his tutor, Sir Nicholas Hussey, attended a Mass there this morning. This afternoon Gaunt took counsel with the Sheriff, Sir Gerard Mountjoy, on measures against the conspiracy amongst the peasants as well as those in the city who favour their cause.' Cranston wiped his white moustache and beard. 'And for my sins,' he breathed in a gust of wine fumes, 'I am to attend this evening's banquet where Gaunt will entertain his new allies.' He made a rude sound with his lips. 'As if I haven't enough problems.'

'Such as, Sir John?'

'Well, besides the death of Oliver, the Regent and Corporation are furious at some rogue who is removing the limbs and remains of executed traitors from London Bridge and elsewhere. After all, my good Brother, what's the use of executing people if you can't display their hacked, bloody limbs as a warning to other would-be traitors?' He linked his arm through the friar's as they went out of the tavern. 'Now, in my treatise on the governance of this city...' He smacked his lips as Athelstan closed his eyes and prayed for patience. Cranston's great work on the Government of London was nearly finished and he never missed an opportunity of lecturing everyone and anybody on his theories on how law and order could be administered in the capital.

'In my treatise I will advise against such practices. Criminals should be executed within the prison walls and the Crown should veto such barbaric practices. In ancient Sumeria…' Cranston pulled an unwilling Athelstan across Cheapside. 'Now in ancient Sumeria…' he repeated.

'My Lord Coroner! Brother Athelstan!'

They both turned. A sweaty-faced servitor, wearing the livery of the city, stood leaning against an empty stall, trying to catch his breath.

'What is it, man?'

'Sir John, you must come quickly. And you too, Brother. The Regent… His Grace the King…'

'What is it?' Cranston snapped.

'Murder, Sir John. Sir Gerard Mountjoy, the Sheriff, has been murdered at the Guildhall!'

Chapter 2

Cranston and Athelstan found the Guildhall strangely
silent. Armed men lined the passageways and corridors,
guarding the entrances and exits to the different courtyards. The servitor led them through these, shaking his
head at Cranston's nagging questions. He brought them
into the garden, one of the most attractive parts of
the Guildhall with its herb plots, fountain and channel,
wooden and stone benches, tunnel arbour and soft green
lawns. A group of men stood round the fountain talking
amongst themselves. They stopped and turned as Cranston and Athelstan came out.

'My Lord Coroner, we have been waiting.'

'Your Grace,' Cranston replied, staring at the swarthy,
gold-bearded face of the Regent, John of Gaunt, Duke of
Lancaster. 'We came as soon as the messenger found us.'

Cranston stared quickly round as Gaunt introduced the
rest. He recognized them all: Sir Christopher Goodman,
the Mayor, red-faced and pop-eyed, then the brilliantly
dressed, proud-faced Guildmasters: Thomas Fitzroy of the
Fishmongers, who always reminded Cranston of a carp

with his jutting lips and glassy eyes; Philip Sudbury of the Ironmongers, red-faced and red-haired, a born toper; Alexander Bremmer of the Drapers, thin and mean-faced, an avaricious grasping man; Hugo Marshall of the Spicers, his head bald as a pigeon's egg; and fleshy-featured Sir James Denny of the Haberdashers, dressed like a court fop in his tight hose and quilted jacket open at the neck.

Cranston nodded at these as well as at Sir Nicholas Hussey, the King's tutor, young-looking despite his silver hair and beard. Finally Lord Adam Clifford, Gaunt's principal henchman, fresh-faced and dressed in a tawny gown which suited the man's clean-shaven, sunburnt face and neatly coiffed black head. Gaunt finished the introductions.

'My Lord?' Cranston declared, angry at the Regent's insulting behaviour in not even acknowledging Athelstan. 'My Lord, I think you know my secretarius and clerk, Brother Athelstan, parish priest of St Erconwald's in Southwark?'

Gaunt smiled patronizingly and nodded. Cranston darted an angry glance at a sniggering Denny.

'We have come at your behest, My Lord Regent. We were told Sir Gerard Mountjoy has been murdered. Where, when and how?'

Gaunt waved a hand towards the small arbour which stood in the far corner of the garden sheltered from Cranston's gaze by the open door of the Guildhall as well as a high trellis covered in ivy.

'There?' Cranston asked.

'Yes, Sir Gerard is there!'

Gaunt's reply was angry but tinged with sardonic amusement. The Regent waved them across.

'I hope you have better luck than we did.'

Mystified, Cranston and Athelstan walked past the fence and looked over a small gate into the arbour. Both jumped as a pair of huge wolfhounds threw themselves against the gate, snarling and barking, lips curled, yellow teeth eager to rend and gash. Cranston and Athelstan stepped back.

The arbour was cleverly contrived, a garden within a garden: a turf seat against the trellised fence, a narrow pavement of coloured stones with a table which also served as a bird bath, and raised banks of fragrant herbs. A peaceful, pleasant place on a late summer's day had it not been for the man sprawled against the fence, a thin dagger thrust deep in his chest. A grotesque sight: mouth gaping, eyes open and slightly crooked as if the corpse was staring down in amazement at the bloody wound staining his russet gown.

Cranston studied the snub, brutish, dead features of one of London's most feared Sheriffs and walked back to the group.

'When did this happen, My Lord?'

Gaunt shrugged his shoulders elegantly as he wiped his hands on his blue samite gown.

'We had Mass this morning followed by a meeting in the council chamber. We were all preparing for the banquet tonight. Sir Gerard was apparently taking the air and a cup of claret in his own private arbour when a guard found him like that.' He pulled a face. 'Those damned dogs won't allow us anywhere near him.'

'If they won't allow you,' Gaunt nodded down the garden, where a group of crossbow men wearing the livery of Lancaster were patiently waiting, 'they will have to be killed.'

Athelstan, standing at Cranston's elbow, stared at these powerful, rich men. They, together with Gaunt, controlled not only London but the kingdom: their silver fuelled the King's armies, provisioned the fleet and controlled Parliament. He sensed they were shocked by Mountjoy's death but quietly pleased to see the demise of a powerful rival, for Mountjoy, a merchant in his own right, had been as power hungry as any of them. The Regent, however, a man of marble face and steely heart, was fighting hard to curb fury, for his attempt to control these powerful merchants had been rudely checked by Mountjoy's death.

'Well?' Goodman snapped. 'Sir John, you are the King's Coroner in the city. Sir Gerard has been murdered and foully so. We know who did it, so get rid of those dogs!'

'Oh?' Sir John smiled wryly. 'You have caught the assassin red-handed?'

'For God's sake, man!' Goodman snarled. 'Look at the arbour. On two sides is the garden fence, the far side is the wall of the Guildhall and the fourth is protected by the pentice.'

Cranston and Athelstan stared at the long narrow lean-to structure built against the buttress of the Guildhall; roofed with old shingles, this covered passageway connected the kitchens to the Guildhall proper.

'How could anyone,' Goodman continued slowly, as if Cranston and Athelstan were dim-witted, 'enter that garden, stab Sir Gerard and walk quietly away without being torn to pieces by those dogs?'

'What My Lord Mayor is saying,' Clifford spoke up, 'is that the two dogs were Sir Gerard's constant companions. Mountjoy was a bachelor. They were his wife, children, family and kinsfolk. The only man who could approach the Sheriff without disturbing the dogs is his retainer and steward, Philip Boscombe.'

Cranston nodded and looked back at the arbour.

'Sir Gerard,' Clifford continued, 'was always fearful of assassination. No one here — no official, no alderman, no burgess — could approach him unless the Sheriff had instructed his dogs to be friendly. Boscombe was the only exception. It must have been him. Servants didn't even hear the dogs bark.'

Cranston walked back. Standing well out of harm's way, he peered into that blood-soaked arbour. The two great hounds lay at their master's feet, now and again looking up as if expecting him to waken and call them. They could sense something was wrong and the smell of blood only made them more aggressive; they turned and growled towards the gate.

'Clifford must be right,' Athelstan whispered, coming up beside Cranston. 'The knife couldn't be thrown. There's no vantage point for that. And see how deeply it's embedded, Sir John.'

Cranston agreed. 'Where is Boscombe now?' he asked.

'Protesting his innocence,' Goodman replied. 'In the dungeons beneath the Guildhall. Sir John, we are waiting! Are you fearful of the dogs?'

'Bring me two hunks of red meat!' Cranston shouted back. He enjoyed keeping these pompous men waiting. 'And a pannikin of water!'

Goodman went into the Guildhall and they stood waiting, listening to his shouted orders. In a short while a servant appeared, bearing a trencher with two bloody steaks and a pannikin of water. He thrust these into Cranston's hands, looked fearfully at the arbour and ran back into the Guildhall.

'Stay where you are!' the Coroner commanded. 'John Cranston fears no one. And those dogs are too noble to be killed.' He walked to the gate and started talking quietly, greeted by the snarling of the dogs. They raised their huge paws and lifted themselves up, their great shaggy heads well above the gate. Cranston stepped back and kept talking softly to them. The dogs continued to bark raucously but then grew silent. They lay down at the gate, looking up at this soft-spoken man holding the delicious-smelling meat and pannikin of water. Athelstan drew closer. Sir John was whispering to the great beasts as if they were old friends.

'You see, Brother,' he muttered out of the corner of his mouth, 'no being, except a human, can ignore kindness.'

He carefully opened the gate. The two great hounds stood still, tails wagging. Cranston whistled softly through his teeth and, taking the meat and water, led both dogs out into the garden. He put the meat down. Whilst the dogs wolfed it, they let Cranston gently stroke their huge heads and fondle their ears.

'Good lads!' he whispered. 'Be good lads for old Jack!'

One of the dogs even stopped eating to nuzzle him. Cranston walked back into the arbour. The dogs stirred.

'Sit!'

The two hounds obeyed and Cranston, followed by a smiling Athelstan, walked into the arbour.

'Close your eyes, Brother.'

Athelstan did so and heard the unmistakable yielding sound as Cranston pulled the dagger out of the dead man's body. Athelstan opened his eyes and stared around.

The corpse had keeled over, lying face down on the turfed seat. A wine cup nestled under the ivy growing up the Guildhall wall and, as Cranston wiped the dagger on the grass, Athelstan realized how mysterious this murder was. Directly opposite where Mountjoy had been sitting was the lean-to pentice or covered walk; the fencing was wooden planks with gaps between, though certainly not wide enough for anyone to throw a knife with such force. The Guildhall wall was an impenetrable barrier and, if the knife had been thrown from the garden, someone would have had to stand at the gate. Athelstan shook his head. Sir Gerard or his dogs would not have allowed someone to stand wielding a wicked-looking knife, and made no protest or resistance.

Athelstan looked down the pebbled path. How it crunched under his sandalled feet. No soft-footed assassin could have stolen along such a path and stood at the gate without sending the dogs into a barking frenzy. He looked up at the buttress of the Guildhall against which the pentice had been built. The only windows there were mere arrow slits and too high and narrow for anyone to throw a knife through them with any force or accuracy. He looked at Cranston who was studying the blade of the knife carefully.

'It must have been Boscombe,' Athelstan muttered. 'That knife was not thrown. See.' He pointed to the trellis against which Mountjoy had been leaning. 'The dagger went right through his chest and scored the fence.'

'Perhaps someone climbed the fence behind Sir Gerard?' Clifford approached them to suggest.

Athelstan shook his head.

'I doubt it, My Lord. Sir Gerard was apparently sitting down when he was killed. Such an assailant would have to climb the fence, swing down with the dagger and take his victim in the chest. Can you imagine the Sheriff or his dogs allowing that?'

The Guildmasters, led by Clifford and Gaunt, gingerly entered the small arbour, looking apprehensively over their shoulders at the two great wolfhounds who now lay, sad-eyed, on the grass.

'Are those dogs safe?' Gaunt muttered.

'Oh, yes,' Cranston replied absent-mindedly. 'They know something's wrong but they do not see us as hostile.' He snorted with laughter. 'Though perhaps we are. One person here definitely is.' Cranston stared around. 'I am Sir John Cranston, King's Coroner in the city,' he declared. 'This is my verdict: I find Sir Gerard Mountjoy murdered by person or persons unknown.'

'What about Boscombe?' Gaunt intervened.

'It may well be he. But have you seen this dagger, My Lord?' Cranston held it up.

At first Athelstan thought it an ordinary Welsh stabbing dirk with its thin, long, evil blade and small grip and hilt. But beneath the smeared marks of Cranston's cleaning, he saw something etched on the blade. Athelstan took it from Cranston's hand and peered down.

'Ira Dei,' he murmured, reading aloud the rudely scrawled letters.

Gaunt kicked angrily at the grass and beat his fists against his side. 'By the Mass.' He glared at the others.

'These peasant bastards threaten us here in our own city, in our own palaces!'

'Ira Dei?' Hussey the royal tutor shoved his way forward. 'The Anger of God. My Lord of Gaunt, what does this mean? The King must be informed!'

'My nephew,' Gaunt replied testily, 'will be told in due course.'

Athelstan caught the deep dislike in the Regent's voice and recalled the whispers about the growing rivalry between the Regent and the royal tutor.

'Ira Dei,' Gaunt replied slowly, 'is a self-styled leader, cloaked in mystery.'

'Leader of what?'

'The Great Community!' Gaunt snarled. 'The name the peasants give to their secret council of leaders who are plotting treason and rebellion, both in and around London. Sir, you should be better informed!'

'My Lord,' Hussey silkily replied, 'like His Grace the King, I only know what I have been told.'

Gaunt looked away in annoyance. 'Mountjoy's dead,' he whispered. 'Stabbed by his servant who must be in the pay or service of these rebels. Sir John, Brother Athelstan, do you agree?'

Cranston was peering at the dagger whilst Athelstan was attempting to lay the bulky corpse of the dead Sheriff out along the turf seat. The man's gown was thickly clotted with blood. Athelstan whispered the requiem and at the same time inspected the wound in the man's chest, and the nick on the fence against which he had been leaning, as well as the blood on the hands of the corpse.

'My Lords,' the friar declared, breathing heavily as he crossed the dead Sheriff's hands over each other, 'I am sure Sir John will agree with me that Sir Roger was murdered by a thrust from that dagger. It cannot have been thrown, the arbour is virtually sealed, and if the assassin stood at the gate, Sir Gerard, not to mention his dogs, would have seen him.'

'All three of them could have been asleep,' Fitzroy boomed stupidly. 'Sir Gerard liked his wine.'

'The dogs didn't,' Denny smirked.

'I doubt it,' Athelstan continued calmly. 'Such hounds would have protected their master from any approach and Sir Gerard knew, at least for a few seconds, that he was dying. See his hands? They are blood-stained.'

'My clerk,' Cranston interrupted grandly, 'is following my train of thought.' He winked at Athelstan and walked back to the gate. 'The dagger was not thrown. The assassin walked through the gate, perhaps with the dagger concealed. After all, it's long and thin with no real hilt. Sir Gerard is sitting drinking his wine. He looks up and the assassin strikes, driving the dagger deep into the Sheriff's heart, piercing his body. In his death throes Sir Gerard scrabbles at the dagger, his hands fall away, he dies.' Cranston beamed round, 'I think the next step, My Lords, is that my clerk and I should interrogate the prisoner.'

Gaunt agreed, an archer was summoned, and both Cranston and Athelstan went back into the Guildhall and down into the dank, musty-smelling cellars. The passage-ways were torch-lit; two archers stood on guard outside a cell with a metal grille high in the door. Cranston peered through this. The dungeon was lit by an oil lamp standing on a battered table and the prisoner lay huddled on a small cot bed. The guards opened the door. Cranston and Athelstan slipped through. The man on the bed moaned and sat up.

In the poor light of the oil lamp he looked as wretched and as miserable as any man could be. Small and fat, with eyes hidden in rolls of fat, he was heavy-eyed with weeping and his hair was thick with dungeon-dirt.

Athelstan squatted down beside him and stared into the soft, pampered face of the dead Sheriff's steward. The fellow crossed his arms and began rocking to and fro.

'What is it now? What is it now?' he muttered, the tears rolling down his cheeks. 'Am I to be tortured? Am I to hang? Sirs, you are not to hurt me.' He whimpered like a child and Athelstan saw the bruise on the side of his head. He touched the man gently on the hand and glanced back at Sir John. Cranston could tell by the look in Athelstan's eyes that the friar had already concluded that this squat, little man with his doughy skin and plump hands was no murderer.

'We are here to help,' Athelstan whispered. He got up and leaned against the table whilst Cranston stood with his back to the door. 'Just tell us the truth.'

The man looked down, still blubbering, shoulders shaking.

'Sir Gerard's dead,' he moaned. 'And I am to hang. Sirs, I am innocent – and, oh, the day began so well!'

'Then start from the beginning,' Athelstan urged. 'Boscombe, Sir John Cranston has the ear of the Regent. If you tell the truth and prove your innocence, you could be out of this cell by nightfall.'

The prisoner looked up and Athelstan saw the hope flare in the steward's dark, tear-filled eyes.

'The day began so well,' the fellow repeated, then coughed and his voice became firmer. 'Sir Gerard was pleased with what was going to happen: how the Regent and he were to seal a bond of friendship between the Guilds. His Grace the King, the Regent and the others arrived mid-morning for the Mass in the Guildhall chapel. Sir Gerard was in attendance. I and the other retainers stood at the back. Mass began: the Guildmasters, the Regent and Sir Gerard shared the kiss of peace; they received the sacrament followed by the blessing of the keys.'

'What was that?' Cranston interrupted.

'As a guarantee of their good intentions,' Boscombe replied, 'the leading Guilds deposited an ingot of gold,

47

as did the Regent, in a specially constructed chest reinforced with iron bars and six separate locks. One key is held by the Regent, the other five by the Guildmasters.' Boscombe rubbed the side of his face. 'After that, we had marchpanes and sweet wines in the porch of the church then the Regent, together with the Mayor, Sheriff and the five Guildmasters, took secret counsel in the Sheriff's private chamber.' Boscombe ran his fingers through his hair, now thick and matted as a wolf-lock. 'The meeting broke up and my master said he would take his pleasure in his private garden.'

'Did you go there?'

'Yes, I took him a stoup of wine. He was sunning himself. He said the morning had gone well and I was not to disturb him again.' Boscombe started to cry. 'Masters, I was in my own chamber when I heard the shouting and the soldiers came for me. I was hustled down to the garden and saw poor Sir Gerard there. And now,' he wailed, 'I am to hang!'

Athelstan touched him lightly on the shoulder. 'Be of good comfort, friend. You are no murderer. Sir John here will see that justice is done. One further question. Sir Gerard, your master, did he have any enemies?'

Now Boscombe smiled slightly. 'Enemies?' he retorted. 'I served my master well but to him I was another dog, to be kicked when I did wrong or thrown a bone when I did well. It would be better to wonder, Father, who was *not* Sir Gerard's enemy, for he had no friends. My

Lord of Gaunt tolerated him. Sir Christopher Goodman the Mayor could hardly abide being in the same chamber as he, whilst the five Guildmasters…' Boscombe sneered. 'They are powerful, dangerous men. They could not abide Sir Gerard, not only for his wealth but for gaining high office in the city.'

Athelstan got to his feet. 'Stand up!' he ordered.

Boscombe pulled himself to his feet.

'Are you wearing the same clothes as you were this morning?'

'Why, yes, of course, though this morning, Brother, they were finery.' Boscombe tugged at his cream-coloured jerkin and tapped the soft, brown, woollen hose, all grimed and stained with dirt.

'Take a look, Sir John,' Athelstan offered. 'Did this fellow plunge a dagger into Sir Gerard's heart?'

'Of course,' Cranston murmured, seizing Boscombe's wrist and looking carefully at the sleeves. 'No sign of blood here.' He clapped the servant so heartily on the shoulder, poor Boscombe nearly collapsed back on the bed again. 'You are no assassin.' Cranston suddenly smacked his lips and Athelstan realized how long the Coroner had been without a drink. 'So come on, lad, let's go upstairs!'

Cranston hammered on the door. The guard opened it but tried to stop Boscombe leaving.

'Sod off!' Cranston roared. 'How dare you interfere with the King's Coroner?'

The man hastily stepped back, mumbling apologies as the Coroner, almost dragging poor Boscombe by one hand, led them back up the passageway and into the Guildhall. They found the Regent and the others still in the garden, seated on wooden benches in a small grassy enclave. They were sipping cool white wine as if it was a fair summer's day and all was well. They totally ignored the household men who had sheeted the Sheriff's body and were now taking it down to lie amongst the wine casks where it would remain cool and not begin to stink.

Cranston and Athelstan stood aside as the servants hurried by, cursing and muttering at their grisly burden.

Over in the far corner of the garden, the two great wolfhounds lay forlornly on the grass as if they knew their privileged life was gone. Sir John swept before the seated men, a wan-faced Boscombe gripped by one hand. Goodman sprang to his feet whilst the others watched Sir John with narrowed eyes and disapproving faces.

An unwholesome bunch, Athelstan thought, men dedicated to power and the amassing of wealth; dark souls with sinister minds and powerful ambitions. They reminded the friar of hawks in a castle courtyard, straining at their jesses, ready to leave their perch to swoop and kill. Goodman advanced dramatically on Sir John.

'This man is a city prisoner.'

'And I am the city Coroner,' Cranston replied. He had never liked Mountjoy but Goodman he detested as a man who would betray his own mother so long as the price was right.

'You had no authority to free him!' Goodman spluttered.

'What is it, Sir John?' Lord Adam Clifford, seated beside the Regent, languidly asked. The young man looked up, shielding his eyes against the late-afternoon sun. 'Good Lord, man, you are not going to hang him now, are you? I haven't eaten and this garden has seen enough violence for one day.'

Cranston bowed his head to the Regent. 'My Lord, a little mummer's play. Would you be so good?'

Without waiting for an answer, Cranston spun on his heel and, winking at Athelstan, hustled poor Boscombe into Mountjoy's private arbour. The Regent shrugged, placed his wine cup on the floor and followed Cranston. Lord Adam smiled at Athelstan.

'Some play,' he murmured. 'Gentlemen, I think we should follow His Grace.'

In the arbour Boscombe's nervousness returned; he shook like a jelly as Cranston led him across to the blood-stained turf seat.

'Right!' Cranston beamed at Gaunt and the others standing at the gate. 'Now, Master Boscombe,' he drew his own long stabbing dirk, 'I want you to murder me.' Cranston slumped down on the turf seat, impervious to the blood congealing there, and smiled across at the Mayor.

'Sir Christopher, of your mercy, a cup of that wine you are drinking?'

The Coroner mopped his brow with his hand and wetted his lips. Goodman was about to protest but Gaunt snapped his fingers. The Mayor hurried away and returned with a cup slopping at the brim, which he thrust into the Coroner's fat paw. Cranston silently toasted the Regent and then gazed at the pathetic Boscombe who stood, gingerly holding the dagger, as if terrified of cutting himself, never mind Sir John.

'Right!' Cranston barked, sipping from the cup. 'Kill me, Boscombe!'

Athelstan stepped forward. 'Go on, man,' he murmured. 'Do it now!'

Boscombe, holding the dagger out, lumbered towards Sir John. Athelstan wasn't sure what happened next. Cranston continued to sip from the wine goblet, Boscombe struck – but the next minute the Coroner had knocked the dagger from his hand and sent the servant sprawling on to the grass. Cranston drained the cup and got to his feet.

'My Lord Coroner has made his point,' Athelstan tactfully intervened. 'Boscombe doesn't even know how to hold a dagger. Like Sir John, Sir Gerard was a fiery man. He, not to mention his dogs, would have put up some resistance. More importantly, My Lord,' Athelstan addressed Gaunt, 'if Boscombe had struck a dagger so deep, he'd bear bloodstains on his hands and sleeves. But,' he added, helping Boscombe to his feet, 'there are no such stains.'

Gaunt stared heavy-lidded at Athelstan, then at Boscombe. He sighed and blew out his cheeks, dug into his purse and flicked a coin at Boscombe who, despite his nervousness, deftly caught it.

'Master Boscombe, a grave injustice has been done. Wait over there!'

He scuttled away as fast as a rabbit to sit with the two great wolfhounds. Gaunt walked towards Cranston and Athelstan, rubbing his finger round the rim of his cup.

'If Boscombe didn't do it,' he whispered, 'then who did?'

Athelstan and Cranston stared back.

'More importantly,' Gaunt continued, 'how was it done? The garden is enclosed. Mountjoy was a soldier, guarded by dogs. We have examined his wine cup. He was not drugged, so how did someone get so close to kill such a man?' Gaunt wagged a finger at Sir John. 'You, My Lord Coroner, and your clerk will be my guests at tonight's banquet. You are under orders to resolve this matter, and do so quickly.' He looked over at his companions. 'Sirs, we must leave this matter in the capable hands of My Lord Coroner.'

'Have you resolved the other business?' Goodman spitefully called.

Cranston blushed with anger at the laughter this provoked. Sir Nicholas Hussey, whom Cranston secretly respected, looked embarrassed.

'What business is this?' Gaunt asked.

'Oh,' Goodman brayed, walking forward, 'the heads and bloody parts of traitors filched from London Bridge and other places. Sir John has been trying to catch the thief for weeks.'

Athelstan would have liked to have smacked the Mayor full in his red, fleshy face but instead looked down and hoped Cranston would not give vent to his fiery temper. Sir John did not disappoint him. He stepped forward, his face only a few inches away from Goodman's.

'I shall not only resolve that matter,' he whispered, yet loud enough for the others to hear. 'But, I assure you, sir, when this business is finished there will be fresh heads on London Bridge!'

They all made to leave and were about to re-enter the Guildhall when Boscombe ran forward to crouch at the Regent's feet.

'My Lord!' the man wailed, raising a tear-streaked face to John of Gaunt. 'What shall I do now? My master's dead. The dogs?'

'Do you have a position?' Gaunt asked the Mayor.

Goodman shook his head. The Regent shrugged.

'Then, Master Boscombe, you should count your blessings. You are at least free.'

'And the dogs?' he wailed.

'Perhaps they should join their master. Unless, of course,' Gaunt glanced sideways at Cranston, 'My Lord Coroner stands maintenance for all three of you?'

Cranston stared at the pathetic little man and the two huge wolfhounds who looked so resigned to their fate. He was about to refuse but then caught Goodman's smirk and the doleful eyes of the hounds.

'I'll stand maintenance!' he retorted before Athelstan could urge prudence.

Cranston pulled Boscombe to his feet, whistled to the dogs and marched away through the Guildhall, grinning evilly from ear to ear as the hounds charged after him, scattering that group of powerful, haughty men.

Chapter 3

'Lady Maude will kill me!' Sir John muttered as he and Athelstan sat on a garden bench watching the two great wolfhounds, who had already terrified the life out of Cranston's household, bound round the garden. Every so often they would come back and place their great paws on the Coroner's fat legs to lick his face until the garden rang with Cranston's ripest curses.

Boscombe, needing no second bidding, had gathered his pathetic belongings into a bundle and followed Sir John home. He now appeared at the door, washed, changed and bearing a brimming goblet of claret.

'Good man! Good man!' Cranston murmured. 'You are already high in my favour.' He wagged a stubby finger at his new steward. 'Five things matter to me,' he growled. 'First, the Lady Maude. She is to be obeyed in all things. Second, take care of my sons, the poppets. Third, Brother Athelstan,' he tapped the friar gently on the arm, 'is my friend. Fourth, my study where I keep my great treatise is my sanctuary. And, fifth, my wineskin. There are two in fact; one hanging behind the buttery door, the other in my chamber. They are to be kept full at all times, but the Lady Maude is never to know there are two.'

'Of course, Sir John.' Boscombe disappeared as silently as he'd appeared.

Cranston sipped the claret. 'He will be a good man,' he murmured. 'But what about those bloody dogs, eh? Satan's balls, Athelstan, they look big enough to eat the poppets and Lady Maude in one gulp!'

Athelstan chewed his lower lip. He could see Sir John's problem but not even the glimmer of a solution.

'It will all depend,' he said slowly, 'on what Lady Maude decides, Sir John.' He held back the laughter. 'If you are lucky, she'll just put the two dogs out of doors. If she's angry, you may go with them!'

Cranston belched. The two dogs turned and looked towards him.

'Hell's teeth, boys!' Cranston growled at them. 'What shall I call you? Do you know, that snivelling bastard Mountjoy, God rot him, didn't even bother to give you names? Well, I have thought of two: the one with the blue collar will be called Gog and the one with the red, Magog.'

The two dogs must have thought it was time once again to thank their new master for they came hurtling back towards him. Athelstan felt his heart lurch with fear but Cranston lifted his hand and the two dogs stopped and lay panting before him, their eyes never leaving his fat, florid face.

'Where did you get this gift with dogs? They'd eat out of your hands,' Athelstan asked, carefully putting his feet under the bench.

'Ever since I was knee-high to a buttercup I've got on with dogs,' Cranston replied. 'My father was a hard man. When I did wrong, he put me out in the kennels.' Ever reluctant to discuss his youth, he pointed to the writing implements on the table in front of Athelstan. 'But it's not as difficult as this problem, eh?'

Athelstan picked up his crude drawing of the Guildhall garden. 'How?' he muttered, conscious of Cranston breathing noisily in his ear. 'How could such a murder occur?'

'Never mind that,' growled the Coroner. 'Let's think about who? Hell's tits!' he muttered, answering his own question. 'The possibilities are legion, and amongst them that group of whoreson codpieces who richly deserve a hempen necklace round their necks!'

Athelstan stared at the Coroner. 'I didn't know you cared so much, Sir John?'

'They are,' Cranston continued, getting into his stride, 'a group of foul, wrinkled, double-speaking, painted turds!' He knocked Athelstan's piece of parchment aside and crumbled the remnants of the piece of bread he had been nibbling. 'At the Guildhall this afternoon, my dear monk…'

'Friar, Sir John!'

'Same thing!' he mumbled. 'This afternoon we met the finest collection of rogues who ever graced this kingdom.' Cranston placed one lump of bread on the table. 'We have the Guildmasters, the devil's own henchmen. So full of oily grease, if you set a torch to them, they'd burn for ever. They hate each other, and resent the Crown whilst each and all would love to control London. Any one of these or all together could have murdered Mountjoy.

'Second,' another lump of bread appeared on the table, 'we have Gaunt's party. God knows what that subtle prince is up to. He may desire the Crown or at least to be its master. He wants to control the London mob and needs the Guildmasters' gold to achieve this. Next,' a third piece of crust appeared, 'we have the King's party. Now our young prince is not yet of age, but followers like Hussey would love to break the power of the Regent and replace him with their good selves. Then we have the Great Community of the Realm, the peasant leaders with their secret council and mysterious leader named Ira Dei. Finally, we have the unknown. Was Mountjoy killed for personal rather than political reasons?'

Cranston lowered his voice. 'Who knows? It could have been Boscombe or, indeed, anyone in London. I wager if you called a meeting of those who hated the Sheriff, there wouldn't even be standing room in St Paul's Cathedral and the line of those waiting to get in would stretch all the way down to the Thames.'

'But, Sir John, the knife bore the name Ira Dei?'

'Oh, come, come, clever friar,' Sir John boomed. 'Don't play the innocent with me. I am sure some assassin turned up when all those notables were gathered in the Guildhall and asked for directions so he could kill the Sheriff! It's obvious,' Cranston stated, drawing himself up, his white whiskers quivering. 'I only speak aloud what that double-faced group of bastards secretly know. The assassin was *already* in the Guildhall. Neither the Regent nor that fat slob Goodman reported any stranger being seen in or around their blessed Guildhall.'

Athelstan grinned. '*Concedo*, O most perceptive of Coroners. So this matter becomes more tangled?'

'Of course.' Cranston picked up the morsels of bread.

'And what if,' he speculated, 'there's an alliance between all these groups? An unholy conjunction, as between Pilate and Herod?'

'If that's the case,' Athelstan replied, 'we have a list of complexities which defies logical analysis. The Guildmasters may not be united. They may be divided or even treacherous, paying court to both Gaunt and the peasant faction.'

'Or worse still,' Cranston intervened, 'the Guildmasters could be courting Gaunt, the King and the peasant leaders.' He waved one podgy hand. 'Perhaps only one of the Guildmasters is a traitor? Or did Gaunt have Mountjoy killed because he was the one worm in their rose?' Athelstan put up both hands. 'I agree, Sir John. How Sir Gerard was murdered is a mystery. Who murdered him… well, it could be anyone? So, we are left with one question: why?'

'And we have already answered that.' Cranston got up, patted his stomach and beamed down at his clerk. 'Perhaps Sir Gerard was too much trouble for Gaunt? One thing we do know.' He drummed his fat fingers on the tabletop. 'The object of this game is power and the prize is to be king of the castle and watch the destruction of your enemies. All I can say is, we must trust no one.'

'My own belief,' Athelstan replied, 'is that as this murder occurred on the very day Gaunt cemented his alliance with the city of London, I must conclude Sir Gerard's death was not the result of a personal feud but a bid to wreck that alliance and sow the seeds of dissension and mistrust. In which case…'

'In which case, what?' Cranston snapped.

'In which case, my dear Coroner, before either of us is much older, there will be another murder.'

Cranston, cursing softly, swept the bread from the table and watched as Gog and Magog lumbered over to discover what their master was offering them. The bells of St Mary Le Bow began to chime. Sir John looked up at the darkening sky.

'Come on, Friar, we are invited to the Regent's banquet at the Guildhall.'

'Sir John, I should return to my parish.'

Cranston grinned. 'The devil's tits! The Regent has invited you, you have to go!'

Cranston strode back to the house, bellowing for Boscombe. Whilst Athelstan washed and cleaned himself in a bowl of water in the scullery, Sir John went up to his own chamber and dressed in a gown of murrey sarcanet, edged with gold, changing his boots for a more courtly, ornate pair. He came back to the kitchen, red face gleaming, smelling as fragrant as any rose from the ointment he had rubbed into his hands and cheeks.

'Sir John, you look every inch the Lord Coroner. I am afraid,' Athelstan looked down at his dusty gown, 'I have no fresh robe.'

'You look what you are,' Cranston retorted, patting him gently on the shoulder. 'A poor priest, a man of God, Christ's servant. Believe me, Athelstan, you can wrap a dog's turd in a cloth of gold, but it remains a dog's turd.'

And, with that pithy piece of homespun wisdom, Cranston roared to the maids, whispered instructions to Boscombe about the dogs, collected his miraculous wineskin and marched down the passageway, Athelstan hurrying behind. Sir John opened the door.

'Oh, bugger off!' he roared at red-haired, one-legged Leif the beggar who leaned against the door lintel, his shabby tray slung round his neck. Leif looked as if he was on the verge of collapsing from fatigue and hunger, but Athelstan knew he was a consummate actor who ate and drank as heartily as Sir John.

'Oh,' whined Leif, 'my belly's empty.'

'Then it suits your head!'

'Sir John, a crumb of bread, a cup of water?'

'Pigskins!' Cranston bellowed. 'You've already eaten my supper! You are a hungry, lean-faced villain, Leif.'

'Sir John, I am a poor man.'

'Oh, get in,' muttered Cranston. 'See Boscombe, he's my new steward. No, on second thoughts – Boscombe!' he roared.

The little fellow appeared, as silent as a shadow.

'This is Leif,' Cranston bellowed. 'He'll eat me out of house and home. Give him some wine but not my claret. There's bread, soup, and Lady Maude has left a pie in the larder.'

'Oh, thank you, Sir John.' Leif hopped down the passageway as nimbly as any squirrel.

'Oh, by the way.' Cranston smiled evilly. 'Leif, my friend, go into the garden. I have two new guests who would love to meet you.' Then, slamming the door behind him, he went down Cheapside laughing softly.

'Sir John, was that wise?'

'Oh, don't worry about Leif, Athelstan,' Cranston shouted over his shoulder. 'He's nimble as a flea, can move faster than you or I. And often has!' he added.

Cheapside was deserted now except for the dung carts, the makers, and the occasional whore dressed in saffron or yellow, hanging round the doors of taverns. Once darkness fell, they and the other city riffraff, the roisterers, the apple squires and what Cranston termed 'the other beasts of the night', would soon make their presence felt.

They arrived at the Guildhall to find the entire building surrounded by royal archers and men-at-arms. Cranston bellowed his name at them and shouldered his way through, up the steps and into the audience chamber where Lord Adam Clifford was waiting for them.

The young courtier's face creased into a genuine smile. 'Sir John, Brother Athelstan.' He clasped their hands warmly. 'You are most welcome!'

Cranston looked at the young nobleman's simple leather jacket, woollen hose and high-heeled leather riding boots.

'But, My Lord, you are not joining us for the banquet?'

The young man pulled a face. 'The Lord Regent has other business for me.'

Athelstan could tell by Clifford's eyes that the young man was displeased to be sent away.

'You are the last guest, Sir John,' he whispered hurriedly. 'The King will arrive soon and the banquet begin. You had best hurry!'

Clifford handed them over to a liveried servant who led them upstairs and along passageways, all lit by flickering torches. Nevertheless, Athelstan could sense uneasiness in the place; archers wearing either the White Hart, the King's own personal emblem, or the Lion Rampant of Gaunt, were everywhere.

'Lord Adam seems a wise-headed fellow,' Athelstan observed.

'One good apple in a rotten barrel,' Cranston whispered out of the corner of his mouth. 'He's a north-erner who has attached his fortunes to Giant's star. I hope he's wise. If the Regent falls, so will he.'

At last they reached the Hall of Roses, the sump-tuous though small private banqueting chamber of the Guildhall. The servant ushered them in, Athelstan and Cranston blinking at the brilliant light from hundreds of candles fixed round the room. The other guests were already seated; they paid little heed to the new arrivals and whispered amongst themselves as a cup-bearer took Cranston and Athelstan to their seats.

'A most noble place,' the friar whispered.

'Don't forget, Brother,' Cranston murmured as they sat down, 'tonight we dine with a murderer!'

Chapter 4

Cranston sat in his seat in the Hall of Roses and lovingly cradled a jewelled wine goblet.

'First time I've been here,' he muttered to Athelstan.

The friar studied his fat friend anxiously; Cranston, deep in his cups, was frighteningly unpredictable. He might either go to sleep or else start lecturing these powerful men. However, the Coroner seemed quiet enough for the moment and Athelstan, who had eaten and drunk sparingly, gazed appreciatively round the Hall of Roses.

A perfect circle, the chamber reminded him of a painting of a Greek temple he had once seen in a Book of Hours. The roof was a cupola of cleverly ornate, polished hammer beams which swooped across the ceiling to meet a huge central red rose, carved in wood and painted in gold leaf. The walls and dark embrasures were of dressed stone and the supporting pillars of porphyry linked by banners of cloth of gold, bearing either the Royal Arms or the insignia of the House of Lancaster. The marble floor was overlaid by a carpet which, from a red rose in the centre, radiated out in strips of purple and white, each ending in the name of one of the knights of Arthur's Round Table. Over each name sat a guest at his own separate table, a small oaken trestle covered with a silver-white cloth. At the top, on King Arthur's seat, was the young Richard, his golden hair elaborately dressed, a silver chaplet round his white brow; the young King was attired from head to toe in purple damask.

Athelstan, ignoring the hubbub of conversation around him, studied Richard who sat gazing unwinkingly across the hall. Then he caught the friar's glance, smiled and winked mischievously. Athelstan grinned, embarrassed, and looked away. He was not frightened of Gaunt, who sat in scarlet robes on the King's right, but Athelstan knew how jealous the Regent was of the King's open affection for Sir John Cranston, as well as his secretarius, Brother Athelstan. The young King turned and talked to Hussey on his left, grasping his tutor's wrist in a gesture of friendship. Cranston, though on his eighth cup of claret, turned and pulled a face at Athelstan; for the King to touch anyone at a formal banquet was a breach of etiquette and the highest mark of royal favour.

Athelstan glanced at Gaunt. He was astute enough to see the flicker of annoyance cross the Regent's saturnine face even though Gaunt tried to hide it by stroking his neatly clipped gold moustache and beard.

'As I have said,' Cranston whispered rather too loudly in Athelstan's ear, 'no love lost there. Hussey is now the

King's favourite as well as his tutor. A university man,' Sir John continued. 'I wonder what Hussey and the King think of Gaunt's friendship with the Guildmasters? Just look at the turd worms!'

Athelstan squeezed Cranston's arm. 'Sir John, keep your voice down. You have eaten well?'

Cranston smiled. 'As I would wish to in Paradise! For God's sake, Brother, just look at the wealth!'

Athelstan stared at his own cup, plate and knives all fashioned from pure gold and silver, whilst his goblet, hardly touched throughout the meal, was encrusted with a King's ransom in jewels, part of the loot Gaunt had brought back from his wars in France.

'What have we eaten so far, Brother?'

'Lamprey, salmon, venison, boar's meat, swan and peacock.' Athelstan grinned. 'And dessert is still to come!'

He was about to tease Sir John further when suddenly Fitzroy, Guildmaster of the Fishmongers, rose to his feet, scrabbling at his fur-lined collar, his habitually red face purple now as he coughed and choked. The rest of the guests watched, astounded. No one moved as Fitzroy staggered against his table, turned slightly and crashed to the floor.

Despite his laden stomach, Cranston sprang to his feet, Athelstan behind him, and hurried across. Fitzroy lay sprawled on his side, eyes and mouth still open, but Athelstan could feel no life beat in the puce-coloured throat. He stuck his finger into the man's mouth, ensuring the tongue was free, thinking Fitzroy might have choked. He hid his distaste, working his fingers downwards, but found no blockage in the man's throat. Cranston felt Fitzroy's wrist and then his heart.

'He's gone!' he growled. 'Dead as one of his bloody fish, God rest him!'

The others hurried across in a hubbub of shouts and exclamations, the young King included. Despite his tender years, Richard shouldered his way forward.

'Is the fellow dead, Sir John?'

'God rest him, yes, Sire.'

'And the cause?'

Athelstan shrugged. 'I am no physician, Your Grace. Apoplexy, perhaps?'

'Nephew, you should not be here.' Gaunt edged his way forward and clapped a beringed hand on young Richard's shoulder.

'We will stay, Uncle, until the cause of death is established. You, man.' The King nodded at one of the royal archers guarding the door. 'You will go for Master de Troyes!'

Gaunt bit back his anger and, nodding at the archer, confirmed his nephew's order. Meanwhile Athelstan stared down at the corpse.

'This is no apoplexy, Sir John,' he whispered, 'I believe Fitzroy's death is not a natural one.'

The rest protested noisily but Sir John, crouching beside Athelstan, lifted a finger to his lips as a signal for silence.

Athelstan leaned down and sniffed at the man's mouth. He smelt wine, roast meat and the bittersweet smell of something else, like that of a decaying rose with the wormwood strong within it.

'Did Fitzroy complain of any illness before the meal?' Sir John suddenly asked.

Bremmer, Sudbury, Marshall, Denny and Goodman, all clustered together, shook their heads.

'He was in the best of health,' Denny squeaked.

'Any family?' Sir John asked, still crouched beside the corpse.

'A wife and two married sons. But they are absent from the city.'

Cranston nodded. Like Lady Maude, many of the wives of leading city officials and merchants left the city during the warm summer for cool manor houses in the country. Athelstan glanced up and carefully watched these clever, subtle men. In his judgement, one of them was a poisoner. He got to his feet and, stepping over the body, sat down at Fitzroy's table. The silver plate still bore portions of meat and other remnants from the banquet. Two cups of wine stood there, each about one-third full with either red or white wine. Athelstan picked up the gold-edged napkin, studied this carefully, sniffing at it, then the cups and the food. The hall grew silent and he looked up to find the rest studying him curiously.

'What is the matter, Brother?' Gaunt's voice was full of suspicion.

'I believe,' Athelstan declared, ignoring Cranston's warning look, 'that Master Fitzroy did not die of a seizure but was poisoned.'

'Murdered?' Goodman snapped.

'Impossible!' Marshall snorted. 'What are you implying, Brother?'

'My clerk is implying nothing!' Cranston retorted, getting to his feet.

Athelstan carefully laid the napkin over the table, covering the plate and cups.

'If my secretarius,' Cranston continued defiantly, 'says a man is poisoned, then he's been poisoned.'

'Now, now, what is this?' the young King intervened. 'If Sir Thomas were murdered here, his assassin would still be in the room.'

Athelstan got up and walked across to a servitor who stood holding a jug of rose water and a bowl, with a small towel over his wrist. Athelstan smiled at the fellow, extended his fingers and carefully washed away the sugary-sweet substance from Fitzroy's mouth. He dried his hands carefully on the towel and walked back to the group.

'I believe Master Fitzroy was murdered,' he declared. 'I have seen seizures before, but not like this one. Death was too sudden and I detect a strange smell on his lips.'

The powerful Guildmasters stared at Athelstan: they believed him now and their arrogant looks were tinged by fear and suspicion.

'Who sat on either side of him?' Cranston asked the unspoken question.

'I did,' Goodman declared. 'I sat to his right.'

'And I to his left,' Sudbury added. 'Why, what are you implying?'

Cranston looked at the servants huddled near the door. 'You, sir.' One stubby finger singled out a frightened-looking steward. 'Come here!'

The fellow scuttled forward.

'Did Sir Thomas Fitzroy eat or drink anything we did not?'

'No, sir. All food was served from the one platter and his wine came from the same jugs as everyone else's.'

'I will stand as surety for that.' Bremmer, Guildmaster of the Drapers, spoke up.

'As will I,' Marshall of the Spicers declared. 'You see, old Fitzroy liked his food and drink. Bremmer and I had a quiet wager that Fitzroy would ask for double portions of everything and his cups be refilled more than anyone else's. I was right,' the spicer added slyly, glancing quickly at Cranston. 'He ate and drank even more than you, Sir John.'

Cranston glared back and belched loudly as if that was the only answer such a statement warranted. He turned to Bremmer. 'You are sure of that?'

'I am, Sir John.'

'And you?' Beginning to sway slightly, Cranston looked sharply at the steward.

Oh, Lord, Athelstan prayed silently, don't let Sir John sit down and go to sleep. Not now. Please, please!

Cranston, however, seemed to have the bit between his teeth as he advanced threateningly on the frightened steward.

'Are you sure that Fitzroy ate and drank only what we did?'

'Of course, Sir John. You see,' the steward turned, bobbing to the King and the Regent, 'all meats and all drinks were served to His Grace the King and My Lord of Gaunt first, then to everyone else. If any servitor had returned for more wine or meat by the time he had reached Sir Thomas, I would have remembered.'

'Can the servants be trusted?' Goodman jibed.

The steward glared furiously back. 'How could any of us,' he retorted, 'whilst serving meat and drink with both hands, stop to sprinkle or pour poison with others, including Fitzroy, watching?'

'I only asked!' Goodman smirked.

Cranston made a rude sound and walked over to Athelstan. He towered above the friar and glared down at him. 'You'd better be right!' he hissed.

'Don't worry, my good Coroner.' Athelstan smiled. 'Ah, here comes the physician.'

Theobald de Troyes, swathed in a voluminous cloak, strode into the room, eyes heavy with sleep and face angry at being disturbed so late. Adam Clifford arrived at the same time, his riding boots covered in mud, the spurs still attached, clinking and jangling. As the physician went to crouch beside the corpse, Gaunt signalled Clifford away from the rest and stood whispering. Athelstan watched Clifford's face and knew that not only was he right about Fitzroy but, from the look of surprised anger on the Regent's face, this second murder was a major blow to Gaunt's political dreams.

Clifford asked the Regent a question. Gaunt drew back his head sharply and shook his head. Clifford strode forward, pushing his way through the group of Guild-masters. Without a by-your-leave, he curtly ordered the physician to stand aside whilst he searched the dead man's wallet, ignoring cries of protest from the others. At last he found what he was searching for and, with a key in his hands, beamed triumphantly at Gaunt.

'We have it, My Lord!'

'Good!' The Regent sighed with relief. 'Keep it for a while.' He turned. 'Master physician, can you determine the cause of death?'

'Oh, yes.' De Troyes got to his feet, wiping his hands on his robe. 'Oh, yes,' the physician repeated sarcastically. 'First, Sir Thomas is dead. Second, the cause is murder. And third, the means is probably white arsenic admin-istered to his food and drink.'

'Impossible!' Goodman shouted, his bulbous eyes glaring at the doctor. 'How do you know he didn't eat or drink something before he came here?'

'Now, now.' The physician held up his slender fingers. 'I am merely the physician, not the poisoner.' De Troyes turned, choosing to ignore Goodman. He smiled and bowed at Sir John and Athelstan. 'My Lord Coroner, Brother Athelstan, so we meet again?' The physician enjoyed seeing Goodman's bubbling fury at being snubbed. 'You are the city Coroner, Sir John. I have been summoned here to determine the cause of death and have given it. May I now ask a question of my own? How long were you feasting here before Fitzroy collapsed?'

'About three hours,' Cranston replied. 'Why?'

'Well, white arsenic would take about an hour to strike at the humours. The patient would feel some discomfort but perhaps dismiss it as wind or a piece of food stuck in the stomach. Death, however, follows rapidly after.'

'Well, he did complain,' Sir James Denny spoke up. 'He mentioned some discomfort but, as is well known, Fitzroy liked his food and ate like a pig.'

'Sir John,' the physician continued, ignoring the Guild-master, 'you have my verdict: Fitzroy was poisoned here. Now, do you need my assistance any further?'

'Yes, we do.' The young King, who had been conversing with his tutor, Sir Nicholas Hussey, tapped his boots until he had everyone's attention. Richard's voice was surprisingly strong. 'We have established certain matters, have we not, dearest Uncle?' He smiled at Gaunt's sullen expression. 'First, Sir Thomas Fitzroy has been murdered by poison. Second, the poison was administered here. Yet, third, Sir Thomas Fitzroy ate and drank what we did.'

Gaunt bowed. 'Your Grace, my dear nephew, you are as usual most perceptive. A wise head on such young shoulders. So what do you advise next?'

'Let My Lord Coroner finish his task.'

Cranston bowed, walked back to Fitzroy's table and removed the napkin. He beckoned the physician over and he, Brother Athelstan and the Coroner carefully examined the remnants of the food, the wine cup, and Fitzroy's napkin and knife. The others looked on, moving restlessly and talking amongst themselves. De Troyes, despite being a fussy man, listened carefully to what Athelstan said as they sniffed, touched and slightly tasted everything on the table.

'Nothing,' de Troyes declared. 'My Lord Coroner, I suggest the remnants of all this food be given to me. There are ways of testing it – perhaps left as rat bait. But I must conclude there's no poison in anything on Sir Thomas's table.'

Athelstan stood perplexed. He was sure that no one had touched anything after Fitzroy's collapse. He and Cranston had been the first to cross to the stricken man and, even as Fitzroy had sprung to his feet, clutching his throat, Athelstan had carefully watched the men on either side of him. Neither Goodman nor Denny had made any move to take or replace anything on the table. Sir John carefully went through the dead man's pouch but could find nothing which would explain Fitzroy's sudden death by poison.

The atmosphere in the hall had now subtly changed. People were drawing apart as the full implications of the day's events sunk in. Sudbury spoke for them all.

'My Lord of Gaunt,' he declared defensively, 'we began this day in such amity, yet within hours two of our company are dead, foully murdered.'

'What are you implying?' Clifford snapped. 'These deaths cannot be laid at the Lord Regent's door!'

'I merely describe what has happened,' the Guildmaster replied smoothly.

'Your Grace.' Determined to take charge of the situation, Gaunt walked towards his nephew. 'Your Grace,' he repeated, 'you should retire. Sir Nicholas!' He glared at the royal tutor.

'We will go now,' Richard declared. 'But, sweet Uncle, two foul murders have occurred in the Guildhall. Someone must account for them.' Spinning on his heel, the young King swept out of the Hall of Roses, followed by Hussey and the physician.

Gaunt waited until they had gone. 'Clear the room!' he ordered the serjeant-at-arms.

'Sir,' the steward spoke up. 'The banquet is not yet finished. Shall I serve the dessert?'

Gaunt's look of fury answered his question and the steward and the other servants scuttled from the hall.

Clifford whispered to the archers and soldiers that they too should leave. He had no sooner closed the door behind them than a loud knocking made him re-open it. Athelstan glimpsed a liveried servant who muttered a few words and thrust a piece of parchment into Clifford's hand. He re-closed the door and walked into the centre of the room, read the parchment then handed it to the Regent. Gaunt studied it and fury flared in his face.

'Take your seats!' he ordered. 'I have news for you.'

They all obeyed, Athelstan and Cranston included. Gaunt sat down in the King's chair, the piece of parchment held before him. They waited until the four archers, summoned by Clifford, came in and bundled Fitzroy's corpse unceremoniously into a canvas sheet, carrying it out of the room with as much care as they would a heap of refuse. Gaunt stared round the now silent, watchful guests.

'I have a proclamation.' His voice rose to a shout. 'From the miscreant traitor who calls himself Ira Dei!' He flung the parchment at Clifford.

The nobleman smoothed it out. '"Sir Thomas Fitzroy",' Clifford read, '"executed for crimes against the people." Signed, Ira Dei.' He looked up and Athelstan sensed the fear in all of Gaunt's guests. Even Cranston, not easily intimidated, bowed his head.

'What is this?' Goodman muttered hoarsely. 'Who is this miscreant who can strike down the greatest in the city?'

'I don't know.' Athelstan spoke up, trying to dispel the atmosphere of fear. 'But now we are assured of three things. First, Fitzroy was murdered. Second, his murder was committed by, or on the orders of, this man who calls himself Ira Dei.' He paused and looked sideways at Cranston.

'And third?' Gaunt questioned.

'Your Grace, it is obvious. Fitzroy's death has not been announced publicly. This proclamation, pinned on the Guildhall doors, proves one of two things: either Ira Dei is present in this room and had one of his henchmen attach such a notice, or one of his henchmen is now with us and this Anger of God, as he terms himself, pinned up the notice himself.'

'What about the guards?' Cranston asked. 'We saw them as we came in.'

'They were withdrawn into the Guildhall once the banquet had begun,' Gaunt replied crossly.

'In which case, my clerk must be right,' Cranston tartly observed. 'Whatever interpretation you put on it, Your Grace, you have a murderous traitor in your midst!'

Athelstan's words had already provoked raised eyebrows. When they were repeated by the Coroner, consternation broke out.

'What are you saying?' Goodman shouted, getting to his feet, all court etiquette forgotten.

'It's imperative!' the foppish Denny shouted. 'Your Grace, we must inspect the gold each of us deposited in the chest in the Guildhall chapel.' He pulled out the key hanging from his neck on a silver chain, very similar to the one Clifford had removed from the dead Fitzroy.

'I agree,' the red-haired Sudbury declared, his face even more flushed from the claret he was gulping. 'Your Grace, this is a disaster. For all our sakes, the chest must be examined.'

Gaunt looked at Clifford who nodded perceptibly. The Regent removed a silver chain from round his own neck. The key which swung from it glinted in the candlelight.

'It's best if we do,' he agreed.

Clifford called the guards and, led by four serjeants-at-arms bearing torches, Gaunt and his now subdued guests, Cranston and Athelstan included, marched along the vaulted passageways, up the wide wooden stairs and into the small Guildhall chapel. They stood for a while just within the door, peering through the darkness, smelling the fragrance of incense; the guards lit flambeaux, as well as the candles they found on the high altar. The chapel, a small jewel with polished marble pillars, mosaic floor and painted walls, flared into life. The marble altar at the far end was covered by pure white cloths. They walked towards it. Gaunt deftly pulled the cloths aside. Beneath the altar, supported on four pillars, sat a long wooden chest reinforced with iron bands. Even in the poor light, Athelstan could see the six locks along one side.

'Pull it out!' Gaunt ordered.

Two soldiers brought it forward so that it stood before the altar. Even this action caused consternation, for the chest seemed surprisingly light. Gaunt shouted for silence as he, followed by Clifford, who held Fitzroy's, inserted and turned their keys. The Guildmasters followed suit, the clasps were lowered and the chest opened. Athelstan and Cranston peered over the shoulders of the others.

'Nothing!' Marshall breathed.

Cranston, quicker than the rest, pushed forward and plucked up the piece of yellow parchment lying on the bottom.

'"These taxes have been collected",' he read aloud, '"by the Great Community of the Realm." Signed, Ira Dei.'

'This is intolerable!' Denny shouted. 'My Lord of Gaunt, we have been betrayed in this matter!'

But the Regent, his face white as a ghost, sat slumped in the sanctuary chair, staring into the darkness, his lips moving wordlessly. Cranston, who had known John of Gaunt since he was a boy, had never seen him look so frightened or bewildered.

'This is the devil's work,' Gaunt muttered.

His words were ignored as the other Guildmasters shouted and cursed. Clifford stood, mouth agape, staring down at the empty chest. Cranston shook him roughly by the shoulder.

'For God's sake, man!' he hissed. 'Clear the chapel. This does no one any good.'

Clifford broke out of his reverie and clapped his hands loudly. 'My Lord of Gaunt must ponder this matter!' he shouted above the hubbub.

'What matter?' Sudbury screamed back. 'My Lord of Gaunt stretches out his hand and we clasp it. He talks of amity between himself and the city – now two of our company are dead. The gold we deposited here has been stolen and the miscreant, Ira Dei, not only murders and robs but makes a mockery of us all. What shall we report to our Guilds, eh? How do we tell our brethren that thousands of pounds sterling are now missing?'

'My Lord of Gaunt will act,' Cranston replied. 'He is Regent, acting for the Crown. Is any man here going to commit treason and claim My Lord of Gaunt is responsible for this?' He stared at Goodman the Mayor, leaning against the altar, a look of stupefaction on his face.

'The chapel is to be cleared. My Lord Mayor, you should stay.'

At last Cranston's authority prevailed and the Guild-masters, muttering amongst themselves and throwing black glances over their shoulders, trooped out of the chapel. Gaunt waited until the door closed behind them then lifted his face from his hands.

'Sir John, Brother Athelstan, I thank you for that.' He got to his feet. 'But what shall we do? The Guildmas-ters are right. Each has lost a thousand pounds sterling.

Mountjoy and Fitzroy are dead, and Ira Dei dances round me as if I was some bloody maypole.' He gestured with his hand. Athelstan and Cranston sat down, Goodman and Lord Adam Clifford likewise. Gaunt covered his face with his hands then rubbed his eyes and looked at Cranston.

'What do you propose, My Lord Coroner?'

Cranston shook his head. Athelstan caught a spark of anger in the Regent's eyes. Sir John would have to move quickly or he might well become the scapegoat for the rage boiling in the Regent's heart.

'Your Grace.' Athelstan rose to his feet. He tried to shake off his own tiredness, curbing his desire to flee back to his own quiet church in Southwark.

'Your Grace,' he repeated, 'two men have been foully murdered, but all assassins make mistakes and we have yet to reflect upon the events of this calamitous day. However, the removal of the gold from a chest which could only be opened by six separate keys is most mysterious. I have a number of questions. First, who made the chest?'

'Peter Sturmey,' Clifford replied, 'a trusted locksmith whose services are retained by the Crown. I doubt very much whether he would act the traitor in this. His own son is an Exchequer official who was recently in an affray at Colchester whilst trying to collect taxes.'

Athelstan held up his hand. 'Then what about the chest itself? My Lord Regent, perhaps we might examine it?'

Gaunt grunted his assent and Athelstan, assisted by Cranston and Clifford, with Goodman looking on, turned the chest over, knocking at the wooden panelling, examining the locks.

Cranston shook his head. 'Good and true,' he breathed, getting to his feet. 'The chest has no secret compartments.' He studied the clasp and locks. 'None of these has been tampered with.'

Athelstan flicked the dust from his robes. 'Therefore, my third question. Could there have been a master key?'

'Impossible!' Clifford snapped. 'Each lock is unique.' He drew out two of the keys which the Guildmasters had left. 'I am no locksmith, Brother, but study these carefully. Look!' He held both of them up against the candlelight. 'See the curves and notches of each key? They are quite separate and distinct. Indeed, My Lord of Gaunt insisted that they be so.'

Athelstan rubbed his mouth to hide his dismay.

'Your fourth question begs itself,' Clifford added. 'Did Sturmey make a duplicate of each key? But that,' he continued hurriedly, seeing the Regent shake his head, 'would make Sturmey a traitor who cheerfully handed over his keys to another for the locks to be opened.'

'Devil's tits!' Cranston murmured. 'How could it be done? Was the chapel guarded?'

Goodman shrugged. 'No, why should it be? The chest was heavy with gold, and with six locks...' His voice trailed off.

'Who planned all this?' Athelstan asked. 'I mean, the gold ingots, the chest?'

Clifford pulled a face and looked at Goodman. 'The idea of the chest and the gold being deposited there,' he replied, 'came from My Lord of Gaunt, though it was myself and Sir Gerard Mountjoy who chose Sturmey.' He smiled. 'The Guildmasters insisted on that.'

'Because they didn't trust me!' Gaunt snapped. 'I had nothing to do with the construction of the chest or the fashioning of its locks or the making of its keys. Both I and the Guildmasters decided we should best leave that to our worthy city officials here. They brought the chest and the keys direct from Sturmey's shop this morning.'

'And, before you ask,' Lord Adam intervened, 'never once did any of them hold all six keys together. My Lord Mayor bought three, Mountjoy the rest. The transaction was witnessed by both Fitzroy and Sudbury and the chest was carried by city bailiffs.'

Cranston looked, narrow-eyed, into the darkness, a gesture the Coroner always used when he was deep in thought.

Sir John Athelstan exclaimed. 'What is the matter?'

Cranston smacked his lips, a sure sign that, even at this very late hour, he was beginning to miss his claret.

'Sturmey,' he said. 'The name of Sturmey means something to me. Now why is that, eh? Why should a reputable locksmith, patronized by the great and the noble, strike a chord in my old memory?'

Athelstan grinned. Cranston's memory was prodigious. He knew the names and most of the faces of London's rogues and, even in a crowded Cheapside, could bellow out warnings to pickpockets and foists.

'What does Sturmey's name mean to you?' Gaunt asked quickly.

The Coroner shook his head. 'It will come.' He bowed. 'My Lord Regent, if you will excuse me and my clerk, it is imperative we call on this locksmith tonight. Where does he live?'

'In Lawrence Lane, just off the Mercery,' Clifford replied.

'Then,' Cranston grinned at Athelstan who just glared back in tired annoyance, 'we'd best call upon master locksmith of Lawrence Lane near the Mercery and ask him a few questions, eh?' He bowed to the Regent once more. Gaunt looked away. Cranston shrugged and walked down the church, a despondent Athelstan trailing behind.

'Cranston!'

Sir John turned. Gaunt was now standing on the altar steps.

'You know the Guildmasters will be back. Oh, they'll be reasonable. They'll demand their gold and their answers within a set time.' He wagged a finger. 'I need answers, too, my Lord Coroner, within ten days at the most.' He left the unspoken threat hanging in the air as Cranston spun on his heel and walked out of the Guildhall chapel.

Chapter 5

Once out in Cheapside Cranston stopped and stared up at the moon. 'The devil's piss on them!' he cursed. 'Cock's blood! What a stinking pot of turds! What a mess! The whoreson, beetle-headed, fat-bellied, treacherous bastards!'

Athelstan smiled. 'You are, My Lord Coroner, referring to our brothers in Christ, the Guildmasters?'

'Yes, monk, I am.' Cranston plucked his miraculous wineskin from beneath his cloak and gulped heartily. 'Lord,' he breathed, 'what a mess! How was Fitzroy killed, Brother? He didn't take the poison before the meal, and his food and all the cutlery bore no sign of any potion.'

Athelstan shook his head. 'You are ahead of me, Sir John. I am still wondering about Mountjoy's death.' The friar stared across the darkened Cheapside, his gaze attracted by the lantern horns fixed outside the great merchants' houses. He recalled the words of his old lecturer, Father Paul: 'The root of all sin,' the old friar had boomed, 'is pride. And the opposite of love is not hatred or indifference but power. Power corrupts; the pursuit of it is the road to Hell.'

We are on that road now, Athelstan thought, thronged by powerful men with a raging thirst for the best things in life. We are all killers, he concluded, and despite the warm evening air, shivered. He felt like a masked swordsman being thrust into a pitch-black tourney thronged by killers. 'I want to go home,' he whispered before he could stop himself.

Cranston looked at him curiously. 'This is your home, Brother.'

Athelstan smiled and shook himself free from his reverie. 'Aye, Sir John, but we have a locksmith to question. Tell me, why are you puzzled by Sturmey's name?'

Cranston blessed himself, took three more swigs from the wineskin, popped back the stopper and, linking his arm through Athelstan's, guided him up the Poultry.

'I don't know,' he muttered. 'But the name rings a bell. It will take time, Brother.'

Athelstan pinched his nostrils, for this part of Cheapside still stank of dead birds. He tried not to look at the rats racing between the cesspits in the centre of the street to forage amongst the juicy morsels of giblets and decapitated heads of chickens, partridge, quail and plover. Two white feathers floated by and Athelstan thought of angels.

'No angels here,' he muttered.

'You're dead bloody right!' Cranston retorted.

They jumped and stepped aside as two old ladies suddenly turned the corner, pushing a hand cart, the corpse of another old harridan sprawled over it. Athelstan sketched a blessing in the air. One of the old crones looked over her shoulder and cackled.

'Gone she has,' she screeched. 'Died of the flux and it's the lime pits for her.'

'I wish I could stop that,' Cranston observed. 'They will dump the body on some church steps.'

The cart trailed away into the darkness and they continued into the Mercery. Two whores stood on the corner of an alleyway, their saffron dresses and red wigs shining like beacons in the gloom.

'Hello, ladies!' Cranston shouted. 'You know the law?'

'What law?' the taller of the two replied. 'We are a prayer group.'

'It's Cranston!' the shorter one hissed, and the two ladies of the night fled like fireflies up the darkened alley.

Athelstan and Cranston turned into Lawrence Lane, a dark tunnel because the houses on either side leaned over so close, a person in the highest story could actually tap on a window opposite.

'Mind your step!' Cranston warned.

Athelstan looked down and realized the sewer in the centre of the street had overflowed, drenching the cobbles with all kinds of putrid filth. The street reeked of sulphur which some good citizen must have poured in to kill the stench. Dark forms edged out of alleyways. Cranston tugged his cloak over his shoulders and pulled out his long Welsh stabbing dagger.

'Good evening, my buckos! I'm Jack Cranston, Coroner.'

The sinister shadows disappeared.

They continued on, Cranston stopping to look at the shop signs which hung on poles just above their heads. At last, just before Lawrence Lane ran into Catte Street, he stopped and pointed to a sign creaking on rusting chains. It bore the legend 'Peter Sturmey, Locksmith'. Cranston stepped back and looked up. He could see candlelight glowing in one of the upper stories so began to hammer on the door.

'Piss off!' someone shouted from across the street.

Athelstan and Cranston moved quickly as the foul contents of a night pot were hurled down.

'Sod off!' Cranston yelled back. 'I am an officer of the law!'

'I couldn't care if you were the King himself!' the voice shouted back, but they heard the casement window snap shut and Cranston went back to his hammering.

At last his perseverance was rewarded. They heard footsteps, the door was pulled back on its chains and the pallid face of a maid, ghostly in the candlelight, peered out at them.

'Who is it?' she murmured. 'What is the matter? Do you have news of my master?'

'Open the door!' Cranston murmured. 'That's a good lass. I am the city Coroner and this is Brother Athelstan. We must have words with your master.'

The chains were loosened and the maid, swathed in a cloak, stepped back to allow them in. In the candlelight the passageway came alive with dancing, flickering shapes.

'I want your master,' Cranston repeated gently.

'Sir, he is not here. He left this afternoon and has not returned.'

Athelstan closed his eyes. 'Oh, God!' he breathed.

'What is it?'

A tousle-haired boy, heavy-eyed with sleep but with the face of an angel, suddenly darted from a room off the passageway, a lantern almost as big as his head held high in one hand.

'And who are you, sir?' Cranston asked.

'Perrot,' he replied. 'Master Sturmey's apprentice.'

The boy came closer. Athelstan judged him to be about thirteen or fourteen summers old and, once again, was reminded of an angel Huddle had painted on the walls of St Erconwald's.

'The master's gone,' the boy said flatly. 'He went out just after noon and he hasn't come back.'

'And the lady of the house?'

'She's gone too and won't be back.'

'Why not?'

'She died five years ago.'

Athelstan grinned and plucked a penny from his purse. He spun it and the boy nimbly caught it.

'And Sturmey's son?'

'He's gone too,' the maid and apprentice chorused.

'He's in York. Some important business of the King.'

Cranston nodded as he looked at the two solemn faces.

'Look,' he said reassuringly, 'we can't discuss things here. You, boy, you sleep in the shop?'

'Aye, I do.'

'Then let's go there.'

The boy blinked and looked at the maid, who nodded.

'Come on then,' Perrot instructed. 'But you mustn't touch anything, otherwise the master will beat me.'

He led them into a room off the passageway, lit candles and pulled out two stools for his unexpected visitors. Athelstan sat down and stared around. He'd never seen so many keys. They hung in bunches on the wall or lay on benches around the whitewashed room, together with pieces of metal, casting irons, pincers. He glimpsed the small forge on the outside wall. The place smelt of burnt wood and charcoal and everything was covered in a fine grey dust. He looked under one table and saw the apprentice's bed: a straw mattress, a bolster, a woollen blanket and a rather battered wooden horseman. Perhaps the boy's favourite toy.

'Would you like some wine?' the maid invited, trying to act older than she was.

'No, no.' Athelstan smiled. 'Sir John never touches wine, do you, My Lord Coroner?'

'No, no,' Cranston gruffly replied, narrowing his eyes at Athelstan. He drew himself up. 'It sets a fine example.'

The boy peered at the large Coroner under lowered eyelashes, as if only half-convinced.

'Where did your master go?' Cranston asked.

'I don't know, he just left the shop.'

'And how was he?'

'Very excited,' the apprentice replied.

'About what?'

'Oh, making the chest for the great lords, and the keys.'

'Tell me.' Cranston leaned forward, trying to keep the wineskin concealed under his cloak. 'Did you help your master make the chest, its locks and keys?'

'Oh, yes.'

'And how many keys did he make?'

'Six.'

'Didn't he make any more just in case one was lost?'

'Oh, no, my master said that was forbidden.'

'And,' Athelstan intervened, 'did he have any visitors to the shop? Someone mysterious, cloaked and hooded?'

'No.' The boy laughed. 'Why should he?'

His eyes flickered and he looked away. You are hiding something, Athelstan thought, but nothing to do with this.

'And which of the great ones came here?'

'Well, they all came here yesterday,' Perrot replied. 'In their cloaks, boots and beaver hats, they nigh filled the house. They had to take the chest and keys to the Guildhall. There were soldiers outside with a cart.'

'Yes,' Athelstan continued. 'But before your master finished the keys and the locks, did any of the great ones come to see him privately?'

'I don't think so,' the boy replied. 'I live here, and sleep here. Master always brings his visitors here except when he is working in his garden. He likes to go there by himself. Says he likes the change.'

'But the visitors?' Athelstan persisted.

'Two large fat ones,' the boy replied, 'the Lord Mayor and the Sheriff. They always came together over the last two weeks to make sure my master was doing his work.'

'And no one else?'

'No, Father.'

Athelstan's eyes turned to the young maid standing next to the boy. 'And you saw nothing mysterious or untoward?'

They both shook their heads.

'What happened to the moulds?' Cranston moved his feet. 'The ones in which the keys were cast?'

'They were destroyed,' the boy replied proudly. 'When the great ones came for the chest and keys, they stood around and watched me smash them with a hammer.'

Cranston gazed at Athelstan who shook his head.

The Coroner lumbered to his feet, stretched and yawned; fishing in his pocket, he took out two pennies which he handed to the boy and girl.

'Very good!' he murmured. 'But when your master returns, tell him to find Sir John Cranston's house in Cheapside. I have to speak to him.'

The maid and apprentice nodded. Cranston and Athelstan walked back into Lawrence Lane and down to the corner of the Mercery.

'You know he'll never come back, Sir John?'

Cranston blew out his cheeks. 'Aye, tomorrow I'll issue an instruction to the officials to search amongst the corpses found throughout the city.' He stifled a yawn. 'Brother, you are welcome to share my house tonight.'

Athelstan looked up at the starlit sky. 'Thank you, Sir John, but I must return.'

He stood and watched as Cranston, shouting farewells, shuffled like some great bear up Cheapside. Suddenly he turned.

'Brother, I'll walk you to the bridge!'

'No, no, I insist, Sir John. I'll be safe. Who'd attack a poor friar?'

Cranston watched the priest cross the Mercery and go down Budge Row.

'Aye!' he whispered to himself. 'Who'd attack a poor friar? This city is full of bastards who would!'

Cranston waited until Athelstan had disappeared out of sight then followed him along Budge Row, down the

Walbrook into the Ropery and along Bridge Street. At the far end in a pool of light, their torches fixed on poles, guards stood at the entrance to the bridge. Cranston heard their indistinct voices as they questioned the friar. One of them laughed and Athelstan was allowed through. The Coroner sighed with relief but strained his ears once more as he heard the slither of footsteps behind him.

'Listen, you nightbirds,' he growled over his shoulder, 'this is old Jack, city Coroner. If you don't piss off, I'll have your balls round your necks!' When he turned, the street was empty.

Cranston went to relieve himself above a sewer, finished what he termed his 'devoir', fastened the points of his hose and smacked his lips. He made the sign of the cross and took a generous swig from the miraculous wineskin. Then he remembered the two dogs, Gog and Magog, and wondered what Lady Maude would think of them. Cranston groaned and decided another generous swig would not go amiss.

-

Athelstan sat at his table in the little priest's house just opposite St Erconwald's church in Southwark. He had returned to find everything in order. The church doors were locked, and someone had left a small jar of honey in one of the recesses; obviously a gift from one of his parishioners. His old horse Philomel was lying on his side, breathing heavily through flared nostrils as he dreamed of former glories when he had been a full-blooded destrier in the old King's wars. Athelstan stood by the stable door, talking to him for a while, but the old horse snored on, so the friar continued his survey of his little church plot. His garden was in good order, or the little he could see of it, whilst Bonaventure, the great mouser, the one-eyed prince of the alleyways, was apparently out on a night's courting or hunting.

Now he stared round the meagre kitchen. The walls had been freshly painted with lime against the flies. He closed his eyes and smelt the fragrant herbs sprinkled on the fresh green rushes and then looked at the cauldron over the fire. He half-raised himself to ensure the porridge he was cooking did not become too thick or congealed. He sighed, went into the buttery and brought back a jug of milk. It still smelt fresh, so he poured this into the cauldron, carefully stirring the porridge as Benedicta had instructed him.

'I wish I could cook,' he muttered.

He had once entertained Cranston to breakfast and the Coroner had sworn that Athelstan's porridge, if thrown by catapults, could break down any city wall. He returned the jug, wiped his hands on a towel and went back to stand over the table which was littered with pieces of parchment. Each scrap of parchment contained the details of a murder.

'What do we have?' Athelstan mockingly asked himself. 'How did Rosamund Ingham kill Sir John's companion, Sir Oliver? No mark of violence. No trace of poison.' He scratched his cheek. 'Was the man murdered? Or was Cranston just furious at seeing an old friend made a cuckold?'

And yet, he thought, Cranston, despite his bristling, white whiskers, florid face, great balding head and even bigger belly, was as shrewd and cunning as a serpent. Cranston had a nose for mischief; if Sir John thought a foul act had been committed, then he was usually right.

Athelstan picked up another piece of parchment and studied his crude drawing of the garden at the Guildhall where Mountjoy had been murdered. 'How on earth?' he muttered to himself. On one side was the high trellis fence against which the Sheriff had been leaning, to his left a sheer brick wall, to his right the garden fence guarded by the dogs and, facing him, the wooden fence of the pentice connecting the Guildhall to its kitchen. How could an assassin enter such an enclosed space and stab the burly Mountjoy to death without any clamour from the Sheriff or his fearsome dogs?

And, finally, there was Fitzroy, killed by an unseen hand. Who could deal poison without revealing how it was done? Who was this Ira Dei? Which of these powerful politicians was the traitor?

Athelstan shook his head and went back to his parish accounts. He felt tired but, since his return from the city, he had snatched only a few hours' sleep before rising, reciting his office by candlelight, washing and dressing upstairs in his small bed chamber. Athelstan pulled the accounts over. He was sick of murder, intrigue and mystery, and the figures had to be totalled before he met the parish council at Michaelmas.

Athelstan nibbled at the edge of his quill. The power struggle on his little parish council was just as fierce as that of any Guildmaster. Watkin the dung-collector, Mugwort the bell ringer, Tab the tinker, Huddle the painter, Ursula the pig woman, Cecily the courtesan, and Tiptoe the pot boy from The Piebald tavern were still fighting off a bitter attack headed by Pike the ditcher. The latter was aided by Jacob Arveld, a pleasant-faced German with a comely wife and brood of children, Clement of Cock Lane, Pernell the Fleming and Ranulf the rat-catcher, whilst Athelstan and the widow woman, Benedicta, tried to keep the peace.

Benedicta... there she was in his mind's eye: her jet-black hair framing a smooth olive face which Huddle the painter always used in his depictions of the Virgin Mary.

Athelstan stared at the hungry flames of the fire and remembered Father Paul's warning: 'Never forget, it's not the physical longing for a woman which will haunt you but the sheer, empty loneliness, the bittersweet taste of longing for someone you can never possess.' He jumped as a dark form slunk through the window.

'Ah, good morning, Bonaventure, my most faithful parishioner.'

The great tom cat padded softly across to his master and looked hungrily at the porridge bubbling over the fire. Athelstan got up and brought him a bowl of milk from the buttery. The cat licked it daintily and nestled down in front of the fire whilst his master went back to considering his troubled parishioners. He had to have peace on the council, particularly if Watkin's daughter was to be wed to Pike the ditcher's son.

'Oh, Lord!' he said to a now snoozing Bonaventure. 'That will put the cat amongst the pigeons!'

Bonaventure moved his head lazily; his one good amber eye seemed full of compassion for his master. Athelstan pulled the accounts closer. He wondered if the woman had come back about her possessed stepdaughter and shivered at what could be awaiting him there. He coughed, dipped his quill in the ink pot and began to fill in the entries, listing what he had spent in decorating the church now the new sanctuary had been laid:

- *Correcting the Ten Commandments 3s.*

- *Varnishing Pontius Pilate and putting in a front tooth 5d.*

- *Renewing Heaven, adjusting the stars & cleaning the moon 20s.*

- *Taking the spots off the Son of Tobias 4s.6d.*

- *Brightening up the Flames of Hell, putting a new left horn on the Devil & cleaning tail 3s.*

- *Jobs for the Damned 2s.6d.*

- *Putting New Shirt on Jonah & enlarging the Whale's mouth accordingly 10s.6d.*

- *Putting new leaves on Adam and Eve 15s.*

Athelstan looked at the list and smiled. He was about to continue when suddenly he heard a gentle tapping on the door. He went across, opened it and looked out. It was the watching time, just before dawn, the sky already lightening and the shadows beginning to disappear.

'Who is it?' he called and looked around. It was too early for any urchin's game. 'Who is it?' Athelstan repeated. Only the wind rattling a loose shutter in the church disturbed the silence. The hairs on the nape of his neck prickled. He felt a shiver down his back. He stared down the track beside the church. Was it some rogue? Some drunk from the stews of Southwark? Suddenly he saw the little wicket gate to the church stood half-open. He grasped the staff Cranston had given him and walked across.

'Brother Athelstan!'

The voice seemed to be coming from behind the church and the friar, followed by an even more inquisitive Bonaventure, warily walked round. Again the voice called his name and Athelstan stared out across the headstones.

'Who is it?' he shouted angrily. 'This is no game but God's house and God's own acre!'

'Turn round, Brother Athelstan!'

'Why should I?'

A crossbow bolt smacked into the church wall beside his head.

'I am convinced,' Athelstan shouted back and turned round, eyes closed, fingers clenched. 'What is it you want?'

'A message from the Anger of God. You are a friar, a priest of the people. Why do you mingle with the fat lords of the soil?'

'If you're his anger,' Athelstan spat back, 'then I am his justice!'

'Take heed of his anger,' the voice said clearly.

Athelstan looked down at Bonaventure who seemed to be enjoying this new game.

'Cranston's right,' Athelstan whispered. 'You *are* no bloody use!'

'Take heed,' the voice repeated.

Athelstan's fiery temper broke at last. 'Oh, sod off!' he shouted and stalked down the church track and into his house, closing the door with a slam.

For a while he just stood with his back to it, trying to calm the trembling in his legs. Who dared taunt him here? What would Cranston do when he heard? Athelstan marched into the buttery and poured himself a cup of wine, which he gulped down before going back to sit at the table.

'God damn it!' he breathed. He closed the ledger book, cleared up the rest of the manuscripts and took them across to the huge, iron-bound coffer. As he placed them inside and made the lock secure, he thought of the daring robbery at the Guildhall. He only hoped Sturmey was still alive. If Cranston and he found the thief, they would discover the murderer. He jumped at a loud knocking on the door.

'Father! Father!'

Athelstan went across and opened the door to find Ursula the pig woman, her usually merry, red, warty face now tear-streaked.

'Oh, Ursula!' Athelstan said. 'It's not your sow? I can't come and bless it again!'

'No, no, Father, it's my mother. She's dying!'

'Are you sure?' Athelstan asked. 'I have given the last rites to Griselda at least three times.'

'No, Father, she says she's going. She can feel she is.'

'Come on then.'

Athelstan locked the door of the house and hurried across to the church. Inside it was cool and dark, smelling fragrantly of candle grease and incense. The morning light was already beginning to brighten Huddle's pictures on the wall as Athelstan hurried under the rood screen and into the sanctuary. He genuflected, opening the tabernacle door to remove the Viaticum and phial of holy oils. Then he collected his stole, cloak, tinder and a candle from the sacristy and gave them to Ursula, waiting in the porch of the church. He lit the candle, wrapped the cloak round himself and, with the pig woman shielding the candle's flame in her great, raw hands, locked the door of his church.

He followed Ursula through the narrow, winding streets of Southwark to the pig woman's house, a small, two-storeyed tenement just behind the priory of St Mary Overy. As usual, the great sow, Ursula's pet and the light of her life, lay basking in front of the fire whilst, behind a curtain in the far corner, Griselda lay on a pallet of straw, head back, her beak-like nose cutting the air, her eyes half-open. Athelstan would have taken her for dead already had it not been for the gentle rise and fall of her skinny chest. As Athelstan crouched beside her, placing the Viaticum and holy oils on a three-legged stool, Ursula stood behind him, still holding the candle. Of course, the sow had to see what was happening and, once she recognized Athelstan, whose cabbage patch she regularly plundered, began to snort and snuffle excitedly.

'Oh, for God's sake, go away!' he breathed. 'Ursula, for the love of God, give her a cabbage or something!'

'She doesn't eat cabbages,' Ursula curtly replied as she grabbed the sow by the ear and pulled her away.

'Aye,' Athelstan whispered to himself. 'The bloody thing only likes fresh ones!'

'Is that you, Father?'

Athelstan bent over the old lady, her cheeks hollow, thick bloodless lips parted. But the small button eyes were still bright with life.

'Yes, Mother Griselda, it's Athelstan.'

'You are a good priest,' the old woman wheezed, 'to come and see old Griselda. Do you want to hear my confession, Father?'

Athelstan grinned. 'Why, what have you been up to, Mother, since I heard it last? How many young men this time?'

The old woman's lips parted in a gumless smile.

'What lechery and wantonness?' Athelstan continued, peering down at the old lady. 'Come, Griselda, you have long made your peace with God.'

Athelstan opened the golden pyx, took out the white host and placed it between the dying woman's lips. Then he began to anoint her head and eyes, mouth, chest, hands and feet, whilst the old woman's mouth chewed the thin wafer host. At last he finished. Ursula went to move across to tend the small fire whilst Griselda took Athelstan's hand.

'Will I go to Heaven, Father?'

'Of course.'

'Will my husband be there?'

'Why not?'

'He loved women, Father! In his youth he was as handsome as the sun. He had hair the colour of corn and eyes blue as the sky. But he wasn't a bad man, Father, and I loved him.' She coughed, yellow spittle drooling out of the corner of her mouth. Athelstan picked up a rag and dabbed gently at her lips.

'God will not reject,' he said slowly, 'anyone who has loved or been loved.'

The old woman coughed again. Athelstan looked over his shoulder.

'Ursula, a cup of water.'

But then he felt the grip on his hand loosen. He looked down. Griselda's head had rolled slightly to the left. He felt for the beat in her neck but there was nothing. He looked up at Ursula, holding the battered cup, tears streaming down her fat cheeks.

'She's left us,' Athelstan murmured. 'She's gone now. Gone ahead of us.'

He stayed for a while to comfort Ursula. Despite his protests, she insisted on giving him a huge flitch of bacon then, with his cope and stole under one arm, the flitch of bacon under another, Athelstan walked back to his church.

Southwark was now coming to life. The petty traders and tinkers trundled their hand carts down towards the bridge whilst sweating, cursing carters tried to get produce from the country across the river before the great markets opened. Two lepers covered in black rags begged for alms outside the hospital of St Thomas whilst the local beadles and bailiffs led the night roisterers they had caught, bound hand and foot, down to the stocks. Two drunks who had pissed out of an upper-floor window had already been tied back-to-back, their breeches about their ankles. They would be forced to walk the streets and be pelted with rubbish until noonday when a friend could cut them loose. The officials had apparently also raided a brothel and a cart load of whores, their heads completely shaven, sat morosely manacled together as they were taken down to the river to be punished. A yellow, lean-ribbed dog snarled at Athelstan, jumping, lips curled to bite the bacon. Athelstan shooed it off, went up an alleyway and knocked on the door of Tab the tinker's house.

His wife, grey-haired and worried-looking, answered. Athelstan thrust the flitch of bacon into her hands.

'Father,' she murmured, 'I can't.'

'Yes, you can.' He pointed to the grubby-faced children clinging to her tattered dress. 'And they certainly will. But you mustn't tell Ursula.'

He continued his journey and was about to pass the door of his church when he saw the piece of parchment fluttering there. Athelstan read the scrawled words:

> The Anger of God will shout out like lightning from the clouds.

He cursed, pulled the parchment down, threw it into the mud and, ignoring Pike's salutations, angrily strode back to his house.

Chapter 6

Athelstan sat in the nave of his church, a group of young adults and children round him; this being a working day, their parents had attended morning Mass and left for their day's routine. Athelstan's school, as Cranston jokingly referred to it, met two hours before noon twice a week so the friar could try to educate the young in reading, writing, and the basics of arithmetic and geometry. Naturally, they were also instructed in their faith and Athelstan had been surprised at how quick and eager some of his students proved to be.

He looked round the group, his heart lurching with compassion as he gazed at their grimy, thin faces, make-shift clothes and tattered sandals. They sat in a circle, Bonaventure included, as Athelstan tried to explain how God was everywhere.

Now and again he stole glances at Pike's son Thomas who couldn't sit any closer to Watkin's beautiful daughter Petronella. Athelstan gazed at the girl's jet-black hair, smooth, white skin and sea-green eyes. How could Watkin and his portly wife have produced such a beautiful girl? Thomas was so deeply smitten by her, he hardly bothered even to glance in Athelstan's direction.

'Go on, Father!' Crim, the altar boy, shouted.

'Of course.' Athelstan rubbed his eyes. He was beginning to feel tired after his previous day's labour.

'Of course God is everywhere, he sees everything, hears everything.'

'Is he in my hand?' Crim asked.

'Of course.'

Crim clapped his hands together. 'In which case he's trapped. I've got him!'

'No, no,' Athelstan laughingly explained. 'It's not like that, Crim.'

'But you said he was everywhere?'

'Crim.' Athelstan leaned back on his ankles, wincing as his knee cracked. 'God is like the air we breathe. He's in us, part of us, yet at the same time outside of us. Like the air which you suck into your mouth and yet, at the same time, it is in your hand.'

Mugwort the bell ringer bounded into the church and Athelstan winced as the little goblin of a man disappeared into the small enclosure and began to tug like a demon at the bell, the sign for the mid-day Angelus. Athelstan said the prayer, got to his feet and dusted down his robe.

'You can play now. Crim, don't drink from the holy water stoup. John and James,' he glanced in mock severity at Tab the tinker's two sons, as like as two peas out of a pod with their grimy faces and greasy, spiked hair, 'the baptismal font is not a castle. You can play on the steps but not inside the church. Petronella and Thomas, stay for a while.'

The rest of the children grinned behind their hands and there was a chorus of 'oohing' and 'ahhing' as Athelstan ushered them out of the church. The two lovebirds were well known in the parish; to everyone, that is, except their parents.

'Father?'

'Yes, what is it?' Athelstan looked at the pinched white little face peering out of the tarry, pointed hood. 'What is it, Roland?'

The little boy whispered something and Athelstan had to crouch to listen as Ranulf the rat-catcher's son explained that his father wanted an urgent meeting with Athelstan.

'Yes, yes,' he replied, straightening up. 'Tell your father I'll see him tomorrow.'

He chewed his lip to hide his smile for the little boy was the image of his father, with the same cast of features as the very rodents he hunted. The boy scampered off to join the rest and Athelstan walked back up the nave where the two young lovers sat in front of the rood screen.

'Father.' Thomas got to his feet. 'You must see our parents soon.'

'Why?' Athelstan looked nervously at the girl. 'Has anything happened?'

She smiled and shook her head.

'Father,' she pleaded, 'we have come and told you our secret. You have checked the blood book, there are no ties between us except Thomas's great-great-uncle was married to a relation of my grandmother.' The girl ticked the points off on her fingers. 'We have agreed to receive instruction. Thomas has a fine job with the port reeve at Dowgate and I am very good at embroidery. Father, it was I who made the altar cloths. So why can't the banns be published?'

Athelstan held up his hand. 'All right. I will see your parents this Sunday after morning Mass. Perhaps they can all come for a glass of wine at my house to celebrate the good news?' He kept the fixed smile on his face as the two lovebirds jumped for joy and almost ran down the nave, hand in hand.

'Oh, Lord!' he breathed. 'There are only five days left till Sunday and the outbreak of civil war!'

'In which case I had better be there!'

Athelstan smiled. 'Benedicta,' he replied without turning round. 'How long have you been here?'

'Long enough to hear you talking to yourself, Father.'

Athelstan turned and walked down the church to where the widow woman stood, one hand on a pillar. She looked as elegant and beautiful as ever. Her smooth, olive-skinned face framed in a cream-coloured wimple, and those eyes which could be mocking, smiling, tearful, generous, sad and soulful, and those lips... Athelstan slipped his hands up the sleeves of his gown and pinched himself as he remembered the words of scripture: 'Even if you desire a woman in your mind's eye...' He unclasped his hands.

'Benedicta, what brings you here?'

She grinned impishly. 'How's the baking going for the autumn festival?'

'That,' Athelstan declared heatedly, 'is the least of my worries.'

He described his previous day's visit to the Guild-hall, breaking off only when Benedicta began to laugh at his description of Cranston and the two wolfhounds. However, as he described the killings, her face grew sombre.

'You should be careful, Father,' she murmured. 'The gossip is spreading through Southwark like fire in dry stubble. There's talk of a great revolt, of assaults on tax collectors, and Pike the ditcher is up to mischief again.'

'Does the name Ira Dei mean anything to you, Benedicta?'

'I have heard it bandied about, that and the Great Community of the Realm. Pike the ditcher knows everything.' She smiled wryly. 'Or at least he says he does. Pike is more full of ale than malice.'

'I expected Cranston,' Athelstan said, wistfully staring at the door. 'You see, one of his old comrades has been murdered, and the city fathers not only want their murders resolved and their gold back, they are also demanding an explanation of why the dismembered limbs of traitors are disappearing from the spikes above London Bridge.'

'A cup of troubles,' Benedicta said. 'But, Father, I have to add to them.'

'How?' he asked sharply.

'A woman came to the church last night.' Benedicta narrowed her eyes, trying to recall the name. 'Eleanor Hobden, that's right.'

Athelstan's heart sank.

'She claims her daughter's possessed,' Benedicta continued. 'She says she will take you to her house tonight after Vespers. What's it all about, Father?'

Athelstan's dark eyes looked mournful, but she resisted the urge to clasp his hand or stroke his cheek.

'Trouble,' the priest muttered. 'Benedicta, when I do go tonight, will you come with me?'

'Are you frightened?' she half-teased.

'No, no. But I'll ask Sir John to accompany me too. In these cases, the salt of common sense can be better than a priest's blessing.'

'Caught you at last, monk!'

Athelstan and Benedicta started and looked round as Cranston, hat off, legs astride, stood at the entrance to the church beaming at them.

'Oh, Lord,' Athelstan whispered. 'He's been at the miraculous wineskin.'

'Caught you at last!' Cranston boomed again, and walked down the nave. He stopped and peered about.

'Where's that bloody cat?'

'He's gone hunting.'

'Good!' Cranston came over, put one bear-like arm round Benedicta and planted a juicy kiss on her cheek. 'Lovely girl!' he whispered. He smiled at Athelstan.

'She'll make someone a lovely wife.'

'Sir John Cranston!' Benedicta cried with mock anger.

'Hold thy tongue, woman,' Cranston teased back.

'Brother, you have to come.'

'Oh no, Sir John, where?'

'To Billingsgate, Botolph's Wharf. They have just fished Sturmey's body from the river – a knife, similar to the one used on Mountjoy, planted deep in his chest. He apparently disappeared yesterday afternoon.'

'What was he doing in Billingsgate?'

'God knows!' Cranston smacked his lips and stared admiringly round the church. 'This is becoming more like a house of God than a barn.'

Athelstan winked at Benedicta as he turned and led Sir John back to the door. 'And how are Gog and Magog?'

'Eating as if there's no tomorrow.'

Cranston stopped, threw back his head and laughed. 'Boscombe's proving worth his weight in gold yet he can't tell me anything more about Mountjoy's death. However, what he did tell me,' Cranston laughed again, 'is that Gog and Magog chased poor Leif up a tree: the silly bastard wouldn't come down for hours!'

His face became serious. 'Gaunt and the Guildmasters interviewed me this morning. They reminded me that I have only ten days to find the gold and trap the murderer.'

'Are they insisting on this?'

'Yes, Lord Clifford is also to seek out what he can.'

'Or else what?' Athelstan asked curiously.

'What do you mean, monk?'

'Well, what happens after ten days?'

'Gaunt loses his allies, his gold and his power.'

Cranston stopped and peered down at the baptismal font. He studied the carving round the rim: St John the Baptist, waist-high in a River Jordan which reminded the Coroner of the Thames rather than any river in Palestine. 'Those Guildmasters... Lady, I beg your pardon,' he also bobbed his head towards the tabernacle, 'but they are murderous villains! Cheek-biters, gull-catchers, marble-hearted, ass-headed dogs!' He breathed out. 'They all sat there like great jellies: pop-eyed Goodman, balding Marshall, foppish Denny, and Sudbury with a face even a pig would despair of. What makes me angry, monk...'

'Friar, Sir John!'

'As I was saying, monk, what makes me angry is I know one or more of those bastards is a murderer. He must be!'

Cranston would have continued his litany of curses, but Athelstan guided him out on to the sun-washed steps of St Erconwald's. He locked the door of the church and that of his house and, after grabbing his saddle and bag of writing implements, went to collect Philomel. Cranston, after taking two generous swigs from his wineskin, forgot what he termed the 'Poxy Guildmasters!' and returned to his perennial teasing of Benedicta. At last Athelstan was able to saddle a protesting Philomel. He slung his bag over the saddle horn and carefully mounted.

Sir John collected his own horse from where it had been chomping the cemetery grass and swung himself into the saddle with such force that Athelstan winced; no wonder, he reflected, Crim called Sir John 'Horse Cruncher'. Athelstan urged Philomel forward and, not the best of horsemen, almost careered into Sir John. The friar glared down at a grinning Benedicta and tossed her the keys to both the church and his house.

'You'll keep an eye on things, Lady?'

Benedicta, biting her lip to stop her laughter, nodded.

'And you'll come back at Vespers?'

Again the nod.

Athelstan urged Philomel on and, with Cranston behind, blowing kisses at Benedicta, they left the church-yard and rode down towards London Bridge.

'What's happening at Vespers?' Cranston abruptly asked.

'We are going to meet the devil, Sir John. You, me and Benedicta.'

Cranston belched like a trumpet blast. 'What the hell do you mean, monk?'

'Wait and see.'

Any further conversation proved impossible; as it was market day, the streets of Southwark were full and Athelstan had to wave to different parishioners.

'Greetings, My Lord Coroner!' Pike the ditcher and Tab the tinker bawled as they sat outside a tavern, stoups of ale in their hands.

'Sod off!' he roared back, sensing the mockery in their voices.

They passed The Piebald. Cranston looked longingly through its darkened doorways and closed his eyes as he smelt the savoury pies baking there. Athelstan, however, refused to stop. Eventually they had to dismount to get through a crowd clustering round a chaunter who was loudly reciting the news of the day.

'The French made a landing at Rye and burnt the church! The Lord Sheriff is dead, struck through the heart in his own garden, as is Sir Thomas Fitzroy, dead and stale as many of the fish he sold. A witch has been seen flying over St Paul's and a boy with two heads has been born in a house near Clerkenwel!'

On and on the chaunter went, reciting what he had learnt, a mixture of half-truths and lies. Athelstan and Cranston passed on. Near the bridge itself the vegetable markets were doing a brisk trade; people walking along with their eyes fixed on the goods, frowning thoughtfully. The stalls were packed with different types of vegetables: crimson love apples, bundles of white glossy leeks, celery with pink stalks and bright green tops, the white knobs of turnips and the rich brown coats of chestnuts. Stall owners shouted: 'St Thomas's onions!' 'Leeks fresh from the garden!' Porters forced their way through, teeth clenched, jerkins wet with sweat as they walked, half-bowed, under the overflowing hampers on their backs. A bird seller, his boots red with the soil of the brick field, stood by a pile of cages, selling linnets, bull finches, gold finches and even nests bearing eggs. A little girl, dressed in black rags, sold watercress from a small tub. She looked so pathetic Athelstan bought tuppence worth and Philomel munched it in the twinkling of an eye.

Cranston and Athelstan, fighting to make their way, passed stalls selling cheesecakes, others combs, old caps, pigs' feet; a hawker of knives, sharpening hatchets, shouted abuse at a market official trying to collect the tax. Whilst outside a tavern, the Pied Powder, a court sat to regulate, or at least try to, the running of the market. The air was thick with the smoke and odour from the tanners as well as the packed mass of sweaty bodies.

'Hell's teeth!' Cranston breathed. 'This is the devil's own kitchen!'

For a while they had to stop whilst a group of exasperated beadles tried to clear a legion of cats and stray dogs which had congregated around a stall which sold offal. Now and again the old lady behind would throw down pieces of stale, dirty meat: this only wetted the strays' appetites and brought down upon the old crone the imprecations and curses of her fellow traders. Athelstan, leading Philomel, edged his way through, smiling at Cecily who sat on the steps of the market cross, talking earnestly to a young fop in tawdry clothes and stained hose. She waved at Athelstan and cooed at Cranston, who turned away and grunted. Suddenly, the Coroner's arm shot out and grabbed a ragged-arsed, balding, little man who was slinking through the crowds with a lapdog in his arms. Athelstan, with Philomel nudging him for more watercress, watched in amazement as the burly Coroner lifted up the little man, still holding the lapdog, by the scruff of his neck.

'Well, well, if it's not old Peterkin!' Cranston gave the ferret-faced beggar a shake. 'Old Peterkin the dog catcher. You snivelling little bastard! What are you up to now?'

'Nothing, Sir John. I found this dog and am trying to find its owner.'

Cranston bellowed across to a beadle and the bleary-eyed official hurried across.

'I am Sir John Cranston, Coroner. And this,' he thrust Peterkin and the dog into the beadle's arms, 'is a little turd who goes across into the city, steals some lady's lapdog and then brings it back to claim the reward. Take care of him!'

Cranston handed Peterkin over without further ado, winked at Athelstan, and they turned the corner and passed down the thoroughfare to London Bridge.

The stocks and pillories on either side of the road were full of miscreants: night hawks, pickpockets, and every rapscallion in Southwark. Some stoically took the humiliation and the dirt pelted by passers-by as if it was an occupational hazard whilst others moaned and cried for water. Athelstan quickly studied their faces, relieved to see none of his parishioners placed there. At the entrance to the bridge Cranston stopped and pounded on the iron-studded door of the gatehouse. There was no reply so the Coroner, ignoring Athelstan's questions, kicked on it, bawling, 'Come on, Burdon, you little bastard! Where are you?'

The door was flung open and a small, hairy-faced little creature appeared. A veritable mannikin. Athelstan smiled at Robert Burdon, father of at least thirteen children and constable of the gate tower.

'Oh, it's you, Cranston. What do you want?'

'Can I come in?' Sir John asked.

'No, you bloody well can't! I'm busy!'

Cranston stared up at the spikes above the gatehouse and their grisly burdens: the decapitated heads of traitors and malefactors.

'Fine,' Cranston breathed. 'But who's stealing the heads?'

'I don't bloody well know!' Burdon replied, sticking his thumbs in his belt, his little dark eyes glaring at Athelstan. 'What am I supposed to do, Father? My job is very simple. I'm to guard the gatehouse and place the heads on the spikes, and I always look after them. However, if some vile viper wishes to come and steal them, what can I do?' He puffed his little chest out till he reminded Athelstan even more of a cock sparrow. 'I am a constable, not a guard.'

'Robert!' The woman's voice inside was soft and alluring.

'My wife,' Burdon explained. 'She'll tell you the same. I don't know what happened, Sir John. I goes to bed, the heads are there. I wakes up and, though there's a guard here, the heads are gone.' He leaned closer. 'I think it's witch hags,' he whispered. 'The night riders.'

'Bollocks!' Cranston roared.

'Well, that's the only bloody answer you're going to get from me, so sod off!' Burdon disappeared, slamming the door behind him.

Cranston sighed, shook his head and took a generous swig from the wineskin. 'Come on, Brother.'

'Who do you think is stealing the heads?' Athelstan asked, threading Philomel's reins round his wrist and riding alongside Cranston.

'God knows, Brother. This city is full of every fiend in Hell. It could be a warlock or witch. The Corporation were particularly angry at the disappearance of the head of that French privateer, Jacques Larue – you remember, the one taken off Gravesend? Mystery after mystery,' Cranston moaned. He stopped outside the chapel of St Thomas built midway along the bridge.

'Forget the stealer of heads,' he muttered. 'Who gives a damn? Burdon doesn't, and the guards of the Corporation are half-sodden with drink.' He nodded at the iron-studded chapel door. 'Years ago, when I was lean and lithe, a veritable greyhound, Oliver Ingham and I came here to take our vows as knights and consecrate our swords to the service of the King. So many years ago.' The tears pricked at Sir John's eyes. 'Now I'm fat and old and Oliver lies murdered, left stinking in his bed, with the rats gnawing at his corpse, by a hard-hearted harridan from hell. She murdered him! You know that, Athelstan. I know that. She knows that.'

'And so does God,' Athelstan added gently. 'Come on, Sir John, leave it be.'

They crossed the bridge and turned right into Billings-gate where the fish market was in full swing. The din of the cries and commotion of both sellers and buyers beat against their ears like the buzzing of a hornet's nest. The whole of the wharf seemed to be covered in hand barrows: some laden with baskets, others with sacks. Alongside the riverbank, the tangled rigging of the fishing boats reminded Athelstan of seaports; the smell of fish, whelks, red herrings, sprats and cod was almost overpowering.

'Handsome cod, best in the market!' a stall owner bawled at them. 'Beautiful lobsters, good and cheap! Fine cock crabs, all alive!' another shouted.

Cranston and Athelstan led their horses past stalls where the white bellies of turbot shone like mother-of-pearl next to blood-scarlet lobsters. Brown baskets full of wriggling eels stood round bowls of whelks being boiled alive above steaming cauldrons.

'Where are we going to?' Athelstan whispered.

Cranston pointed to a large tavern which stood in splendid isolation at the far end of the market. 'The Ship of Fools,' he said.

Athelstan groaned. 'Oh, Sir John, you have had claret enough.'

'Sod that!' Cranston shouted back above the din. 'We are here to see the Fisher of Men.' But he refused to elaborate any further.

In the tavern yard an ostler took their horses and they walked into the great taproom which stank of beer, ale and salted fish.

'Your servant.' A bandy-legged tavern keeper touched his forelock, his small, greedy eyes never leaving the heavy purse on Sir John's belt.

'A cup of claret for me, some...'

'Ale,' Athelstan supplied.

'Ale for my clerk, and another cup of claret for the Fisher of Men. I, Sir John Cranston, Coroner, wish to see him.'

The landlord's manner became even more servile. He conducted Cranston and Athelstan as grandly as he would any prince to a small alcove with a table beneath a window overlooking the river. He fetched two deep bowls of claret, a stoup of ale, and gushingly assured Sir John that he had already sent a boy for the Fisher of Men.

'Who is this?' Athelstan asked.

'The Fisher of Men,' Cranston replied, sipping from his cup, 'is a Crown official. There are five in all, working the banks of the river. This one has authority from the Fish Wharf near St Botolph's down to Petty Wales next to the Tower.'

'Yes, but what do they do?'

'They fish bodies from the Thames. Murder victims, suicides, those who have suffered accidents, drunks. If a man's alive, they are paid twopence. For a murder victim threepence. Suicides and accidents only a penny.'

'Sir John.'

Athelstan looked up as a tall, thin figure silently appeared beside them. Cranston waved to the stool and cup of wine.

'Be our guest, sir.'

The man stepped out of the shadows. As he sat down Athelstan fought to hide his distaste. The fellow had red, lanky, greasy hair which fell to his shoulders and framed a face as grim as a death mask, alabaster white, a mouth like that of a fish, a snub nose and black button eyes. Cranston made the introductions and the Fisher of Men glanced expressionlessly at the friar.

'You have come to view the corpse?'

Athelstan nodded.

'Bobbing he was,' the man replied. 'Bobbing like a cork. You see, most murder victims are loaded with stones but this one was strange.'

'Why?'

'Well, you see, Sir John,' the man sipped from his wine cup, face rigid, eyes unblinking, 'it's very rare I meet my customers before they die,' he explained. 'But yesterday, later in the afternoon, just after the market closed, I came out of St Mary at Hill for my usual walk along the wharf. I like to study the river, the currents, the breeze.' The strange fellow warmed to his theme. 'The river tells you a lot. If it's rough or the wind is strong, the corpses are taken out mid-stream. Yesterday I thinks: The river's calm, she means me well. The corpses will be lapped into shore.'

Athelstan hid a shiver.

'Now there was a man walking up and down, up and down, as if he was waiting for someone. Oh, I thinks, a suicide if ever I saw one. However, I didn't wish to be greedy, so I walks away. The man was standing behind the stalls, between them and the riverside. I hears a cry. I looks around. The man has gone.' The fellow sipped from his wine cup. 'I runs back along the quayside and there he is, bobbing in the river, arms extended, blood gushing from a wound in his chest. I had my fishing line.'

The fellow tapped the leather pouches round his waist. 'I had him in, clipped my mark on his chest and took him to my shop.'

'Shop?' Athelstan queried.

'You'll see.'

Cranston looked warningly at Athelstan.

'But there was no one else?' the Coroner asked. 'You saw no one around?'

The fellow shook his head. 'No one at all. I tell you, Sir John, the place was deserted. I saw no one. I heard no one.'

'But how?' Athelstan broke in. 'How can someone approach Sturmey, stick a knife in his heart then disappear like a puff of smoke?'

The Fisher of Men shrugged and drained his wine cup. 'I only takes the bodies out,' he replied. 'I don't account for why they died. Come, I'll show you.'

He led them out of the tavern, down a side street and turned into a narrow alleyway. He stopped beside a long barn-like structure and opened the padlocked door. Athelstan immediately covered his face and mouth against the terrible stench. The Fisher of Men lit torches, the pitch spluttered into life and Athelstan gazed round at the trestle tables, about a dozen in all, which filled the room. Some were empty but others bore bundles covered by leather sheets.

'Now, which one's Sturmey?' the Fisher of Men muttered to himself. He pulled back one sheet. 'No, that's the suicide.' He stopped, a finger to his lips, and pointed to another covered bundle. 'And that's the drunk. So this,' he said triumphantly pulling back the sheet, 'must be Sturmey!'

The dead locksmith lay sprawled there, his face a ghastly white, his hair and clothes sodden. In the centre of his chest was a dark purple stain. Beside the corpse lay a long knife. Athelstan picked it up gingerly.

'The same type,' he murmured, 'as used on Mountjoy.' He took another look at the corpse. Cranston turned away and busily helped himself to his wineskin.

'How do you know it's Sturmey?' Athelstan asked.

'He had a list of provisions in his wallet with his name on,' the Fisher of Men replied. 'And My Lord Coroner had already directed myself and others of my Guild to search for this man.' His face became even longer. 'The rest you know. Have you seen enough?'

'Hell's teeth, yes!' Cranston snapped. 'Cover his face!'

'When you pay the threepence, Sir John, I'll release the corpse.'

Cranston took another swig from the miraculous wineskin. 'All right! All right!' he exclaimed crossly. 'Oh, for God's sake, Athelstan, let's get out of here!'

Chapter 7

Cranston and Athelstan walked back to collect their horses from the stable.

'A cup of claret, Brother?'

'No, Sir John. Sufficient unto the day is the evil thereof. Tell me, have you remembered why you knew Sturmey's name?'

Cranston shook his head. 'But one thing I do know: Brother, Sturmey was killed because he knew something. He could solve the mystery of how the chest was robbed.' Cranston stared as two lepers, garbed completely in black, crept along the street, fearful of being recognized. 'Sturmey was lured,' he continued, 'down to Billingsgate. But why? What forced a reputable locksmith to become involved in treason and robbery?'

'There's only one answer, Sir John. I doubt if he was bribed so the answer must be blackmail. If you search your prodigious memory, I am sure you'll find something rather unsavoury about Master Sturmey.'

Cranston nodded and they led their horses further up the street, where their attention was drawn to a huge crowd which had assembled around a sinister figure dressed in goatskin. The man had long, grey hair falling down over his shoulders, and the lower half of his face was hidden behind a thick, bushy beard; strange mad eyes scanned the crowds, fascinated by this latter-day prophet and the tall, burning cross he was holding. The latter, coated with pitch and tar along the cross beam, burnt fiercely, the flames and black smoke only emphasizing the mad preacher's warnings.

'This city has been condemned like Sodom and Gomorrah! Like those of Tyre and Sidon and the fleshpots of the plain to bear the brunt of God's anger!' The man flung one sinewy arm towards Cheapside. 'I bring the burning cross to this city as a warning of the fires yet to come! So repent ye, you rich who loll in silk on golden couches and drink the juices of wine and stuff your mouth with the softest meats!'

Cranston and Athelstan watched the man rant on, even as soldiers wearing both the livery of the city and of John of Gaunt began to make their presence felt, pouring out of alleyways leading down to the Tower. The soldiers forced their way through the throng with the flats of their swords in an attempt to seize the mad prophet. The mob resisted, their mood sullen; fights broke out and, when Athelstan looked again, the preacher and his fiery cross had disappeared.

'Come on, Sir John, I have a confession to make.'

He led the Coroner further away from the tumult.

'What is it, Brother?'

'This leader of the Great Community, Ira Dei. He has sent me a warning.' Athelstan carefully described his strange visitation earlier in the day as well as the proclamation pinned to his church door.

Cranston, tight-lipped, heard him out, so concerned he even forgot his miraculous wineskin.

'Why would they approach me?' Athelstan asked.

Cranston blew out his lips. 'Fear and flattery, Brother. Fear because he knows you are my clerk and secretarius.'

'And secondly, Sir John?'

Cranston gave a lopsided smile. 'You are rather modest for a priest, Athelstan. Haven't you realized how in Southwark, amongst the poor and the downtrodden, you are respected, even revered?'

Athelstan blushed and looked away. 'That's ridiculous!' he whispered.

'Oh no, it isn't!' Cranston snapped, moving on. 'Forget Ira Dei, Brother. When the rebellion comes, it will be priests like yourself, John More and Jack Straw, who will lead the commons.'

'I'll hide in my church,' Athelstan retorted. 'Speaking of which...' He stopped outside St Dunstan's, looping Philomel's reins through one of the hooks placed on the wall.

'What's the matter, Brother?'

'I want to think, Sir John, and pray. I advise you to do likewise.'

Muttering and cursing, Cranston hobbled his own horse, took a generous swig from the miraculous wineskin and followed Athelstan into the cool, dark porch.

Inside the church was lit by the occasional torch with candles placed around statues of the Virgin, St Joseph and St Dunstan, as well as the sunlight pouring through the stained-glass windows which made the pictures depicted there flare into life in glorious rays of colour. Athelstan stared admiringly up at these.

'I'd love one of those!' he whispered. 'Just one for St Erconwald!'

He looked again and, as he did so, Cranston took one small nip from his wineskin and followed the friar down the nave to sit on a bench before the rood screen. Behind this, in the choir stalls, the master singer and his choir were rehearsing the Mass of St Michael. Athelstan sat on the bench, closed his eyes and listened to the words.

'I saw a great dragon appear in the heavens, ten heads and on each a coronet, and its great tail swept a third of the stars from the sky. Then I saw Michael do battle with the dragon.'

The powerful, three-voiced choir triumphantly sang in Latin the description of Archangel Michael's great triumph over Satan.

Athelstan closed his eyes and prayed for God's help against the evil he now faced: Mountjoy, blood-stained in that beautiful garden; Fitzroy, choking his life out above the gold and silver platters of John of Gaunt; Sturmey, dragged out of the river like a piece of rubbish by the Fisher of Men, his corpse displayed like that of a dead cod or salmon.

Athelstan remembered the warning delivered to him earlier that day and felt his own temper fray. The man who called himself Ira Dei was a blasphemer! How could God or his just anger be associated with sudden murder and evil assassination? All those souls sent into the great darkness unprepared and unshriven. And the other wickednesses of the city? This possessed girl at the Hobdens. The malefactor who stole the severed limbs of traitors. And old Jack Cranston's friend, subtly murdered and left to be gnawed by rats. What had these things to do with God's creation? With the stars spinning in the skies? The green, lush meadow grass? The basic honesty and goodness of many of his parishioners? Athelstan half-murmured the words of his mentor, Father Paul: 'God is never far away. He can only act through us. Man's free will is God's door to humanity.' So what about these murders? He tried to direct his thoughts and search for a common thread. The singing stopped and he opened his eyes as Cranston, emitting a loud snore, crashed back against the bench.

'Sir John, come!'

Cranston opened his eyes and smacked his lips. 'Mine's a deep bowl of claret!' he bellowed.

'Sir John, we are in church.'

Cranston rubbed his eyes and lumbered to his feet. 'I find it difficult to pray, Brother. So let me show you what I do.'

Like a great bear he lumbered across into the side chapel and stood before the wooden carved statue of the Virgin, her arms wrapped round the shoulders of the boy Jesus. Cranston dropped two coins into an iron-bound chest and fished out ten candles, arranging them like a row of soldiers on the great iron candelabra before the statue.

'Ten prayers,' he muttered. 'One for myself, one for the Lady Maude, one for each of the two poppets, one for Gog and Magog, one for you, one for Boscombe and Leif, one for Benedicta and one for old Oliver.'

'That's nine, Sir John.'

'Oh, yes.' Cranston lit the last one with a taper. 'And one for any other poor bugger I should have prayed for!' He blew the taper out with a gust of wine-drenched breath and charged back down the church. 'That's it, Brother. Now it's The Holy Lamb of God for me!'

They unhitched their horses and walked into a busy thronged Cheapside. Sir John expected his usual rapturous welcome at his favourite tavern but was disappointed. The landlord's wife was waiting in quivering anticipation.

'Sir John, a message from the Guildhall! A servitor has been here at least twice. You are to go there immediately!' Her voice dropped to a reverential hush. 'The Lord Regent himself demands your presence!'

Cursing and muttering, Cranston forced his way back across Cheapside with an even more subdued Athelstan trailing behind. At the Guildhall a chamberlain took them to the small privy council chamber which over-looked the gardens where Mountjoy had been killed. He tapped on the door and ushered them in. Cranston swaggered through and glared at the Regent who sat directly opposite, Goodman and the Guildmasters flanking him on either side. Athelstan looked up at the silver and gold stars painted on the blue ceiling then around at the wooden panels. A soft, luxurious room, he thought, where the great ones of the city plotted and drew up their subtle plans. Gaunt beckoned them forward to two quilted, high-backed chairs.

'Sir John, sit. We have been waiting.'

'Your Grace,' Cranston snapped, lowering his great weight into the seat. 'I have been busy! The locksmith Sturmey has been—'

'I know, I know,' Gaunt interrupted. 'Murdered! By person or persons unknown. His body lies in a shed in Billingsgate. And you, Brother?' The hard, shrewd eyes stared at Athelstan. 'The traitor Ira Dei has made his presence known to you.' Gaunt smiled at the friar's surprise. 'We have the means, Brother, of discovering what is happening in our city. As for Sturmey, Sir John, I understand you sealed his workshop?'

Cranston nodded.

'My men broke the seals,' Gaunt retorted. 'We have searched his house but can find no trace or mention of Sturmey making a second set of keys.'

'But he did make them,' Cranston replied.

'How do you know that?' Goodman spitefully snapped.

'Why else would he be killed?'

Goodman pulled a face.

'I believe,' Cranston continued slowly, 'Sturmey was blackmailed. Like many such men, he led a secret life.'

Athelstan glimpsed a glimmer of fear in Goodman's eyes, but the Mayor lowered his head as Cranston passed on to other matters.

'Your Grace, I could question everyone here, with your authority of course, about their whereabouts yesterday afternoon when the Lord Sheriff and Master Sturmey were killed. However, I suspect that would be fruitless.'

'Yes, it would be,' Denny drawled. 'We were all busy, My Lord Coroner. Even if Sir Gerard Mountjoy could sit sipping wine and talking to his dogs.'

Beneath the table Athelstan suddenly gripped Cranston's wrist and the Coroner quickly bit back the question he was about to ask.

'Then, Your Grace,' he said instead, 'why am I summoned here? Do you have news?'

'Yes, of two things,' Gaunt replied. 'First, a proclamation has been pinned on the Guildhall door. A simple message from Ira Dei. It reads: "Death follows death".

What do you make of that, Sir John? Or should I ask Brother Athelstan, who is so strangely silent?'

The friar gently tapped the top of the table. 'A warning, Your Grace, that someone else in this room might be murdered.' Athelstan glanced at the Guildmasters but they seemed unperturbed by his reply.

'Has another murder occurred?' Cranston asked. 'Where is My Lord Clifford?'

'A third was planned,' Gaunt replied. 'Lord Adam was attacked this morning by a group of malefactors near Bread Street but, thank God, managed to escape. He is now resting at his town house. I suggest you visit him there.'

'Is that all?'

'Oh, no.' Gaunt rose quickly to his feet but his eyes never left those of Athelstan. 'You are, Brother, a loyal servant of the Crown?'

'Under God, yes.' He tried to control his panic: he was the real reason this group of powerful men wanted to see Cranston and he half-suspected what lay behind their smug, complacent looks. Gaunt stood, smoothing his moustache between finger and thumb.

'Brother, you have been approached by Ira Dei. You are a priest working amongst the poor of Southwark. You are, strangely enough, much loved and respected. If we asked, indeed if the King ordered, would you reply to Ira Dei, join the Great Community of the Realm and…?'

'Betray them?' Athelstan snapped.

'Your Grace!' Cranston shouted, pushing back his chair. 'The notion is both foolish and rash. Brother Athelstan is my secretarius. I am an officer of the Crown. He would always be held suspect.'

Gaunt shook his head. 'Sir John, you contradict yourself,' he replied, choosing his words carefully. 'Yesterday, both you and Brother Athelstan claimed that Ira Dei, or one of his henchmen, was present at my banquet. If this so-called Great Community of the Realm can turn even the most powerful into a traitor, why not a Dominican who works amongst the poor?'

'Yes, why not?' Goodman spoke up, and Cranston softly groaned at the way both he and Athelstan had slipped into this neatly laid trap.

'After all, Sir John, what are your thoughts on this matter?' Goodman continued. 'Are you not for the poor? Have you not advocated reform in the city and the shires? To ease the burden of the petty traders and peasants?'

'You cannot force me,' Athelstan interrupted quietly. 'My obedience is to my Father Superior and to God!'

'And your allegiance to the Crown?' Gaunt shouted back. 'As for your Father Superior, I have already obtained his permission.'

'Your Grace, you cannot force me to act against my conscience!'

Gaunt sat down and smilingly extended his beringed hands. 'Now, now, Brother, what are we asking for? We do not wish you to be a traitor, to the Crown or to this so-called Great Community or to yourself.'

'What is it you want?' Cranston quietly asked.

'Nothing much,' Gaunt murmured. 'Ira Dei has communicated with Brother Athelstan. Let our faithful loyal friar write back. Who knows? This mysterious traitor may reveal his hand.' Gaunt smiled. He sat down and spread his hands. 'I am sure this traitor is no fool and Brother Athelstan would never be trusted. But, as the old proverb puts it, Sir John: "If you shake the apple tree, it's wonderful what might fall out".'

Athelstan remained tight-lipped, refusing to commit himself further, and only gave vent to his anger once they had left the council chamber and were returning downstairs to the ground floor of the Guildhall. Cranston was more sanguine, aided by another swig from his wineskin.

'Take heart, Brother.' He patted Athelstan on the shoulder. 'Remember, My Lord Regent must be desperate.'

Athelstan stopped at the foot of the stairs. 'The meeting was quite fruitful, Sir John, yes?'

Cranston grinned. 'Yes. Two juicy morsels. First, how did Denny know that My Lord Sheriff was sipping wine and talking to his dogs? Quite a detailed observation from someone who supposedly never went near the Lord Sheriff when he was sunning himself in his private garden.'

'And Goodman's embarrassment?' Athelstan asked.

'Yes, yes. I think our dead master locksmith had some dark secret which My Lord Mayor shares.'

Cranston looked sharply at Athelstan. 'There's something else, isn't there, Brother?'

The friar looked away but Cranston glimpsed the turmoil behind his troubled eyes. Athelstan murmured something.

'What's that, Brother?'

'Tell me, Sir John, My Lord Regent has a legion of spies?'

'Legion is the correct word, Brother. More like a swarm of ants across the city. No one can be trusted, and that even includes people like Leif the beggar. Such people are not evil, it's only that being so poor they can be quickly bought.' Cranston stepped closer and Athelstan tried not to flinch at the gust of wine fumes.

'Of course,' the Coroner whispered, 'you are wondering how Gaunt knew about Ira Dei?'

Athelstan was about to reply when they both heard a sound and turned to find Sir Nicholas Hussey, the King's tutor, standing behind them.

'My Lord Coroner, Brother Athelstan.' The suave, silver-haired courtier bowed slightly. 'We heard you were in the Guildhall. His Grace the King requests a moment of your time.'

Athelstan looked curiously at this dark-skinned scholar, a lawyer by profession. Hussey's quiet control of the King, his subtle manipulation of the young boy, was now making itself felt. He noticed the bright blue of the man's eyes, clear as a summer day. He also saw the cunning in his face and quickly concluded Hussey might be even more dangerous than the Regent they had just left. Cranston, too, stayed silent, quietly wondering how much Hussey had heard. Then the Coroner smiled.

'It would be an honour,' he murmured.

Hussey led them down a corridor and, surprisingly enough, into the Guildhall's private garden where Mountjoy had been killed. The young King, dressed in a simple Lincoln green tunic, his blond hair tousled, sat on a turf seat, a leather baldrick and a pair of spurred hunting boots alongside him. A toy crossbow lay propped at his feet and, by the mud-marks on his face and hands, Cranston realized the young man had been hunting, probably in the woods and meadows north of Clerkenwell. Both he and Athelstan bowed but Richard dismissed the pleasantries and waved to the seat beside him, pushing the baldrick and boots unceremoniously aside.

'Sir John, Brother Athelstan.' Bright-eyed, the King gestured them to sit. 'Uncle's not here so I can do what I want. Sir Nicholas, you will stay?'

The tutor bowed. Athelstan was quick enough to catch the glance exchanged between the young King and his mentor. Richard seized Cranston's huge hand and leaned forward so that Athelstan could hear his conspiratorial whisper.

'Have you found the murderer yet?'

'No, Your Grace.'

'Or who this Ira Dei is?'

Again Cranston shook his head. Richard smiled.

'But my uncle's upset. I have heard him shouting,' he continued. 'He blames everyone. Goodman, My Lord Mayor, and even his creature Lord Clifford have not escaped censure. Do you think Uncle will be murdered?'

Cranston gazed severely at the boy. 'Your Grace, how can you say such a thing?'

'Oh, quite easily, for Uncle would like to be King.'

'Your Grace, whoever tells you that is a traitor and a knave. One day *you* will be King. A great prince like your father.'

Richard's eyes clouded at Cranston's mention of Gaunt's brother, the famed Black Prince.

'Did you know Father well, Sir John?'

Cranston's gaze softened. 'Yes, I did, Sire. I stood beside him at Poitiers when the French tried to break through.'

And, urged on by Richard's pleading, the Coroner gave a blow-by-blow account of the last stages of the Black Prince's famous victory. Richard sat listening, round-eyed, until Hussey intervened, pointing out the Lord Coroner was a busy man and had other matters to attend to. Richard gave them leave to go, thanking both Athelstan and Cranston warmly. They were just about to leave when Richard, tiptoeing over the grass, ran up and caught them both excitedly by the sleeve.

'If you find Ira Dei,' he whispered excitedly, 'bring him to me, Sir John!'

Cranston smiled and bowed. He and Athelstan walked back through the Guildhall and out into the heat of Cheapside.

'Now what was all that about?' Cranston muttered to himself.

Athelstan shook his head. Only when they were safely ensconced in a window seat of The Lamb of God, each with a tankard of cool ale in their hands, did the friar comment.

'You asked a question as we left the Guildhall, Sir John. Have you considered the possibility that these deaths may not be the work of the peasant leader Ira Dei but of another court faction trying to bring the Regent into disrepute?'

'You mean Hussey and the like?' Cranston shook his head. 'In answer to that, good friar, all I can reply is: have you considered the possibility that, if Gaunt goes, the young King may fall with him?'

Athelstan sat back, surprised. 'It's as close as that, Sir John?'

'Oh, yes. When and if the revolt comes, do you think the peasant leaders will distinguish between one prince and another? Haven't you heard their song, Brother? "When Adam delved and Eve span, who was then the gentleman?".' Cranston gulped from his blackjack of ale. 'What worries me more, Brother, are the likes of

Goodman, Denny and Sudbury, who would like to see London without a King, ruled by merchant princes like the cities they trade with: Florence, Pisa and Genoa. So many players,' he murmured. 'God knows, Brother, it's hard to distinguish between the good and the bad.' He roared for another tankard. 'But you were saying, before Hussey arrived, you think Gaunt has a spy in your parish?'

Athelstan's face became closed and tight-lipped and Cranston glimpsed the gentle friar's rare anger.

'You have your suspicions?'

'For the moment, Sir John, by your leave, I'll keep close counsel and a still mouth. But, yes, I do.'

They sat for another hour, Cranston deciding to eat at the tavern rather than return to his empty house. The shadows began to lengthen. Outside the market closed and the stalls were taken down. As the tavern began to fill with sweat-soaked apprentices and hoarse-voiced tinkers, desperate to quench their thirst, Cranston and Athelstan collected their horses and returned through the emptying streets towards London Bridge.

The crowds had now gone home so they found their passage easy and Athelstan began to prepare himself for his visit to the Hobdens and the exorcism of the young girl, Elizabeth.

'Have you ever done this before?' Cranston asked curiously, half an eye on a well-known pickpocket who was trailing a tired-looking tinker.

'Done what, Sir John?'

'An exorcism, a real one?'

Suddenly Cranston turned away and shouted across Bridge Street: 'Foulpie!'

The pickpocket spun round, a startled look on his face.

'Foulpie, me boy!' Cranston roared. 'I've got my eye on you, you bloody little thief! Now be a good lad and piss off!'

The one-eyed tinker stopped and turned, startled. 'What's the matter?' he shouted.

Cranston grinned and pointed to Foulpie, haring back towards East Cheap as fast as any whippet.

'A rapscallion interested in your takings.'

The tinker smiled his thanks and the Coroner turned back to his subdued companion.

'Well, Brother?' he asked between swigs from the miraculous wineskin. 'Have you ever exorcized the Lord Satan or one of his minions?'

Athelstan half-grinned and shook his head.

'I've seen an exorcism,' Cranston continued. 'A real one. Fifteen years ago at St Benet Sherehog. You know the church?'

Athelstan nodded.

'A young boy was taken there from the hospital of St Anthony of Vienne. Well,' Cranston helped himself once more to the wineskin, 'Brother, I still have nightmares about it! You see, the exorcist was one of those rare men, a really holy friar.' Cranston sniffed at his own joke. 'And I was one of the official witnesses appointed by the Bishop of London. They brought this lad, no more than fourteen summers, and chained him in the sanctuary chair next to the rood screen.' The Coroner stopped to clear his throat, now Athelstan was listening eagerly. 'This boy,' he continued, 'could speak in strange tongues, raise himself from the ground and, worse, tell people their secrets.'

'What happened?' Athelstan asked curiously.

'Well, the exorcist began the ceremony and the boy suddenly changed. He became violent and abusive, cursing the exorcist with every foul word he knew. Now there's a part of the ceremony, you know, when the exorcist...'

'Solemnly invokes?' Athelstan asked.

'That's it, solemnly invokes the devil and asks him by what name he is called. The boy's voice, usually thin and reedy, became deep and rich, "I AM THE SWINE LORD," he replied.' Cranston shook his head. 'That sanctuary became dark and there was the most offensive stink of putrefaction. Then the exorcist reached the end of the ritual where he was supposed to tell the demon who possessed the boy to leave, and the demon answered: "WHERE SHALL I GO? WHERE SHALL I GO?"' Cranston stopped and reined in his horse.

'Go on, Sir John, please.'

'Well, there was another witness there. A young lawyer from the Inns of Court in Chancery Lane. He had watched the proceedings in a half-mocking fashion and, when the demon cried, "WHERE SHALL

I GO? WHERE SHALL I GO?" this young bright spark suddenly whispered, "Well, he can come to me.'"

Sir John turned in the saddle. 'Brother, I do not lie. The possessed boy threw himself back in a dead faint. I heard a rushing sound as if a huge bird was swooping for the kill and this young lawyer was suddenly lifted off his feet and thrown bodily against a pillar. He was unconscious for days.' Cranston urged his horse on.

'Why do you tell me this, Sir John? Are you trying to frighten me?'

'No.' Cranston's face remained serious. 'That's the only occasion I have ever witnessed such a scene and it taught me a lesson. I can distinguish, Brother, between the real forces of darkness and the countless tricks of charlatans. Believe me, I have seen them all. Voices in the night, footsteps on dusty stairs, clanking in the cellars.' He grinned. 'So, put your trust in old Jack Cranston, Brother. Bring your oils and holy water, by all means, but leave old Jack to his own devices.'

Chapter 8

Cranston and Athelstan arrived back at St Erconwald's. Whilst the Coroner relaxed in the priest's house, Athelstan unlocked the church and knelt at the entrance of the rood screen to recite Divine Office. He found it difficult to concentrate on the words of the psalmist and was taken by the phrase, 'A sea of troubles'. He stopped to reflect on the problems which faced both himself and Cranston as well as the possibility that, even in this little parish of St Erconwald's, the Regent had his spies. The friar leaned back on his heels and stared up at the crucifix. He hoped tonight's visitation would be the first and the last; Athelstan quietly vowed that, if it was, he would apply all his energies to this Ira Dei and the horrible murders perpetrated in the Guildhall and elsewhere.

He stared across at the new, beautifully carved statue of St Erconwald, the patron saint of his parish. Athelstan smiled. Erconwald had been a great bishop of London, a man who had faced many problems here in this bustling city, before retiring to the solitude of a monastic house at Barking. The friar could feel sympathy with him and stared at the fixed, pious face, so lost in his thoughts he jumped at a soft touch on his shoulder.

'Father, I am sorry.'

Athelstan turned to see Benedicta anxiously looking down at him.

'Father, you did say to return at Vespers?'

Athelstan rubbed his eyes and smiled. 'Benedicta, it's good of you to come. Wait here.'

He mounted the sanctuary steps, opened the tabernacle, took out the sacred oils and collected from the small sacristy a stoup of holy water with an asperges rod. These he placed in a small, leather bag and went back to Benedicta.

'I suppose,' he said with mock severity, 'everything is well enough in the parish?'

'As quiet as the sea before the storm,' she teased.

They left the church, locked it and went across to find Cranston seated in Athelstan's one and only chair, head back, mouth wide open, snoring his head off, whilst Bonaventure lay curled in his generous lap.

'Oh, foolish cat,' Athelstan whispered, and gently lifted him off before shaking Cranston awake.

The Coroner awoke, as usual, lips smacking, greeted Benedicta then, at Athelstan's urging, went into the buttery and dashed cold water over his hands and face. Cranston returned refreshed and bellowing that he was ready to do battle with the devil and anyone else.

All three left St Erconwald's, each lost in their own surmises of what might happen, and made their way through the narrow alleys and runnels of Southwark. It was just before dusk. Shops and stalls now closed, the crowds were dispersing to their own homes. The day's business was done and Southwark's violent night hawks, roisterers and denizens of the underworld would only emerge from their rat holes once darkness had fully fallen. They stopped before crossing the great thorough-fare leading down to London Bridge and watched a party of mounted knights pass, bright in their multicoloured surcoats, their great war helmets swinging from saddle horns. Squires and pages rode behind holding shields and lances. After them came two long lines of dusty archers marching through Southwark towards the old road south to Dover.

'There's a lot of such toing and froing,' Cranston observed. 'The French are now attacking every important seaport along the Channel and the Regent is desperate for troops. If he withdraws any more from Hedingham and the other castles north of London, it might spark off the revolt.'

Cranston watched as the archers trooped by – crop-haired, hard-bitten, with weather-beaten faces – veterans who would make short work of any peasant levies.

'What will you do?' he suddenly asked Athelstan. 'I mean, when the revolt comes?'

The friar pulled a face. 'I'll send Benedicta away with anyone else who wishes to escape the eye of the storm. I'll stay in my church.'

Athelstan, too, studied the soldiers. They stirred memories of his brother Francis and himself during their short and inglorious foray with the English armies in France. He had come home, leaving Francis to be buried in some communal pit. As usual, when thinking of his brother, Athelstan closed his eyes and breathed a quick requiem for the repose of his soul.

They continued their journey and at last arrived at the Hobdens' narrow, three-storeyed house. Athelstan looked up. He glimpsed a single candle glowing in an upper-storey window, and shivered.

'Christ and all his angels protect us!' he breathed as he knocked on the door.

'Don't worry!' Cranston urged. 'Jack Cranston's here!'

'Yes,' Benedicta whispered. 'I suppose angels come in all shapes and sizes!'

Cranston was about to make a tart reply when the door swung open. Walter and Eleanor Hobden greeted them. Athelstan took an instant dislike to both of them. The man seemed sly and secretive, whilst the sharp-featured, gimlet-eyed Eleanor looked a veritable harridan.

'Father, you are welcome.'

The Hobdens stood aside and ushered them in. Athelstan entered the darkened passageway, trying to control his anxiety, as well as a shiver of apprehension which made him flinch and tense as if expecting a blow.

'I have brought Sir John,' he declared haltingly. 'Sir John Cranston, Coroner of the city. And this is Benedicta, a member of my parish council.' He smiled sheepishly. 'In these cases, it's best to have witnesses.'

The Hobdens, standing on either side of the fire, just stared hard-eyed and Athelstan fought to control his mounting unease. What was happening here? he wondered. Why did this house make him feel so apprehensive? He scarcely knew the Hobdens and yet he found the atmosphere in their house oppressive, redolent of an unspoken evil.

'Where is your daughter?' he asked, conscious of how subdued both Cranston and Benedicta had become. He glanced over his shoulder. Cranston's usual cheery expression was now grave and sombre as if the house had taken some of his usual ebullience away.

'Elizabeth's upstairs,' Waiter muttered. 'Father, have you brought the oils and water?'

'Of course.'

'It will begin soon,' Eleanor Hobden spoke up. 'Once darkness falls the demon manifests itself.'

'In what ways?' Cranston snapped before Athelstan could stop him.

Walter shook his thin shoulders. 'Father Athelstan knows that,' he whined. 'Elizabeth speaks but with her mother's voice. Then there's the knocking on the walls, the smell, the accusations.' His voice trailed off.

'How did your wife die?' Athelstan asked. 'I mean, your first wife?'

'Of an abscess inside her,' Eleanor replied brusquely. 'We called the best physicians, but they could do nothing. She just faded away. I was a distant cousin of Sarah's and, when she fell ill, I came to nurse her. Father, there was nothing that could be done.'

Athelstan turned as a bent old woman crept, like a shadow, into the room.

'This is Anna,' Walter announced. 'Elizabeth's nurse.'

The old woman drew closer, her wrinkled face creased into a hapless smile.

'Elizabeth has driven even me away,' she moaned. 'She will have nothing to do with me at all.'

Athelstan studied Anna's black button eyes, wispy grey hair and narrow nose, and sensed a malice which only deepened his unease.

'Do you want some wine?' the Hobdens offered.

'No, no.' Athelstan grasped the bag holding the oils and stoup of holy water even tighter.

'Can I assist?' Anna offered.

'No,' Eleanor Hobden intervened harshly. 'Anna, go back to the scullery. Walter and I can deal with this.'

Athelstan tensed as he heard a voice calling: 'Walter! Walter!'

He looked at Hobden whose face had become even more pallid.

'It's beginning again,' the man whispered. 'It begins like this every night.'

'Tush, man, it's only your daughter calling you.'

'No.' Hobden's eyes rolled like a frightened animal's. 'Sir John, I swear that's my dead wife's voice.'

Athelstan concealed the trembling which had begun in his legs.

'We'd best go up,' he said firmly. 'Master Hobden, if you will show me the way?'

Like a condemned man treading the gallows steps, Hobden led them up the darkened, winding staircase to the second floor and along a passageway to a half-open door. He pushed this slowly open and stood, one hand on the lintel, staring into the candle-lit room. Athelstan, Cranston and Benedicta, close behind him, gazed at the young woman lying in the centre of the great four-poster bed, her dark hair bound behind her, the skin of her white face drawn so tight it emphasized her high cheek bones. She stared glassily at her father and the others.

'So, you have brought visitors, Walter? Witnesses to your crime.'

Athelstan watched, curious, as the lips moved but the voice seemed hollow, disembodied.

'Elizabeth!' Hobden moaned. 'Stop this!'

'Stop what, Walter? You murdered me, killed me with red arsenic, poisoning me so you could marry another woman!'

'That is not true!'

Walter was about to continue when the knocking began. At first slow, indistinct, but then it spread up from the bottom floor of the house as if some dark creature from Hell was scrabbling up behind the wainscoting.

Benedicta stood back. 'Father,' she whispered. 'Be careful!'

Athelstan walked into the room and headed towards the foot of the bed. He was fascinated by the girl's dark, glassy eyes and those lips spouting out their litany of accusation. The knocking continued like a drum beat and Athelstan gagged at the awful stench pervading the room. He gathered his courage.

'Elizabeth Hobden, in Christ's holy name, I beg you to stop! I command you to stop!'

Athelstan undid the neck of the bag and, hands shaking, took out the stoup of water and the asperges rod. He sprinkled holy water in front of him and made the sign of the cross, but Elizabeth kept talking, her voice strident as she repeated over and over again the accusations against her father. Athelstan tried to hide his fear as he began the exorcism ceremony proper with the solemn litany of invocation, calling on Christ, His Blessed Mother and all the angels and saints. His words were drowned by the girl's shouts and that awful pounding on the walls whilst the smell became even more offensive.

Athelstan tried to continue even as a small inward voice began to question his own faith. He glanced over his shoulder and glimpsed Benedicta's white face and Hobden standing terrified at the doorway. Of Cranston there was no sign. Oh, Sir John, Athelstan thought, now in my hour of need!

He looked back at the girl – those hate-filled eyes, shoulders and head rigid against the white bolsters. She seemed oblivious to his presence, staring past him at her father. Then suddenly, in the room below, as Athelstan began his prayers again, he heard a scream, a shout and the noise of running footsteps on the stairs. Cranston, breathing heavily, burst into the room, almost knocking Athelstan aside.

'You bloody little bitch!' he roared at the girl.

Athelstan stared at him in astonishment. He was aware that the pounding on the walls had stopped. The girl, however, continued to screech accusations until Cranston strode across to the bed and slapped her firmly across both cheeks. He then grasped her by the shoulders and shook her.

'Stop it!' he roared. 'Stop it, you lying little hussy!' He gazed angrily at Athelstan. 'You have been tricked, Brother!' He shook the girl again. 'A subtle little conspiracy between this wench and her maid.'

His words had the desired effect. The girl became silent. The glare of hatred in her eyes faded as she glanced fearfully at Athelstan and then Sir John. Cranston sat on the edge of the bed and wiped the sweat from his brow.

'This little minx,' he breathed heavily, 'and her nurse concocted this medley of lies and deceits. Come on, man!' He waved Walter Hobden forward. The girl's father stepped gingerly into the room whilst she hid her face in her hands and sobbed quietly. 'Didn't it ever occur to you,' Cranston taunted Hobden, 'that this was all mummery?'

'But she drove Anna away,' he wailed.

'Listen, tickle brain,' Cranston replied, getting to his feet, 'that was part of the masque. The two only appeared estranged! Whilst Elizabeth held court up here, her good nurse, banished to the scullery, used chimney holes and gaps between the wainscoting to create the knocking sounds.' He walked over to the small hearth. 'This is an old house,' he explained. 'There are funnels and smoke flues, chimneys and other old gaps. If you go down to the scullery where the main cooking hearth is, you can, by rattling rods carefully placed up the chimney stack, create a disturbance all through the house. I have seen it done before. A children's game, played on the eve of All Hallows.' Cranston tapped the wainscoting. 'And this probably helps. It makes the echoes even louder. I went down to the scullery and there was old Anna seated like a night hag beside the hearth, busy with her metal rods.'

'But the voice?' Eleanor Hobden came into the room.

'Oh, for God's sake, woman!' Cranston scoffed. 'Haven't you ever heard anyone imitating a voice?' He stared up at an astonished Athelstan. 'I believe Crim, your altar boy, small as he is, can give a very good imitation of me?'

Athelstan smiled faintly. He felt relieved at Cranston's abrupt revelation and curt dismissal of all this mummery and trickery, yet still he felt a deep unease.

'But the smell?' Athelstan sniffed.

'Oh, I am sure there's an answer for that.'

Cranston knelt down, put his hand under the bedstead and drew out two small unstoppered pots. He then went to the other side of the bed and found the same. Cranston picked one up, sniffed at it gingerly and recoiled in distaste as he handed it to Athelstan.

'God knows what it is! I suspect goat's cheese.'

Athelstan sniffed and turned away in disgust. 'Goat's cheese,' he coughed, 'and something else.'

'A well-known trick,' Cranston observed. 'Take off the stoppers and a pig sty would be sweet compared to it.' He grinned. 'Put the jars open under the bed, move the blankets, and a stench is wafted from Hell.'

Athelstan gazed down at the sobbing girl whilst the sound of a commotion outside indicated that the fearsome Eleanor Hobden was now dragging the old nurse upstairs. Eleanor entered, cast a look of disdain at her husband and threw the struggling Anna, who looked on the point of fainting with fear, down on to the rushes. She went across and grasped Elizabeth's hair, pulling back her head. Despite her evil game, Athelstan felt a pang of compassion for the girl. Her face looked ghastly: red-rimmed eyes and pallid, tear-soaked cheeks. Elizabeth had bitten her lips and a trickle of blood ran down her chin.

'Leave her alone!' he ordered.

Eleanor gave another vicious tug to the girl's hair. Athelstan grasped her by the wrist.

'For God's sake, woman, leave her!'

Eleanor reluctantly obeyed but glared at Cranston.

'She is guilty of a crime, isn't she? The pretended raising of demons and the use of such trickery is almost as grave a charge as dabbling in the Black Arts themselves.'

Cranston, who had taken a deep dislike to the woman, nodded. 'Are you saying I should arrest her?'

'If you don't, I'll throw her and that bitch of a nurse out into the street!'

'Eleanor!' Walter moaned. 'Don't!'

'Oh, shut up!' she spat back. 'I told you this little minx was a liar and a cheat.' She went across and shoved her face only inches from her husband's. 'Either they go or I do.'

Cranston stole a glance at Athelstan. The friar looked helplessly down at the sobbing girl whilst Anna still crouched like a dog amongst the rushes. Eleanor walked back and dug the girl in the shoulder.

'Get out of this bed and leave the house as you are!'

'Oh, for pity's sake!' Cranston snapped.

'My Lord Coroner,' the Hobden woman replied, 'you were not invited to this house. You are here as an officer of the law. You have seen a crime committed yet you have no sympathy for its victims, only the perpetrator.'

Cranston glanced across at Walter Hobden, but that man of straw just stood rubbing his hands together with all the courage of a frightened rabbit.

'For God's sake!' Benedicta walked across the room and, though she'd been frightened by Elizabeth's acting, betrayed no fear of Eleanor Hobden. 'For God's sake!' she repeated. 'Woman, the girl may well be witless.'

Athelstan went and sat down on the bed, put his arm round the sobbing girl and looked at her father.

'Why did your daughter make such accusations?'

'Because she hates me,' Eleanor retorted. 'She always has and she always will. Now she can get out!'

Benedicta's eyes pleaded with Athelstan. He nodded at her to help the old nurse back to her feet.

'Listen,' he declared, 'I insist, Mistress – no, I demand this because I came here at your invitation. True, Sir John was not invited but he is owed something too for delving into the truth.'

The woman nodded.

'Accordingly,' Athelstan continued, 'Elizabeth and her nurse will stay here tonight. Tomorrow morning the Lady Benedicta will return and take both of them to the Abbey of St Mary and St Frances, which lies at the junction of Poor Jewry and Aldgate Street.'

Walter murmured his approval. His wife chewed on her lower lip, glowering at her stepdaughter.

'Agreed,' she snarled eventually. 'But the bitch is to be gone by noonday!'

–

Cranston stood at the corner of Bread Street and West Cheap and stared across at his house.

'Oh,' he moaned, 'I wish Lady Maude was back.' He stroked the muzzle of his horse, licked his lips and looked at the welcoming warmth and light of The Holy Lamb. He had left Benedicta and Athelstan in Southwark and made his own way back to Cheapside, talking loudly to himself as he often did about the hardness of the human heart and the stubborn hatred of the likes of Eleanor Hobden. His horse snickered and nuzzled his chest.

'I suppose you are right,' Cranston muttered.

He led his horse down a side street and into the yard of The Holy Lamb where he and the Lady Maude stabled their horses. Once the horse was settled, and resisting all temptation, Sir John strode across a deserted Cheapside back to his own house.

He had his hand on the latch when he heard his name called. Two figures detached themselves from the alleyway at the side of the house and stepped into the pool of light provided by the lamp hung on a hook next to the door. Cranston's smile faded.

'What the bloody hell do you want?' he snarled.

Rosamund Ingham pushed back the hood of her cloak with one hand, the other resting lightly on the arm of the slack-faced Albric. Her face was as imperious and harsh as Eleanor Hobden's. Cranston quickly noted the similarity between the two women: beautiful but hard-eyed, with a sour twist to their mouths. He put his hand back on the latch.

'I asked what you wanted?'

'Sir John, leave us alone. Tomorrow morning, as you know, my husband will be buried. I don't suppose you'll be there?'

'No, I won't! I loved Sir Oliver as a brother. I won't stand before God in the presence of his murderers!'

'That's a lie!'

'That's the truth and I'll prove it!'

'And if you don't,' Rosamund pushed her face forward, 'I'll see you in the courts, Sir John.'

'Piss off!' he replied, his hand falling to his dagger as he saw Albric move forward.

'Go on,' Cranston sneered. 'Draw your sword and I'll tickle your codpiece.'

Rosamund waved her lover back with one hand. 'Take the seals off my husband's room,' she demanded. 'And leave us alone or...'

Cranston stepped forward. 'Or what, My Lady?'

Rosamund sneered. 'I am asking you, Sir John. And I'll not ask again.'

'Good night, My Lady.' He pushed open the door and slammed it behind him.

He sniffed the air appreciatively and walked into the kitchen. A red–faced Boscombe was removing a golden-crusted pie from the oven next to the hearth.

'Just in time, Sir John,' the little man beamed. 'Beef stew pie, garnished with onions and leeks. A glass of claret?'

Sir John beamed. 'Philip, if you were a woman, I'd marry you tomorrow.'

He washed his hands in a bowl of rose water and went to sit at the table. 'You have not entered the bliss of nuptial grace?'

Boscombe shook his head. 'No woman would have me, Sir John, and Sir Gerard was the harshest of task masters.'

'In which case,' Cranston muttered, 'you haven't met the Lady Maude.'

He was about to lift his cup when suddenly Gog and Magog, who had been resting in the garden, burst into the kitchen. Gog knocked Cranston flying off his chair whilst Magog, skilful as a falcon in flight, leapt up and plucked the pie right out of Boscombe's hands. Cranston, cursing, got to his feet but the two dogs now had the pie and, even before he could reach them, were wolfing it down without a by-your-leave. Boscombe stood and wailed. Cranston stared at the dogs and, if animals could smile their thanks, he was sure these two had.

'Lovely lads!' he whispered.

Both hounds broke off their unexpected feast and leapt up to lick his face and nibble at his ears until Cranston roared, 'Enough is enough!' and pushed them down.

He looked across at Boscombe who stood, tears trailing down his cheeks. Cranston went over and patted him on the shoulder, almost knocking him to the floor.

'Come on, man!' he growled. 'At least they fed well.'

The pie had now disappeared. The two dogs, licking their lips, gazed admiringly at the new master who was so liberal with his food. They sat like carved figures as Cranston shook a warning finger at them.

'Don't ever,' he admonished them, 'try that with the Lady Maude!'

The two dogs seemed to sense the significance of the word 'Maude' and Gog even looked fearfully at the door, but it was only Leif stealing into the house, attracted by the rich savoury smells.

'Time for supper, Sir John?'

Cranston grinned. 'You'll be lucky.'

Leif looked nervously at the dogs. 'But, Sir John, I have scarcely eaten all day.'

'Oh, for God's sake!' Cranston went back to the hallway, picked up his cloak and, with the threatening face of Rosamund Ingham still in mind, wrapped his sword belt around him. 'Come on, Boscombe. And you, Leif, you lazy bugger! We're off to The Lamb of God!'

The two dogs made to follow.

'No, no, lovely lads! Stay!'

Both animals crouched down as Cranston pushed a protesting Boscombe and more eager Leif towards the door.

'Shouldn't we lock it?' Boscombe asked, once they entered Cheapside.

'Listen, man,' Cranston replied. 'What do you think the lovely lads would do if some night hawk made the mistake of walking in there?'

Boscombe smiled.

'Come on,' Cranston urged. 'That pie smelt delicious. Let me give you your just reward.'

Two hours later, full of claret and mine host's onion pie, Cranston, with one arm round Boscombe and the other hugging Leif, walked out of The Lamb of God and gazed expansively across Cheapside.

'So you were at Poitiers?' Boscombe asked.

'Oh, yes,' Cranston replied. 'Slimmer and more hand-some then—'

He was about to continue when he heard a faint cry for help from a nearby alleyway. Ignoring Boscombe's warning, and despite the cups of claret he had drunk, Cranston sped like an arrow into the darkness. He glimpsed two figures in black holding a torch above another sprawled on the ground. Cranston caught the glint of steel and heard another piteous moan. He wrapped his cloak round his left arm and carried on like a charging bull.

'Aidez! Aidez!' Cranston shouted, the usual hue-and-cry call for help.

The two figures looked up and he knew something was wrong. They didn't retreat and they had masks on their faces, whilst their 'victim' suddenly sprang to his feet. Cranston stopped, breathing heavily, and wiped the sweat from his forehead.

'You are never too old to learn,' he muttered. The Coroner cursed himself for falling into a well-known trap, hastening to a supposed victim's help only to blunder into an ambush. He gazed quickly over his shoulder, back up the alleyway where Boscombe and Leif were beginning to make their way down.

'Go back!' he roared.

He drew his own sword and gingerly began to retreat. He dared not turn and run. He might slip or a thrown dagger might wound him and bring him down. Anyway he was old and fat whilst these three assailants crept like macabre dancers towards him. Cranston kept moving backwards then suddenly sideways to protect his back against a narrow, jutting buttress of the alley wall.

The three black-garbed assassins crept closer. Each carried sword and dirk. They separated as they advanced. Cranston recognized them as professional killers, much more dangerous than the street rats who would run a mile at the sight of naked steel. He tried to control his breathing. Who had sent them? he wondered. The Ira Dei? Cranston blinked. No, no, that was too obvious.

Then he remembered Rosamund Ingham's hate-filled face, her unspoken threats, and rage replaced any fear.

The three slithered forward, arms out, legs spread, the elaborate street dance of professional fighters. Cranston watched the middle figure, catching a glimpse of an eye, then shifted his gaze to the two companions as if he was more concerned about them.

'Come on, my buckos!' he taunted. 'So you have brought old Jack on to the floor. Come on, let's tread a measure together!'

The two killers on the outside crept forward. Cranston kept shifting his gaze but knew this sort. They were only feinting. He looked to his right then quickly back as the middle killer closed in, sword low, dagger high. Cranston suddenly shifted his long sword back, then forward in a blinding arc of steel. The assassin died before he even knew it as the pointed, sharp edge of Cranston's sword severed his exposed windpipe.

Cranston, now smiling, parried forward, first to the right, then the left. He sensed one of the attackers was inexperienced, moving further back than he should. Cranston turned and charged at the other, knocking the wind out of him. Then, standing back, the Coroner shoved his sword with all his strength straight into the man's stomach. He looked round but the third attacker was now running like the wind back into the darkness. Cranston stood back, resting on his sword as he sucked in the night air and looked at the two dead assailants.

'Killing blows,' he muttered to himself.

One man was lying face down on the cobbles, the other sprawled against the wall like a broken doll. Boscombe and Leif came hobbling up and stared in horror at the two corpses as well as a different John Cranston. His face looked as hard as iron by the spluttering light of the torch which still lay on the cobbles where one of his assailants had dropped it.

'Sir John.' Boscombe touched his new master. 'Sir John, I am sorry we could not help.'

Cranston shook his head. 'You were wise,' he whispered. 'But, Master Boscombe, I thank you for your concern. Nothing old Jack couldn't deal with.'

'Why?' Leif spluttered.

Cranston gazed down the alleyway, a bitter smile on his lips. 'Oh, I know why,' he brooded. 'And now it's old Jack's turn to play!'

Chapter 9

Athelstan, too, brooded as he knelt on the altar steps the next morning after Mass. There had been only three in the congregation, not counting Bonaventure: Pernell the Fleming, Cecily the courtesan in her bright taffeta dress, and Benedicta who had just left. The widow had assured Athelstan she would take Elizabeth Hobden and her nurse Anna to the Friar Minoresses later in the morning.

Athelstan chewed on his knuckles and watched the half-open door of the church. He felt angry and hurt, and hoped he could control himself during the coming meeting.

He blessed himself and rose at the sound of footsteps, walking down the nave to meet Pike the ditcher, who stood uneasily by the baptismal font.

'Father, you sent for me?'

'Yes, Pike, I did. Please close the door.'

Pike went back, closed it, then turned in astonishment to see his gentle parish priest bearing down upon him like a charging knight. Athelstan seized Pike by his grimy jerkin and pushed him up against the door. The man didn't resist, terrified of the rage blazing in Athelstan's eyes.

'Father, what is it?' he stammered.

'You bloody Judas!' Athelstan shook him. 'Pike, I am your priest and you betrayed me!'

'What do you mean?'

But Athelstan glimpsed the truth in the ditcher's nervous eyes. He let go, pushed him away and walked back up the nave.

'Don't lie, Pike!' he shouted, his words ringing through the church. 'You know damned well what I am talking about! You were the only one who saw me take down the proclamation pinned to my door by Ira Dei.' Athelstan rounded on him. 'In fact, I suspect *you* put it there. And that's fine, Pike. You play your stupid, dangerous games of revolt and building God's kingdom here in London. But, tell me, do your fellow communards, does the Great Community of the Realm, does Ira Dei know you are a traitor? John of Gaunt's spy?' Athelstan walked back. 'And what would happen to you, Pike, if they found out, eh? How does your secret society treat traitors?'

Pike stood with hands hanging helplessly and Athelstan's anger began to drain away at the sheer terror in the man's face and posture. The priest pushed his face close to the ditcher's.

'For God's sake, Pike, I baptized your children! I give you the sacrament. I admired you, working from dawn to dusk for a mere pittance to feed your family.' Athelstan drew his breath. 'You are not like me, Pike. I have no family to worry about. But you are a good worker, a good husband, a good father. For God's sake, why play the Judas with a man who is not only a priest but your friend? Couldn't you trust me?'

Pike flailed his hands ineffectually as tears coursed down his dirty cheeks.

'Oh, for God's sake!' Athelstan muttered. 'Pike, I don't mean to threaten you. Your secret's safe with me. Not even Sir John knows.'

The ditcher shuffled his feet. 'It's not like that, Father.'

'What do you mean?'

'Three months ago,' he replied, 'I and a few others from Southwark were listening to that mad priest – you know, the one with the fiery cross, outside St James Garlick-hythe. Then the soldiers came and we were arrested. I had a choice: pay a fine or become Gaunt's spy. The fine would have crushed me and...' His voice trailed off.

'And what?'

Pike looked up defiantly. 'Don't believe everything you hear, Father. I am not one of your zealots. Oh, at the beginning I was, but not now. Not when they talk of slaughter, of killing every priest, of burning the good with the bad.' He laughed sourly. 'It's not difficult, Father, to betray something you don't believe in any more. And as for My Lord of Gaunt, he had discovered I am not the most capable of spies. So, I tell him about a notice pinned on the door of the church. Or that a member of the Great

Community of the Realm has visited Southwark, three days after the man has left. Don't worry, Father, Gaunt never profits from what I tell him.'

Athelstan looked at the great, burly ditcher standing there, hanging his head. You represent the common man, Athelstan reflected, caught between the demons who want to destroy everything and those who wish to keep everything. Athelstan walked forward, hands extended.

'I am sorry. You are no traitor, no Judas!'

Pike grasped his hand. 'Can you help me, Father?'

Athelstan pursed his lips. 'Yes, I think I can. But it will take time. Meanwhile don't do anything rash, man. And...'

'And what, Father?'

'What do you know of Ira Dei?'

Pike laughed. 'Father, I am a very small leaf low down on a very tall tree. I don't even know who the rebel leaders are. No one knows who Ira Dei is. He comes, shrouded in darkness, delivers his message, and just as mysteriously leaves. He could be anyone. The Lady Benedicta, Watkin, even Sir John Cranston!' Pike grinned. 'Though I think people would recognize *him*. Father, I know nothing. I swear on the life of my children!'

'But could you get a message to him?'

'I could tell certain people. Why?' Pike's face became concerned. 'Father, take care. Have no dealings with such violent men, be they nobles or peasants. Do you know what I think? It's a fight between the rats and the ferrets over who will rule the chicken run.'

Athelstan smiled, touched by Pike's concern.

'The message is simple. Say Athelstan of St Erconwald's would like to meet Ira Dei.' He made Pike repeat the message.

'Is that all, Father?'

'Yes, it is. I have kept you long enough. I am sorry for my temper.'

Pike shrugged. 'You get what you deserve, Father. But you will help me?'

'Of course!'

'I'll never forget, Father.'

Pike disappeared. Athelstan thought of the ditcher's gangling son, deeply in love with Watkin's daughter, and stared at Bonaventure, who had been watching them with close attention.

'Well, well, my cunning cat,' he whispered. 'Perhaps Sunday morning won't be so terrible after all, eh?'

Athelstan stared round the church and remembered his promise to another parishioner. He locked St Erconwald's and hurried through the streets to Ranulf the rat-catcher's house, a small, two-storeyed tenement on the corner of an alleyway. The pale pinch-faced rat-catcher was waiting for him. His brood of children, all resembling him, gathered behind their father at the door to welcome the priest to their house. As Athelstan entered the darkened passageway, he recalled that Ranulf was a widower whose wife had died in childbirth five years previously. Ranulf, his brood trailing behind, ushered Athelstan into his small solar or working shop. Athelstan sniffed as he sat on the stool. The rat-catcher was on the chair opposite, children around him, eyes intent on the priest.

'Do you like the smell, Father?'

'Why, yes, Ranulf, it's not offensive.'

Ranulf patted his black-tarred jacket. 'I rub aniseed and thyme into this. Rats like that.'

He paused as his eldest daughter, dressed in a ragged black dress, solemnly served Athelstan and her father pots of tasty soup. As she did so, the friar gazed round: in one corner was a cage with sparrows; in another hung fishing lines, a badger's skin, lead bobs and eel hooks.

'Do you like rats?' Ranulf suddenly asked.

Athelstan stared back.

'There are four types, Father. Barn rats, sewer rats, river rats and street rats. The worst are the sewer rats – they are the black ones.' He pulled back the sleeve of his tarred jacket, displaying an arm badly pocked with the marks of old wounds. 'The black rats are bastards, Father. Sorry, but they are real bastards! I have been dead near four times from bites. I once had the teeth of a rat break in my finger.' He extended his hand. 'It was terrible bad, swollen and rotted. I had to have the broken bits taken out with pincers. I have been bitten everywhere, Father.'

Athelstan jumped as a small, furry animal, which seemed to come from nowhere, ran up the rat-catcher's leg and sat on his lap.

'This is Ferox,' Ranulf announced, 'my ferret.'

Athelstan stared in disbelief at the creature's little black eyes and twitching nose.

'Ferox means ferocious,' Ranulf continued, not giving Athelstan a chance to speak. 'Now, ferrets are very dangerous but Ferox is well trained. He has sent at least a thousand rats to their maker.'

Athelstan hid his grin, finished his soup and handed the bowl and pewter spoon back to the girl. The rest of Ranulf's children stood staring at their father with eyes rounded in admiration. The priest looked at the rat-catcher's slightly jutting teeth, pointed nose and white whiskery face, and recalled his recent conversation with Pike. Ranulf was the same: a hard-working man, a good father, one of the small ones of the earth, so far from power and wealth and yet so close to God.

'Ranulf, you wanted to talk to me about the Guild?'

'Yes, Father, we'd like our Guild Mass at St Erconwald's.' Ranulf swallowed nervously. 'The Guild would meet in the church and then we'd have our feast in the nave afterwards. If that's all right with you, Father?'

Athelstan nodded solemnly.

'Every month on the third Saturday we'd meet at St Erconwald's for our Mass and use the nave for a meeting.'

Athelstan again nodded.

'And we'd pay you two pounds, fifteen shillings every quarter.'

Athelstan guessed the rat-catcher thought the amount rather low.

'That will be most satisfactory,' he replied quickly.

'Are you sure, Father?'

'Of course.'

'And wives and children can attend?'

'Why not?'

'And you'll bless our ferrets and traps?'

'Without a doubt.'

'And do you know of a patron saint, Father?'

Athelstan stared back. 'No, Ranulf, that puzzles me, but I am sure I can find one for you.'

Ranulf gave a sigh of relief and got to his feet.

'In which case, Father, you have our thanks. Osric, he's the chief rat-catcher in Southwark, will draw up the indenture. He knows a clerk at St Paul's.'

'I can do that with no fee,' Athelstan answered, getting to his feet.

Ranulf crowed with delight and clapped his hands whilst his children, catching his good humour, danced round Athelstan as if he was their patron saint. He glimpsed a trap hanging on the wall and suddenly thought of Cranston's poor friend Oliver Ingham.

'Tell me, Ranulf, have you ever heard of a rat gnawing a corpse?'

'Oh yes, Father, they'll eat anything.'

'And you kill them with traps or ferrets?'

'Aye, and sometimes with poisons such as belladonna or nightshade, if they are really cunning.'

Athelstan smiled his thanks and walked to the door.

'Father!'

Athelstan turned. 'No, Ranulf, before you ask – Bonaventure is not for sale. But we can always enrol him as a member of your Guild.'

Athelstan took leave of Ranulf and his family. He was halfway down the alleyway, his mind full of rats, poisons, traps and ferrets, when suddenly he stopped, mouth gaping at the idea which had occurred to him. He smiled and looked up at the brightening sky.

'O Lord, blessed are you,' he whispered. 'And your ways are most wonderful to behold.'

He almost ran back to the rat-catcher's house and hammered on the door. Ranulf appeared quite agitated as Athelstan grasped him by the shoulder.

'Father, what is it?'

'You must come with me. Now, Ranulf! You must come with me now to see Sir John! Ranulf, please, I need your help!'

The rat-catcher needed no second bidding. He went back indoors, shouted instructions at his daughter, kissed each of his children and, with Ferox firmly penned in a small cage, allowed Athelstan to hurry him through the streets of Southwark down to London Bridge.

Rosamund Ingham paled as she answered Sir John's insistent knocking. She stood with the door half-open and glared at the Coroner then at Athelstan, with Ranulf standing behind him. 'What's the matter, Mistress?' Cranston greeted her. 'You look as if you have seen a ghost!'

'What do you want?'

'You asked me last night to remove the seals from your dead husband's room and that's why I am here.' He pushed the door further open. 'We can come in, can't we? Thank you so much.'

He glimpsed Albric standing further up the stone-flagged passageway and, from where he stood, Cranston could see the young fop was visibly frightened.

'I'd best take you up to the room.' Rosamund recovered her composure quickly, her pert face showing some of its old icy hardness.

Athelstan waved her on. 'If you would, Mistress.'

Cranston winked at him.

'For a monk, Brother, you are as sharp as a new pin.'

'Friar!' Athelstan hissed.

'Well, even better,' Cranston whispered back as they climbed the stairs.

Athelstan lowered his eyes so as not to glance at Mistress Ingham's swaying hips. A born flirt, he thought, and knew Cranston would use a cruder word. He glanced at his fat friend walking just behind him. Although the Coroner had a smile on his lips, his light blue eyes were hard with fury. They reached the top of the stairs. Cranston removed the seals and pushed the door open.

'Why are they here?' Rosamund pointed a dainty finger at Athelstan and Ranulf.

'First, because they are fellow officers!' Cranston snapped. 'And, second, Mistress, because I want them here. You have no objection surely?' Rosamund moved herself in between Sir John and the open door.

'You have removed the seals,' she snapped. 'Now, get out!'

'Oh, didn't you know?' Cranston raised his eyebrows. 'When the King's Coroner unseals a room, he has to ensure, to his own satisfaction, that the chamber is as he left it. Surely you have no objections?'

The woman's lips tightened and Cranston gave up all pretence.

'I am not here because I am the late Sir Oliver's friend,' he muttered, glancing at Rosamund's black dress. 'I suppose the requiem was both short and sweet?'

'It finished an hour ago.'

Cranston shoved her aside. 'I am the King's Coroner,' he declared, 'I wish to see this room, and I should be grateful, Mistress, if you and that thing downstairs would make yourselves available to answer certain questions.'

Rosamund flounced away, though Athelstan saw the fear in her face and knew that Sir John was right. She was a killer and undoubtedly responsible for the previous night's murderous assault on the Coroner. As he followed Cranston into the chamber, Athelstan quietly prayed that both Rosamund and her weak-willed lover would fall into the trap prepared for them and that Ranulf would justify their expectations.

Cranston stared round the bed chamber, quiet and sombre, the dust motes dancing in the sunlight pouring through a glazed window. He opened the shutters of another, took a swig from his wineskin and, in an act of outstanding generosity, allowed Ranulf a drink as well.

'Right, my lad.' Cranston clapped the rat-catcher on the shoulder. 'How would you like the right to be appointed chief rat-catcher in the city wards of Castle Baynard, Queenhithe and the Vintry?'

Ranulf beamed his pleasure.

'In time, my lad, perhaps. But now, find me some rats – preferably dead ones.'

Ranulf brought Ferox out of his little cage from beneath his cloak. Cranston stepped back immediately.

'You know what we are looking for, just keep that bloody thing away from me! I have a horror of ferrets. I knew a man once who allowed one to get inside his hose. He ended up being castrated!'

Ranulf grinned as he stroked the inquisitive ferret between the ears. The ferret gazed unblinkingly at Cranston.

'Oh, bloody hell!' the Coroner said.

'Sir John, if you are really afeared,' Ranulf replied, pointing to a small bench, 'perhaps it's best if you stand on that.'

Cranston gazed suspiciously at him but Ranulf remained sombre-faced.

'Lord Coroner, I always advise nervous patrons to do that.'

'You'd best do as he says, Sir John,' Athelstan added with a smile. 'You know how Bonaventure loves you. Ferox may be of the same ilk.'

Cranston needed no second bidding but stood like a Colossus on the small bench. He leaned his back against the wall, fortifying himself with generous mouthfuls from the miraculous wineskin. Ranulf held Ferox to his lips and whispered in his ear.

'What are you doing?' Cranston bellowed.

'Telling him what to do.'

'Oh, don't be bloody stupid, man!'

Ranulf carefully put Ferox down on the floorboards. For a few minutes the ferret sniffed before darting like an arrow beneath the great four-poster bed. Athelstan went across to the small table and picked up the unstoppered earthenware jug.

'You say this contained the foxglove?'

Cranston, his eyes intent on the bed, just nodded.

'And you say it was found knocked over and the medicine drained?'

'Yes, yes, Brother, but leave that. What's that bloody ferret up to?'

Cranston got his answer. Suddenly there was a violent scuffle under the bed and Ferox emerged, his small snout bloodied as he dragged a fat, long-tailed, brown rat out into the open.

'Good boy!' Ranulf whispered.

'The bloody thing's as stupid as you are, Ranulf!' Cranston roared. 'He's not here to kill bloody rats but find dead ones!' Ranulf picked up the dead rat, opened the window and tossed it into the street. Again Ferox went hunting. The minutes passed. Athelstan watched the industrious little ferret and tried not to look at Cranston who, having taken so many swigs from the wineskin, was beginning to sway rather dangerously on the bench. Ranulf kept picking the ferret up and putting it under cupboards and behind chests. Sometimes the ferret would return, other times there would be an eerie scuffling, a heart-stopping scream, and he would re-emerge with a rat. Athelstan had to look away as Cranston began to bellow imprecations. On one occasion Rosamund came and rapped on the door. Cranston roared at her to bugger off and instructed his 'grinning monk', as he called Athelstan, to bolt the door.

At last Ranulf was finished. Ferox was put back in his cage. Cranston came down from his perch and all three began to move the bed and bits of furniture, Ranulf even lifting floorboards, but they could find nothing.

Eventually, all three went, red-faced and perspiring, to stand in the centre of the room. Cranston's elation was obvious. He clapped both Athelstan and Ranulf on the shoulder and apologized for bellowing at Ranulf.

'I'll buy you the best claret in London!' he swore. 'And a drink for your little friend.'

'He likes malmsey, Sir John.'

'Well, as far as I'm concerned, he can have a bloody bath in it! But you are sure?'

Ranulf nodded.

'In which case, we should try the jar.'

He went across, took up the small jug and, using his wineskin, filled the jug to the brim, then raised it to his lips.

'Sir John, are you certain?'

'Oh, for God's sake, Athelstan, I am about to find out.' He drank from the jug, draining every drop from it. '*Alea iacta!*' he declared. 'The die is cast! Let's see the bitch downstairs.'

They all trooped down to the solar where a tight-faced Rosamund and a much more nervous Albric sat waiting for them.

'Sir John.' The woman got to her feet. 'You have been a good hour in my house. Now get out!'

'I haven't finished yet,' he snapped, advancing within a few inches of her.

'Why, what else do you want? These ridiculous allegations!'

Cranston breathed in deeply. 'Rosamund Ingham, and you Albric Totnes, I, Sir John Cranston, King's Coroner in the city, do arrest you for murder and treason!'

Rosamund went white and gaped. Albric slumped wet-eyed and slack-jawed. Athelstan recognized him as an easier quarry. 'O, Lord,' he reflected, quoting from the psalms, 'Stretch out your hand and show your justice.'

Rosamund soon regained her composure. 'Murder? Treason? What nonsense is this?'

'You know full well, Mistress.' Cranston produced from his voluminous sleeve the small jug which he had taken from the chamber above. 'You agree, Mistress, in the presence of witnesses, that this is the jug containing your late husband's medicine, an infusion of foxglove or digitalis? A medicine, I understand, which can strengthen the heart if taken in small doses?'

'Yes, it is. What are you going to say, Sir John, that my husband took too much? He insisted on pouring it himself. No one else was allowed to touch it.'

Cranston nodded. 'And would you agree, in the presence of witnesses, that this is the jug that was left in your husband's chamber when I sealed it, and that in your husband's death throes he knocked over?'

'Yes, yes!'

Cranston turned at a sound near the door and summoned over the old manservant.

'Just in time, me lad!' he boomed. 'I could do with another witness. Tell me, Mistress.' He turned back to the woman. 'Have you ever tasted foxglove?'

'Of course not! Sir John, you have been drinking!'

'Yes. Yes, I have. I even drank from this jug.'

Athelstan gazed quickly at Albric, who might be a coward but, by the look on his face, had already guessed the direction of Cranston's interrogation. It seemed only to increase his terror.

'Well,' Cranston continued evenly, 'foxglove is fairly tasteless. And that's how you murdered your husband. He kept the main supply of the potion in a stoppered flask in the buttery. What he didn't know is that, perhaps a month before his death, you poured the potion away and replaced it with nothing more harmful than water.'

'Don't be stupid, my husband would have noticed!'

Cranston smiled. 'Where is that flask?'

'I've thrown it away!' Rosamund stammered.

'Well, well,' Cranston snapped. 'Why should you do that?'

'It wasn't needed!'

'Rubbish. You wished to hide the evidence! It would never have occurred to him. After all,' Cranston continued, 'we see what we expect to see. I understand from my medical friends that foxglove in its liquid form is both clear and tasteless. Perhaps you added something to thicken it a little? What do we have, woman, eh? A man with a weak heart, worried sick about his faithless wife, being deprived for weeks of a life-giving medicine. Oh, yes, Sir Oliver, God rest him, died of a heart seizure – but one brought about by you. Now, Brother Athelstan here is a theologian.' Cranston glanced quickly at Albric who sat slumped in his chair, arms crossed tightly over his chest. 'Athelstan will tell you that there are two types of sin. The first is an act, the second an omission. Albric, do you know what omission means?'

The young fop shook his head.

'It means, you treacherous little turd, that you commit evil by not doing something. You can kill a man by throwing him into the river. You can also kill him by refusing to help him out.'

'What proof do you have?' Rosamund demanded.

'Enough to hang you,' Cranston answered sharply, coming forward. 'You see, as your husband died, in the middle of his seizure, his hand flailed out and he knocked over the medicine jar, allowing the liquid to spill out. Now, this house is plagued by rats, hungry and inquisitive.' Cranston was so furious he found it hard to speak.

'What My Lord Coroner is saying,' Athelstan intervened quietly, 'is that if a rat would gnaw a dead man's body, it would certainly drink any liquid left lying about. I have looked at that table,' he lied. 'As has the professional rat-catcher here. There are signs of rats on that table. Their tracks, as well as their dung, are all over the chamber.' He glanced quickly at Ranulf who nodded wisely. 'More importantly,' he continued, 'as my good friend here will swear, any rat who drank foxglove would soon die but we discovered no dead rat in that chamber.' Athelstan schooled his features. He was bluffing and no Justice would convict anyone on the evidence they had produced. His heart skipped a beat as he heard Albric moan. The young man uncrossed his arms and made to rise.

'This is nonsense!' Rosamund snapped, a gleam of triumph in her eyes. 'First, the rat could slink away to die anywhere and we have found dead rats in the house, haven't we, Albric?' The young man, white-faced, just nodded.

'That's impossible!' Ranulf, entering the spirit of the occasion, now spoke up. 'Foxglove would kill a rat immediately. I would swear to that. Indeed, I could show you.'

Albric sat down again and stared fearfully at Athelstan.

'You also mentioned treason.' Rosamund rushed her words to hide any confusion.

'Yes, I did,' Cranston replied softly. 'Last night I was attacked by footpads. I beat them off and took one prisoner,' he lied. 'He confessed how you hired them to kill me.'

'Nonsense!'

'He named you.'

'Oh, this is ridiculous!' she sneered. 'Are you also accusing me of hiring three footpads?'

Cranston smiled. 'How do you know there were three?'

The sneer died on Rosamund's face.

'They also named you.' Cranston nodded at Albric.

'That's not true!' the young man snapped and glared furiously at Rosamund. 'You said it would be safe!'

'Oh, shut up, you fool!' She sat down, covering her face with her hands.

Athelstan relaxed, aware that he had been digging the nails of his fingers into the palms of his hand. He went to stand over the young man.

'Confess,' he said quietly. 'Turn King's evidence and who knows what the Coroner will do for you?'

Athelstan crouched and patted the young man's hand then stood up as Albric stared at the floor.

'I'll confess,' he muttered.

Rosamund pushed her tearful, hate-filled face at Athelstan. 'Shut up, you bloody priest! You ragged-arsed half-man! I did it for you!' she hissed at Albric. 'I did it for you!'

He shook his head. 'We're finished,' he whispered.

Cranston turned and beckoned Robert over. 'Quickly, go down the street. At The Moon and the Cage tavern you'll find four serjeants. You are to bring them here immediately!'

The steward scurried off. Athelstan and Cranston walked to the front door and waited until the four city serjeants came. Cranston whispered instructions to them then he and his companions left even as Rosamund's rage turned to hysteria. She screamed her fury at Cranston and

Athelstan as the serjeants began to load her and Albric with the chains they had brought.

Outside in the street Cranston stood still, his eyes full of tears. 'I can't say anything,' he said. He shook Athelstan's hand very formally and then Ranulf's. He wiped a tear away. 'Come on. I did not go to Oliver's requiem mass but let me buy you the funeral toast.' He pointed down to Ferox, now dozing quietly in his cage. 'And our little friend here can go home drunk.'

Chapter 10

An hour later, a rather drunk Ranulf with an even tipsier ferret staggered out of The Moon and the Cage tavern, muttering that he had to get back to Southwark. Cranston watched the rat-catcher disappear out of the door of the tavern and grew expansive.

'A fine man, Brother. I've always called your parishioners a gang of sinners but there goes a good man.'

'We are all sinners,' Athelstan replied. 'But, God knows, thinking of Mistress Rosamund, I'd draw a line between those who fall due to weakness and those who sin out of malice.'

'Which brings us,' Cranston trumpeted, keeping a wary eye on the relic-seller feasting on his ill-gotten gains in the far corner of the taproom, 'back to the deaths at the Guildhall, eh?'

Athelstan quickly told him about his meeting with Pike the ditcher. Cranston heard him out, smacking his lips and sniffing at the savoury smells from the tavern kitchen.

'Pike should watch himself,' he growled. 'A man who stands with a foot on either side of a flame ends up getting his balls burnt. Oh, by the way, talking of danger, has the Lady Benedicta collected that minx of a girl?'

'By now, Sir John, she should be safely at the Minor-esses.'

'A bad business that,' Cranston muttered. 'Do you know, Brother, there was something evil in that house?'

'Well, it's finished,' Athelstan declared half-heartedly. He agreed with Cranston's conclusion but still felt guilty about what had happened. 'However, this business at the Guildhall.' He ran a finger round the rim of his cup. 'You realize, Sir John, those murders are not like the ones we usually investigate? You knew Sir Oliver had been murdered. Someone in that house had killed him. The same is true of the other crimes we have resolved, be it the business at the Springall manor or the murder of Sir Ralph Whitton at the Tower last Christmas.'

Athelstan warmed to his theme. 'You see, Sir John, such crimes originate not from bad blood but hot blood. Political assassination, however, is different. There's no personal rancour, no malicious glee at the destruction of an enemy, just expediency. This is what we are dealing with now: Mountjoy and Fitzroy's deaths were coldly decided, seized as a means to bring My Lord of Gaunt's plans into confusion.'

Athelstan rubbed his lips and, before Cranston could order more wine, told the pot boy to go away. 'Remember, Sir John, murder is like chess. You move a piece, your opponent counter moves. Sooner or later a mistake will be made or a path opened in order to discover the truth and bring the game to an end. But here our opponent could be anyone.' Athelstan brushed crumbs from his robe. 'Three murders,' he muttered. 'We know they died but little else. How was Fitzroy poisoned when he ate and drank what the rest did? How could Mountjoy be stabbed to death in the privacy of his own garden? And Sturmey? One minute on the quayside, the next floating in the Thames with a dagger in his chest.' Athelstan paused as a loud snore greeted his words. He turned to see Sir John, head back, eyes closed, with a beatific smile on his face. 'Sir John! Lord above!' Athelstan breathed. 'I can't even find your ribs, you're so fat!'

'Portly,' Sir John answered, opening his eyes and licking his lips. 'I am portly, Athelstan.' He tapped his red, fleshy nose. 'Remember, Brother, the Lord Coroner may doze but he never sleeps. What is it you want to know?'

'Sturmey… you knew something from his past?'

'God knows! I can't place it,' Cranston growled, getting to his feet. 'But we've got to visit his shop again.'

'I thought Gaunt's men had sealed it?'

'Yes, they have, but I've received permission from the Regent to remove the seals as long as My Lord Clifford is present.'

'I was hoping to return to Southwark.'

'Well, you can't. There's God's work to be done here. Come on, Brother.'

Athelstan followed Cranston out, noting how the Coroner deliberately knocked against the hard-drinking relic-seller.

'I hate such bastards!' he whispered outside the tavern. 'If I had my way, I'd clear the lot from the city. They sell enough wood from the true cross to build a fleet of ships!'

Athelstan, seeing the fat Coroner was becoming evil-tempered, linked his arm through his and gently diverted the conversation to a more even keel by asking when he thought the Lady Maude would return. They soon found Lord Clifford's house, a handsome, three-storeyed building in Parchment Lane, but the young nobleman was not at home.

'He's gone to see the physician,' a liveried servant explained as he ushered them into the small, comfortable solar. 'However, he is expecting you, Sir John.'

Athelstan courteously declined the offer of refreshment, but Cranston needed no second urging. He sat back in a quilted chair, sipping the claret and openly admiring the luxury of the room. Athelstan, quietly praying Sir John would not drink too much, also looked at the pieces of armour tastefully arranged around the walls. A pair of crossed gauntlets, a shield and two halberds, and a number of intricate, beautifully carved arbalests and crossbows.

'A wealthy man,' Athelstan observed.

'Of course,' Sir John replied. 'I served with his father. He took a group of bowmen to France. A fierce soldier, God rest him, and now his son aims high.'

Athelstan glanced at the thick, woollen rugs on the shining oak floor, the silverware on the polished table glinting in the sunlight pouring through a painted glass window. Athelstan wondered why men like Lord Adam, who had so much, always wanted more. His meditations were rudely interrupted by Clifford himself bursting into the room. He tossed his cloak at a servant and strode across to shake their hands warmly. Athelstan saw the bruises and marks on the young man's face and noticed how stiffly he moved his shoulders.

'You were injured sorely?' the friar asked as the greetings were finished.

Clifford grinned then grimaced. 'Some cuts and bruises to my face. The worst is a dagger wound in my shoulder.'

'The work of Ira Dei?'

'Undoubtedly. I was beaten unconscious before the watch rescued me. The bastards even left a note pinned to my cloak.'

'What did it say?'

'"Do not provoke the Anger of God."' Clifford moved his shoulder gingerly. 'I couldn't give a fig. It will take more than those ruffians,' he remarked drily, 'to hinder me.'

He offered more refreshment but Athelstan said the day was passing.

'Sir John,' he explained, 'wishes to visit Sturmey's shop, remove the Regent's seals and search the place.'

Clifford agreed and they went out into the bustling marketplace, Clifford chatting to them about Gaunt's determination to restore his alliance with the Guildmasters.

'Keep your voices down and your hands on your wallets,' Cranston intervened. He smiled at Athelstan. 'I think all Southwark's here.'

The friar glanced around. The stalls were busy, the noise deafening with the apprentices' raucous cries of 'St Thomas' onions!' 'Fresh bread!' 'Hot pies!' 'Pins and needles for a mistress!' 'A cap for you, sir!' All of London, the silk-clad nobles and serge-clothed peasants, swirled around the stalls and Athelstan glimpsed the sharp-faced foists, pickpockets and cut-purses at work. He'd walked so many times through the city with Cranston, he'd acquired the Coroner's skill in detecting how these sneak thieves worked, constantly moving round the marketplace looking for a victim. These petty law-breakers were now busy, seemingly oblivious to the punishments being carried out around the stocks and whipping posts of Cheapside: market beadles chained men and women, crude placards slung round their necks describing their litany of crimes, be it cutting buttons from precious robes to bone-pickers and rag-gatherers who were not above helping themselves to any items which fell from a stall.

A pardoner stood beneath the market cross, greasy scrolls in his hand, offering remission for sins in return for donations to the Pope's coffers. Hawkers sold battered spoons, rusting tin cups and other paltry articles. The whores paraded themselves, keeping a wary eye for the ward constables; tipplers offered fresh water whilst beating off dogs lapping in their buckets or ragged-arsed urchins begging for a free drink. The execution cart forced its way through, preceded by a dark-cowled monk, muttering the prayers for the dying. Three condemned felons sat on their cheap arrow-chest coffins shouting farewells at the sparse, ragged crowd of friends and acquaintances. These accompanied the condemned felons to the gallows to hang on their feet and so ensure a speedy death. Now and again Cranston would be recognized with 'Hellos' from the worthy city burgesses or black looks and a stream of obscenities from those who had felt the Coroner's fat hand on their collar.

At last they turned up Lawrence Lane. Sturmey's shop was all boarded up but the whey-faced maid and chattering apprentice let them in.

'His son has not come south yet,' the young boy told them. 'But the sooner he does, the sooner I can move on to another master.'

Cranston patted him on the head and slipped a penny into his hand. Clifford drew his dagger, sliced through the Regent's seal and, taking the keys the Corporation had seized, opened the workshop. Inside, ably assisted by the young apprentice, they began to sift through the bits of discarded keys. Athelstan went through the dead locksmith's ledger but, after an hour, they could find nothing of interest.

Clifford, grimacing at the pain in his shoulder, stamped his foot in annoyance.

'Sturmey must have made a second set of keys. But how and where is a mystery, Sir John.'

Cranston was staring at the young, angelic face of the apprentice. A vague memory stirred in his mind.

'How long did you serve Master Sturmey?' he asked.

'It's three years, sir, since my mother drew up indentures with him and I have another three years left.'

Cranston nodded his head sagely. 'And your master always worked here?'

'Oh, yes, here or in the garden.'

'And he had no visitors?' Cranston smiled. 'Like this young noble lord here?'

The lad stared at Clifford and shook his head.

'No, no, it was always the Lord Mayor and the Sheriff.'

Athelstan walked out of the workshop and down the passageway. He smiled at the young maid in the scullery and went through the back door into the garden. A neatly kept place with a small rose patch, a green garth, and the rest flowers or herbs: iris, lily, cowslip and corn-flower growing around a small pond. The air was sweet with fragrance from the herb banks: camomile, fennel, lavender, even some hyssop and marjoram. Athelstan noticed a small brick house at the end of the garden and followed the path down. He was surprised to see the sturdy door heavily barred and padlocked so returned to the house and asked the young boy for the key. The apprentice shook his head.

'Master Sturmey kept that separate,' he declared. 'We was never allowed in there.'

Now curious, Cranston and Clifford followed Athelstan back into the garden. The Coroner took a hammer and chisel from one of the work benches and soon made short work of the lock. Inside, the stone shed was musty, rather airless. Cranston knocked open the shutters and stared round. There was a bench and some chests. Cranston grinned and pointed to the small forge near the fire-hearth.

'This is where he made the keys,' Cranston declared, and using the mallet and chisel, soon opened the chests. Inside were all the implements a locksmith would need: strips of lead and steel, casting irons and bits of keys. Cranston rummaged amongst the contents of the chest and brought out a mould which had been deliberately shattered. He handed this to Clifford.

'If you take that to the Lord Regent, as cats love milk, I am sure you will find Sturmey used this and others to fashion a second set of keys.'

'For whom?' Clifford asked.

'Ah, that's the mystery.'

A small book, deep in the shadows of the chest, caught Cranston's eye. He pulled this out whilst Clifford walked back into the garden to study the fragments of the mould more closely. Cranston flicked through the pages. At first, he thought it was a small Book of Hours but then he looked at the illustrations, cleverly drawn, and slipped it up his sleeve. He now knew Master Sturmey's dark secret.

Clifford was excited by Cranston's find and could hardly wait to hurry off, leaving Cranston and Athelstan to thank the apprentice and maid. Once outside the house, Cranston showed Athelstan the book. He turned over the finely grained parchment pages and whistled under his breath as he studied the paintings some clever artist had depicted there. Boys and young men, as naked as they were born, in a variety of poses. Some fought with swords; one group lounged on cloth of gold couches; two practised spear-throwing. Other pictures were more daring – young men washing each other or exchanging embraces and kisses.

'Master Sturmey did have his secrets,' Athelstan whispered. 'Such a book could condemn a man to be burnt alive.'

Cranston tapped the side of his nose. 'I knew I had it. Come on, Athelstan!'

He strode back into Cheapside, the friar having to trot to keep up with the Coroner's surprising spurt of speed. Leif the beggar, however, stopped them only a few yards from the Coroner's house.

'Be on your guard, Sir John!' he whispered dramatically. 'Be on your guard!'

'What are you talking about, you silly bugger?'

'The Lady Maude's back.'

Cranston's jaw sagged. 'She's come back early,' he whispered. 'Oh, my God, she'll see those bloody dogs!'

'She's in a strange mood,' Leif declared sombrely, trying hard to hide his glee.

'Domina Maude is always in a strange mood,' Cranston growled. He stared longingly across Cheapside at The Holy Lamb.

'Oh, no, Sir John!' Leif warned, now thoroughly enjoying himself. 'The Lady Maude was most insistent. I was to stand guard on The Holy Lamb and tell you to go home immediately.'

Chapter 11

Athelstan felt sorry, for all the life seemed to have gone out of old Cranston. He just stood scratching his bald pate like a little boy caught stealing apples.

'Come on, Sir John,' Athelstan whispered. 'I'll be with you. Lady Maude will scarcely lay a hand on Holy Mother Church.'

'Domina Maude would challenge God himself if she thought the cause was right!' Cranston blinked, drew in his breath, pushed Leif aside and walked like a condemned felon into his house. In the doorway he stopped for one last generous swig, then, raising his fingers to his lips, tiptoed down the passageway and peered into the kitchen.

'Be still!' The Lady Maude stood by the table. Gog and Magog sat like two carved statues before her. Domina Maud was in full spate, giving the dogs a pithy lecture about the rules of the house. Athelstan, peering over Cranston's shoulder, could see that both wolfhounds were as terrified of Domina Maude as their newfound master was. Behind the dogs Boscombe stood fixed like a candle-stick, now and again nodding his head in approval of every word the Lady Maude uttered. Cranston coughed and walked into the kitchen. Lady Maude turned. She was only just over five foot high.

Athelstan had never before met a woman who could seem to be twice her height.

'Sir John,' she cried sweetly. 'I arrived home early.'

Cranston gingerly walked forward, his beaver hat clenched in his hands.

'Lady wife,' he stammered, 'you are most welcome. And the poppets?'

'Upstairs with their nurse, sleeping soundly. And no, Sir John,' as Cranston turned, 'you will leave them at peace. I decided to return,' she walked forward, 'because I missed you, Sir John.' She smiled. 'And good news! My brother Ralph, his wife and children might be joining us after Michaelmas.'

Cranston daren't let his fixed smile slip. 'Oh, rat's arse!' he breathed.

Lady Maude came closer. She stood on tiptoe and kissed her husband on either cheek before turning to clasp Athelstan's hand. The friar saw the merriment dancing in the little woman's eyes.

'Sir John has been behaving himself, Father?'

'A man of righteousness, Lady Maude.'

Her smile widened at the gentle sarcasm in Athelstan's voice. Cranston stood stock-still, staring at Gog and Magog then at Boscombe. The dogs ignored him, their eyes on Lady Maude, whilst Boscombe gazed glassily back.

'You have met our visitors, Lady Maude?'

'Visitors!' his wife cried. 'Sir John, they are part of our family. Master Boscombe is a rare jewel.'

'And the dogs?'

'They now know their place, as should everyone in this house.'

Cranston stiffened even further at the hint of warning in his wife's words. Maude suddenly gripped Sir John's hand.

'You are a kind and generous man,' she whispered. 'I would have been angry if you had done any other. How could a man like Boscombe be turned into the streets and two of God's beautiful creatures be cruelly destroyed? I do not like My Lord Regent, and Boscombe has told me about the business at the Guildhall.'

Cranston shot a glance at him. The servant had been sworn not to utter one word about the attack in the alleyway. Boscombe, still glassy-eyed, shook his head imperceptibly. Cranston relaxed and, seeing how the wind blew, took off his cloak, threw it over the table and embraced his wife in a bear-like hug.

This was the signal for all chaos to break out. The dogs started howling, and Boscombe became solicitous. The Lady Maude insisted on Cranston sitting in his high-backed chair, Athelstan opposite him, whilst she served 'Her Lord and Master' with suitable refreshment.

At last the confusion died down. Sir John and Athel-stan exchanged news and gossip with Lady Maude. A perspiring maid brought down the two poppets to bawl lustily at their father, who dangled them on his knees, turning both even more red-faced with fury. Athelstan gazed at the strapping babies, then admiringly at Lady Maude: he secretly wondered how such a delicate little thing could have given birth to what he privately considered to be the burliest babies he had ever seen. They looked like peas out of the same pod, even more so now, with their fat cheeks and balding heads.

Gog and Magog came over to sniff, nudge and lick – until even Cranston, who revelled in such loving chaos, declared enough was enough and beat a retreat to his Chancery. Once he and Athelstan were inside what Cranston termed his 'sanctuary', the Coroner leaned back against the door and mopped his sweating brow.

'God save us!' he whispered. 'Thank God the Domina chose to be merciful. Believe me, Brother, old Jack Cranston is afeared of nothing except Domina Maude's fury.'

Not to mention Ferox and Bonaventure, Athelstan silently added, but kept his own counsel.

'Now,' Cranston declared, 'let's look amongst my records.' He threw back the lid of a huge, iron-bound coffer and dug like a great dog, sending pieces of parchment flying over his shoulder. Cranston muttered to himself, cursing as he unrolled one scroll after another only to toss it aside.

'At last!' he crowed in triumph, squatting on the floor with his back to the wall. He read the scroll, greedily studying its contents, now and again crying out and slapping his thigh.

'Dirty little secrets!' He tossed the parchment down and rubbed his hands. 'And old Jack knows them.' He got up, threw the parchment at Athelstan and went to the top of the stairs to bellow at Boscombe.

'Go up to the Guildhall,' he ordered. 'Tell My Lord Mayor and the Guildmasters that the Lord Coroner wishes to have words with them immediately about Master Sturmey's secrets.' He grinned at the whey-faced servant. 'Don't look so bloody frightened! You just tell them what I said and watch their faces. I'll be in the council chamber within the hour.'

Cranston returned to restore order to his room whilst Athelstan sat on a stool, reading the parchment.

'I can't believe this,' he muttered.

'Oh, yes.' Cranston grinned evilly down at him.

'Where there's wealth, there's sin. And they were all involved one way or the other.'

Athelstan read on. The parchment was two feet long, the writing small and cramped: it encapsulated memoranda, reports, messages and accounts. Athelstan had to take it over to the window to study it more closely.

'Did you notice another name, Sir John?'

'Who?'

'A Master Nicholas Hussey, a chorister at St Paul's.'

Cranston went over and studied the line just above Athelstan's finger.

'Devil's bollocks!' he breathed. 'Brother, you are right.'

Athelstan read on. Boscombe returned, grinning from ear to ear, to say the Guildmasters and the Mayor would see Sir John immediately. Cranston, snorting like a bull, seized his cloak and almost ran downstairs, shouting his farewells to the Lady Maude. He walked up Cheapside with a wicked smile on his face. Athelstan hurried behind, still trying to finish reading the report, but at last he gave up and put the scroll into his leather writing bag.

'I am going to enjoy this,' Cranston breathed. 'Just watch their faces, Athelstan.'

The Mayor and Guildmasters were waiting in the council chamber. Athelstan noticed how the servants were dismissed and no refreshments were offered as Cranston and he were summarily invited to sit at the great oval table. Goodman looked even more pop-eyed and anxious. Sudbury and Bremmer were visibly sweating. Marshall scratched his bald head and wouldn't meet their eyes whilst Denny had dropped any foppish manners and stared fixedly at Sir John like some terrified rabbit confronted by a stoat.

Goodman cleared his throat. 'Sir John, you wished to see us?'

'Too bloody straight I do!' Cranston leaned his great arms on the table. 'Let's not beat about the bush. Master Sturmey the locksmith was hired to build a special chest to hold the gold bars. It was furnished with six different locks. Each of you held a key but the gold has been taken,

Sturmey's dead, and before you ask, yes, he was murdered because someone forced him to make a second set of keys.' Cranston wiped his mouth with the back of his hand. 'Now you may ask why? What would force a reputable merchant like Sturmey to become involved in robbery and treason? The lure of gold? No, Sturmey wasn't like that. Advancement? No, sirs. He was the victim of blackmail.'

The Mayor and Guildmasters stared at Cranston like a line of felons before a hanging judge.

'Fifteen years ago,' he began, 'I was a junior Coroner in Cordwainer and Farringdon. Surely, Sir Christopher,' Cranston smiled at the Mayor, 'you recall my days in office, for you too were a law officer? There was a scandal, was there not? Certain allegations laid before the King's Council about powerful merchants being involved in the carnal seduction of choir boys and pages at St Paul's Cathedral? Surely you all remember it well?' Cranston cleared his throat. 'Two merchants were hanged, drawn and quartered, for these filthy practices caused the death of one young boy. Now,' Cranston leaned back, holding his hands across his stomach, 'the investigation led to a number of well-heeled, powerful burgesses being questioned and this list included the late Sir Gerard Mountjoy, the late Sir Thomas Fitzroy, Philip Sudbury, Alexander Bremmer, Hugo Marshall and James Denny.'

'We were innocent!' Bremmer snapped. 'Prattling gossip from malicious tongues!'

'I never said any different,' Cranston replied. 'Except there's one other name – Peter Sturmey, locksmith. Anyway, the investigation was eventually brought to an end, otherwise every gallows in the city would have blossomed with its rotting fruit. Now, during this investigation, Sturmey, against whom no charges were brought, revealed the existence of a male brothel in an alleyway off Billingsgate. Well, sirs, I ask you to reflect on this. First, the names I have just listed are all involved in this present business. Second, Sturmey, also involved, has been found murdered, floating off the quayside near Billingsgate.'

'Come to the point,' Goodman said softly.

'Oh, I think it's obvious,' Athelstan spoke up. 'Of course, everyone here was innocent of the charges levelled fifteen years ago. However, Sturmey was guilty, at least in the eyes of God. Once the scandal blew over, he kept silent. He worked hard at his trade, at which he was very good, but kept up his secret life. The years passed. Sturmey's reputation as a locksmith grew and he was entrusted with this special task. Unfortunately, someone remembered the past, kept a close eye on Master Sturmey, and realized he was still living a double life.'

'My clerk has the truth of it,' Cranston continued. 'Sturmey was blackmailed on two counts: on the past but, more importantly, on the present. He probably fashioned a second set of keys out of fear and, on the day he died, was summoned to Billingsgate, a place our locksmith knew very well, for what he thought was his final meeting with the blackmailer.' Cranston spread his hands. 'The rest you know. The blackmailer had no intention of allowing Sturmey to talk. He had served his purpose and was brutally murdered. We do not know the name of the murderer nor how he stabbed Sturmey and tossed his body into the river.'

'So,' Marshall squeaked, 'what has this to do with us, Sir John?'

'Well, you all know the scandal lurking in Sturmey's past. He was hired at your insistence to build the chest and fashion the locks and…'

'And what?' Sudbury snapped, leaning forward. 'Are you implying, Sir John, that one of us, some of us or all, are involved in treason, blackmail and murder?'

Cranston smiled falsely. 'Sir, I did not say that. All I am doing is describing the facts. But, yes, now you have raised the matter, I will ask you, were any of you in Billingsgate the day Sturmey died? Or did any of you visit him secretly?'

A chorus of defiant nos greeted Cranston's questions. Nevertheless, the Guildmasters looked so relieved Athelstan suspected they had a great deal to hide whilst Goodman looked embarrassed. After all, Athelstan reflected, he had known about Sturmey's past and yet had gone along with the rest, choosing the dead locksmith as their craftsman.

'Other people knew,' Denny spoke up. 'Why question only us?'

'Who else knew?' Cranston retorted. 'His Grace the King was not yet born, My Lord Regent was only a boy and the Council would protect his ears from such scandal. I have a copy of the investigation and I don't suppose any other record exists. So, yes, please tell me, who else knew?' Cranston shrugged. 'Perhaps other people did but they are not powerful Guildmasters, they are not witnesses to treason, the robbery of treasure, the murder of one of their colleagues, not to mention the secret assassination of a London Sheriff.' Cranston pushed back his chair and got to his feet. 'But I tell you this, sirs, old Jack Cranston will dig out the truth and justice will be done.'

Once outside the Guildhall, he clapped his hands with glee.

'The buggers are frightened,' he chortled. 'Lord, Brother, you can smell their fear.'

'What happens,' Athelstan asked, 'if these murders have more to do with ancient crimes than the ambitions of the Regent or the dark designs of Ira Dei?'

Cranston shook his head. 'No, those men, Athelstan, are gluttons for power. They are neck deep in vice. Corruption is their second name. Old sins play a part here but only as a device rather than the cause. Mark my words.' Cranston smiled. 'I have shaken the apple tree. God knows what may fall down!'

The Coroner peered across the marketplace. 'Let's leave this matter,' he breathed. 'Tomorrow is Saturday and

I must play dalliance with the Lady Maude. You have my manuscript?'

Athelstan nodded.

'Then keep it. Study it carefully, Brother.'

Athelstan vowed he would and, with Sir John's salutations ringing in his ears, made his way back down the Mercery, across London Bridge and into Southwark.

Benedicta was waiting for him in the priest's house. She looked rather subdued.

'I took the girl Elizabeth and her nurse Anna to the Friar Minoresses. The sisters were good and kind, even though the two were hysterical. Elizabeth calls her father and stepmother assassins: she claims the truth was revealed to her by her mother in a dream. Brother, what will happen to them?'

Athelstan slumped wearily on to a stool and shook his head.

'Benedicta, I don't know. I thank you for what you have done but only God knows what the future holds.'

She went to the buttery and brought back a flagon of ale.

'You look tired.' She pushed the tankard into his hands. 'Come on,' she urged. 'Drink and have something to eat. You'll have some bread and dried meat? I'll prepare enough for both of us.'

Athelstan, embarrassed at her care and concern, mumbled his thanks and sat staring into the weak flames of the fire. Benedicta bustled around the kitchen laying the table. The widow deliberately kept up a litany of gossip about the parish in an attempt to distract Athelstan from what he so aptly described to her as his 'sea of troubles'. During the meal he tried to respond but felt weary, his head buzzing with all he had seen and heard that day. Benedicta took her leave, saying she would see him at Mass tomorrow. Athelstan watched her go then put his head on his arms and fell fast asleep.

When Athelstan awoke it was dark. He felt cold and cramped so he built up the fire. He was about to go into the buttery when he was startled by a gentle knocking on the door.

'Who is it?' he called. Getting no answer, he took his ash cudgel from the corner and placed his hand on the latch. 'Who is it?' he repeated, trying to calm his anxieties. He strained his ears but only heard the gentle swishing of the trees in the cemetery and the ghostly hooting of an owl. He opened the door and stared into the darkness. He was about to walk out when his foot caught something. He bent and picked up a small loaf of bread with a scrap of parchment attached to it. Athelstan looked round once again, closed and bolted the door behind him, lit the candle and read the scrawled hand.

'Incur the wrath of God and you will incur the bread of bitterness.'

Athelstan picked up the small loaf and sniffed it carefully. He could see the sprinkled salt and caught the bitterness of some crushed herb. He read the scrap of parchment again and tossed both it and the loaf into the fire. 'The bread of bitterness,' Athelstan muttered to himself and half-smiled at the apt quotation from the Old Testament. He sat for a while staring at the candle flame; Ira Dei had made his reply, taunting him with the knowledge that he knew Athelstan only wished to communicate with him at the behest of his enemy, John of Gaunt. The friar recalled Cranston's confrontation with the Guildmasters earlier in the day. The Coroner probably hoped that his words might provoke Ira Dei into some stupid error.

Athelstan rubbed his eyes. 'Ah, well!' he muttered. 'Cranston and I now have his answer.' And he wearily climbed the stairs to his small bed chamber.

Chapter 12

Athelstan awoke fresh and invigorated the next morning. He washed, shaved, changed his robe, fed Bonaventure and ate a hurried breakfast. Athelstan then went across to celebrate the Requiem for Ursula the pig woman's mother. Benedicta was waiting for him at the entrance to the rood screen after he had finished in the sacristy.

'What is it, Benedicta?'

'I am sorry to trouble you, Father, but I've received messages from the Minoresses. You've got to come. Last night Elizabeth Hobden tried to hang herself!'

Athelstan bit back his curse, said he would lock the church and meet her within the half-hour on the steps of St Mary Overy. Athelstan quickly made sure all was secure, left oats and hay for a snoring Philomel and hurried down to where Benedicta was waiting for him.

'What else did the message say?' he asked breathlessly as they hurried on to London Bridge.

'Nothing, Father. Apparently the girl kept repeating the same story. Late last night a sister heard a crash from her cell and, when she went to investigate, discovered the girl had tried to hang herself with the sheets from her bed.'

Under the gateway of London Bridge, Athelstan stopped and looked up at the severed heads of traitors spiked there. Benedicta followed his gaze.

'Father, what on earth…?'

Athelstan shrugged. 'I find it difficult to believe, Benedicta, that Cranston is actually hunting someone who steals such grisly objects.'

She crossed her arms and stared out at the mist still floating over the middle of the river.

'Sometimes,' she muttered, 'I hate this place. I have thought of moving away to some country place – more peaceful and clean.'

'You can't.' Athelstan bit his lip. He looked at her squarely. 'If you went, Benedicta, I'd miss you.'

'True, true.' She grinned back. 'And who would then look after you and Cranston?'

They hastened across the bridge and into East Cheap, following the alleyways along Mark Lane into Aldgate and turning right on to the street leading to the gleaming sandstone buildings of the Minoresses. The sun was beginning to rise and Athelstan wiped away the sweat from his brow.

'We should have come by horse,' he muttered. 'God knows why I am here.'

'She has no one else.'

'Aye,' he replied. 'That's as good a reason as any.'

The nuns greeted him warmly and insisted both he and Benedicta refresh themselves in the refectory before the novice mistress, a stout but very pleasant-faced nun, described what had happened the previous evening.

'We found her lying on the floor,' she began. 'Half-choked by the sheet she had wrapped round her neck. If it hadn't torn, if the commotion hadn't been heard…' She spread her hands. 'I'd be sadly reporting her death now. Brother Athelstan, what can we do? We have a girl here, a mere child, who might commit suicide!'

The friar got to his feet. 'Let me see her.'

The novice mistress took them along a cool, porti-coed passage and knocked on a cell door. Another nun answered and the novice mistress took them in to where Elizabeth Hobden sat on the edge of her bed, dark-eyed and pale-faced, a purplish bruise round her soft, white neck.

'How is Anna, the nurse?' Benedicta asked.

'Oh, she's well enough, eating and drinking as if there's no tomorrow,' the nun replied.

Athelstan picked up a stool and sat beside Elizabeth. He looked up at the two nuns.

'Sisters, will you please leave us for a while? The lady Benedicta will stay.'

The nuns left. Benedicta stood by the door as Athelstan gently took the girl's listless hand.

'Elizabeth, look at me.'

She raised her eyes. 'What do you want?' she muttered.

'I want to help.'

'You can't. They murdered my mother and now I am an outcast.'

Athelstan stared at the girl and then at the crucifix nailed on the wall behind her. He took this down and held it up before the girl.

'Elizabeth, do you believe in Christ?'

'Yes, Father.'

'Then put your hand on the crucifix and swear that your accusation is true.'

The girl almost grabbed the cross. 'I swear!' she said firmly. 'By the body of Christ, I swear!'

Athelstan put the crucifix back and crouched beside her. 'Now, promise me one thing?'

The girl stared at him.

'Promise me that you'll do nothing foolish again? Give me a week,' he pleaded. 'Just one week. I'll see what I can do.'

The girl nodded and Athelstan flinched at the hope which sparkled in her eyes.

'I'll do what I can,' he repeated, patted her gently on her hand and left.

'What can you do?' Benedicta asked as the gate of the Minoresses closed behind them.

'I don't know,' Athelstan replied, 'But perhaps Cranston will.' He sighed. 'I had intended to leave Sir John alone, at least until Monday. I'll just have to remind him there's no rest for the wicked.'

They walked back into the city, down Aldgate and Cornhill. At the corner of Poultry, the stocks were full of malefactors taken after roistering on a Friday evening whilst the huge iron cage on the Great Conduit was full of night hawks and bawds who raucously jeered as they glimpsed Athelstan pass by with a woman. Poultry, Mercery and West Cheap, however, were quiet because the market bell rang late on Saturday. Apprentices were laying out stalls whilst rakers and dung-collectors made a half-hearted attempt to clear the refuse and rubbish of the previous day. A maid answered their knock on Cranston's door and blithely informed them that Lady Maude was still abed, for Sir John had gone to Mass at St Mary Le Bow.

Athelstan hid his smile and led Benedicta straight across to The Holy Lamb of God where they found the Coroner in his favourite corner breaking his fast on a meat pie and a jug of ale. He greeted them rapturously, refusing to be satisfied until Athelstan and Benedicta agreed to eat something. He then listened attentively as Athelstan described his visit to the Minoresses.

'What can we do?' Athelstan asked softly.

Cranston drowned his face in his tankard. 'Well, first, we have no proof that Walter or Eleanor Hobden committed any crime, so under the law we have no right to question them. However, I am the King's Coroner in the city. I do have the authority to exhume a corpse.

Hobden said his first wife is buried at St James Garlick-hythe?'

Athelstan nodded.

'Right, we'll begin there.'

'Can we do that, Sir John? What will it prove?'

'First, I can do anything. And, second, who knows what we'll find?' Cranston stared out of the window. 'We'll have to wait until early evening. Part of the cemetery there is used as a market.'

Athelstan closed his eyes and sighed in exasperation. There was so much to do at St Erconwald's but, as Sir John would say, '*Alea iacta*', the die was cast.

'Well, aren't you pleased?' Cranston asked, a tankard halfway to his lips.

'There's something else, Sir John.' And Athelstan briefly described the message left by Ira Dei the previous evening, trying to ignore Benedicta's gasps of annoyance at not being told of the danger.

Cranston wiped his lips on the back of his hand. 'It makes no difference,' he said. 'Gaunt was stupid. Ira Dei would scarcely trust you.'

'Yes, but why reply so quickly?' Athelstan replied. 'Who knew about the Ira Dei message?'

'Gaunt and the Guildmasters. They told us at the same time as they did about the attack on Clifford.'

The conversation stopped as the taverner's wife brought across a bowl of sugared plums for Sir John. Athelstan absent-mindedly picked one up and popped it into his mouth. He was about to speculate further when he realized the plums were so heavily coated with honey and sugar they stuck to his teeth and gums. He excused himself as he walked to the door and tried to prise the cloying morsels free. Suddenly he stopped and stared down at his fingers.

'When did I do that last?' he murmured to himself.

He looked back over his shoulder at Benedicta and Cranston, heads together, whispering, the Coroner undoubtedly explaining what had happened at the Guild-hall. Athelstan walked to the lavarium in the far corner of the tavern, dipped his hands in the rose water and wiped them on a napkin. He felt slightly elated; for the first time since these dreadful murders had started, he began to see a flicker of light in the darkness. He stared at a cured ham hanging from the rafters of the tavern and recalled the words of his mentor, Father Paul.

'Always remember, Athelstan,' the old man had boomed, 'every problem has its weakness. Find it, prise it open and a solution will soon follow.'

'What's the matter with you, Friar?' Cranston bellowed.

Athelstan sat down again. 'Sir John, are you busy today?'

'Of course I am! I'm not some bloody priest!'

Athelstan smiled. 'Sir John, let us retrace the steps of our murderer. Let me go back to the Guildhall, to the garden where Mountjoy died and the banqueting chamber where Fitzroy was poisoned. Benedicta, do you wish to come?'

The woman nodded.

'What's the matter, Friar?' Cranston asked curiously.

Athelstan grinned. 'Nothing much, Sir John, but a sugared plum could hang a murderer!'

He refused to be drawn further as a grumbling Cranston led them across Cheapside, into the Guildhall, down passageways and across courtyards until they had reached the small garden where Mountjoy had been stabbed. A pompous official tried to stop them but turned and fled when Cranston growled at him. Benedicta stared around, admiring the bronze falcon on top of the fountain, and the clear water pouring from leopards' mouths into a small channel lined with lilies and other wild flowers. She slipped down the tunnel arbour, made of coppice poles tied with willow cords, and openly admired the grape vines and roses which had wound themselves around these. She came out, her face flushed with excitement.

'This is beautiful,' she cried.

Athelstan pointed to the small enclosed arbour. 'The seat of murder,' he said flatly. 'That's where Mountjoy was killed.'

They all stood by the fence. Once again Athelstan wondered how any murderer could approach Sir Gerard and get past those fierce hounds.

'Look, Sir John, let's play a mummer's game.'

Athelstan tugged at the Coroner's sleeve, opened the small gate and led him into the garden. 'You sit on the turf seat.' He grinned. 'Benedicta, you must pretend to be a wolfhound.'

Both smiled, shrugged, but did what Athelstan asked. Cranston slumped on the turf seat and took a generous swig from the wineskin.

'Now,' Athelstan whispered, 'Sir Gerard is sunning himself in the garden with his dogs. Sometime that same afternoon he is stabbed to death, the dagger driven deep into his body, yet he made no resistance and those fierce dogs made no attempt to defend him.' Athelstan walked back to the wicket gate and pointed to the brick wall of the Guildhall which bordered one side of the garden. 'Now, a murderer couldn't come through there.' He changed direction. 'He could scarcely climb the fence behind Sir Gerard because both the Sheriff and his dogs would have noticed him. Nor could he come through the wicket gate, knife drawn.'

'What happens if he did?' Benedicta asked. 'What happens if he was a friend, whom the dogs would accept, as their master cordially greeted him?'

'Mountjoy had no friends,' Cranston muttered.

'No.' Benedicta waved her hands. 'The assassin gets very close, he draws a knife and plunges it into Sir Gerard?'

Athelstan shook his head. 'It's possible,' he replied. 'But hardly probable. Sir Gerard would at least have seen the dagger being drawn; the assassin would scarcely enter the garden carrying it. There would have been a fight which would have alarmed the dogs. Remember, Sir Gerard was killed without any sign of a struggle.'

Benedicta stuck her tongue out at him.

'There's only one way,' Cranston growled, pointing to the fence paling at the bottom of the garden. 'The pentice between the kitchens and the Guildhall.'

'There are gaps in the fence,' Benedicta added.

Athelstan shook his head. 'Too narrow for a man to throw a dagger with such force and accuracy. Look, wait here.' He took Cranston's dagger, rather similar to the one the assassin used, walked back into the Guildhall and down the darkened pentice. He stopped and, through gaps in the fence, could see Cranston sitting opposite him on the turf seat. He pushed the dagger through; the gap was wide enough, but he was right, no man could hurl a dagger through it. Scratching his head, Athelstan went back into the garden. 'A mystery,' he muttered. 'Come, let us visit the banqueting chamber.'

Cranston pulled a face at Benedicta but followed the rather bemused friar up to the banqueting hall. The room was deserted and the tables still left as they were on that fateful night. Athelstan badgered Cranston with a string of abrupt questions.

Who had sat where? What had they eaten? How late had it begun?

Then, without explanation, he wandered off, saying he wished to talk to the steward who had been present that night.

Cranston didn't mind. He knew his 'little friar' had started some hare and would become engrossed until he had resolved the problem facing him. Moreover, the Coroner was only too willing to sit and chat with the lovely Benedicta who questioned him closely about Athelstan's story of a thief stealing the severed heads of traitors from above the gatehouse at London Bridge. At last Athelstan returned.

'Well?' Cranston bellowed. 'Have you found anything? Would you like to share your thoughts with mere mortals?'

Athelstan grinned and tapped the side of his head. 'It's all a jumble,' he explained. 'I need to sit, write and think.'

'No better place than The Holy Lamb of God,' Cranston mumbled.

He led them out of the Guildhall, and down the steps into a busy marketplace. The stalls were now laid out for a day's trade. Apprentices shouted goods and prices or tried to catch the sleeves of passers-by. On the corner of the street, Cranston's hated relic-seller was busy proclaiming his litany of goods for sale. He stopped as the fellow listed his different relics from the stone which killed Goliath to the arm of St Sebbi.

'I have the relics,' the fellow bellowed, 'in a secret place, bought specially at a great high price from the Archbishop of Cologne. The head of St John the Baptist, miraculously fresh as on the day the great martyr died. I tell you this, good sirs and ladies all, you pious citizens of London, his hair is red and soft, his skin as supple, as that of a child!'

Cranston sneered and shook his head. 'Why don't you bloody priests,' he muttered, 'put an end to this stupid trade?'

'I wonder where he would obtain the hair of John the Baptist?' Benedicta muttered.

Cranston just gaped at her. 'What did you say?' he whispered.

'How could he get the head of St John the Baptist? And how does he know the prophet had red hair?'

Cranston grabbed the surprised woman and kissed her on both cheeks.

'Come on!' he whispered. 'To The Holy Lamb of God!'

The Coroner forced his way through the throng. Athelstan could see how excited he was by the way Cranston kept bellowing at people to get out of his way. Once in the tavern he dug into his broad purse and drew out a silver coin.

'Benedicta, take this across to the relic-seller. Say you have five more to purchase the head of St John the Baptist.'

'Oh, for God's sake, Sir John!' Athelstan interrupted. 'You know the man's a fraud. There'll be no head, just some stupid trick or device. Who knows, Benedicta may even be robbed!'

'Shut up, Athelstan!'

'But, Sir John,' he pleaded. 'You know! I know!'

'What?' Cranston snapped.

'He can't have the head of the Baptist...' Athelstan's voice trailed away and he grinned at Cranston. 'Ah! To quote the good St Paul, My Lord Coroner, I see in a glass darkly.'

Cranston clapped his hands like a child and Benedicta, with the assurances of both men ringing in her ears, walked back across Cheapside with Cranston's silver clasped firmly in her hand. Athelstan and Cranston watched her go. Benedicta stopped and whispered to the relic-seller and the man left his perch as quickly as any hungry gull. He led her off, down an alleyway with Athelstan and Cranston following quickly behind. Cranston was excited, Athelstan fearful for Benedicta's safety, but the man seemed harmless enough. At last he turned off an alleyway going down to Old Jewry. He stopped before the door of a house, said something to Benedicta, she nodded and they both went in. Cranston and Athelstan hurried up.

'Give the bastard a few minutes,' Cranston whispered.

Athelstan nodded. Cranston counted softly and, when he reached thirty, kicked with all his might against the rickety door and sent it flying back on its rusty hinges. The house was dingy and smelly and, as they hurried along the passageway, Athelstan gagged at the terrible stench. They heard raised voices, Benedicta's exclamations. They found her in a small chamber at the back of the house with the relic-seller and the latter's young assistant. Benedicta looked white, the two tricksters paled with fright at the commotion and Cranston's shouts, whilst on a table in front of them lay the severed head of a red-haired man, eyes half-closed and purple lips agape. If the two relic-sellers could have escaped they would have but they just huddled together in a corner as the Coroner grabbed the severed head and lifted it up. Benedicta had seen enough and, hand to mouth, hurriedly left the chamber for the street beyond.

'Well, well, my buckos!' Cranston grinned. 'You are both under arrest!'

'What for?' the relic-seller shouted.

'Theft of Crown property, my lad, counterfeiting, deceptive practices and blasphemy. This is not the head of John the Baptist but of Jacques Larue, the French pirate taken off the Thames and legally executed!' Cranston gazed round the chamber. 'Lord, this smells worse than the shambles at Newgate!'

He walked out of the door, pushing Athelstan before him, and took the key from the inside lock, imprisoning the two very subdued relic-sellers within.

'There are no windows or other doors, Athelstan. The rogues can stay there until I hand this key over to the ward officials. Now, let us see what this house of treasures contains.'

Athelstan followed him around but, after a while, gave up in disgust at the different grisly objects discovered and went to join Benedicta in the street outside.

'Hell's teeth!' he whispered, quoting Cranston. 'The place should be burnt from top to bottom.'

Cranston, however, came out full of himself. He pulled the house door closed then locked it.

'Benedicta,' he grinned, 'you are an angel. Where else would a relic-seller get a head to sell as that of a saint except from the execution yard?' The Coroner rubbed his hands together. 'One more small victory for old Jack, eh?'

They walked back into Cheapside and waited whilst Cranston summoned officials and sent them to the house. One of the beadles was eating a meat pie, munching insolently as Cranston talked to him. The Coroner grinned as he watched the men stride away.

'I haven't told them what they'll find,' he joked. 'But the insolent one with the meat pie will soon receive a short, sharp lesson on eating when the King's Coroner is giving him instructions!'

He led them back to The Holy Lamb of God, loudly guffawing at Benedicta's wondering how anyone could be so stupid as to trust such rogues.

'Stupid!' Cranston laughed. 'If you go to any city in England, France or beyond the Rhine, you'll find men, Princes of the Church, the most intelligent and educated of priests, spending fortunes on pieces of dirty bone and rag. Do you know, here in London, I heard of a merchant who paid a hundred pounds sterling for a napkin on which the Blessed St Cuthbert wiped his mouth. Devil's balls!' He mumbled an apology to Benedicta. 'But hell's teeth! I wish everything was as easy. Brother, did our journey to the Guildhall clarify anything?'

Cranston eased his great backside down on to the stool and stared pitifully at his clerk. 'Athelstan,' he pleaded. 'Sooner rather than later, the Regent is going to ask me to account.'

The friar stared at the tabletop. 'Let us see,' he began slowly. 'We know why Mountjoy and the other two were murdered. Not because of any secret sin or personal rivalry but to upset the Regent, to block his ambitions, to build up support amongst the powerful merchant class of London. Well, that has been achieved so there will be no more murders. At least, not for the time being.' Athelstan paused. 'I am sure the murders can be laid at the door of the Ira Dei, but suspect he is only the architect. There's a traitor and a killer in Gaunt's party – Goodman or one of those powerful Guildmasters.'

'Why, Sir John?' Benedicta interrupted. 'Why hasn't the assassin struck at Gaunt himself?'

'Because the devil you know, My Lady, is better than the devil you don't. Someone has to be Regent or, to put it more bluntly, someone has to be there to take the blame. If Gaunt were removed, his chair would merely be filled by one of his younger brothers. No, these murders are to clip Gaunt's wings.'

'Has there been any reaction to our meeting with the Guildmasters about Sturmey's private life?' Athelstan asked.

Cranston shook his head. 'Not as yet.'

'Sir Nicholas Hussey was a boy when the scandal occurred?'

'Only very young,' Cranston replied. 'God knows, he may remember whispers, but according to the records there is no indication that he was involved, even as a victim. Ah, well.' He put his tankard down on the table.

'What are we going to do now?'

'Wait, Sir John, think, reflect. As I have said, the murders at the Guildhall are not crimes of passion but cold and calculating. I doubt if we will discover any further clue or sign. We must gather all we know, apply logic, and so squeeze out the one and only solution.'

'If there is one,' Cranston added wearily.

The conversation became desultory. Cranston's elation at the arrest of the relic-sellers dissipated under a cloud of gloom as the fat Coroner began to sink into a sulk. Benedicta took her leave, saying she had no wish to stay, she'd had her fill of cadavers and mystery. Sir John took Athelstan back to his house, but Lady Maude was busy and the poppets out with the nurse in the fields north of St Giles. Cranston became impossible so Athelstan left him for a while, deciding to visit his brethren at Blackfriars.

The friar returned just as the market in Cheapside drew to an early end and people hurried home to prepare for Sunday. Cranston, more refreshed, clapped him on the shoulder and they went back to The Holy Lamb of God to meet Cranston's friend and physician, Theobald de Troyes, whom the Coroner had visited earlier in the afternoon.

'Are you sure you wish to come?' Cranston asked.

'Sir John, I am always at your disposal,' the physician replied. 'Does the priest at St James know?'

'I have already sent a constable down there. There will be labourers to dig out the grave and lift Sarah Hobden's coffin.' Sir John licked his lips. 'Perhaps a drink first?'

Both Athelstan and the physician flatly refused and, one on either side of him, escorted the reluctant Coroner out of West Cheap across Watling Street into Cordwainer and then along Upper Thames Street to the rather sombre church of St James Garlickhythe. The priest, Father Odo, cheery, red-nosed, and much the worse after a generous lunch, came out of the priest's house and took them into a rather overgrown graveyard where three labourers were resting under the cool shade of a yew tree. At first there was absolute confusion as Father Odo tried to read the burial book and discover where Sarah Hobden had been buried.

'I can't find it,' he mumbled, swaying dangerously on his feet.

Athelstan peered over his shoulder, realized the inebriated priest was reading it upside down, and took it out of his hand.

'Let me help, Father,' he offered gently.

Glaring defiantly at Cranston and daring him not to laugh, the friar sat on a tombstone and leafed through the pages until he found the entry: 'Sarah Hobden, obiit 1376, North West'.

'Where's that, Father?'

Odo pointed to the far corner of the graveyard. Athelstan smiled and returned the burial book.

'Father, you sit down and take your rest.' He patted the old priest gently on the shoulder 'Don't you dare!' he hissed at Cranston as the Coroner's hand went to where his miraculous wineskin was hanging beneath his cloak. 'The poor man has had enough and, to be quite frank, Sir John, so have I!'

They called the labourers and crossed to that part of the cemetery Father Odo had pointed out. After some searching, they found Sarah Hobden's grave, derelict, overgrown and neglected; the wooden cross, battered and lopsided, still bore her faded name. Cranston snapped his fingers and the grumbling labourers began to hack at the hard-packed earth.

'What will this prove?' Athelstan asked.

'Ah.' Cranston leaned on the gravestone, cradling his wineskin as if it was one of the poppets. He tapped his nose and pointed at the physician. 'Master Theobald, instruct our ignorant priest!'

The physician winked at Athelstan. 'When I received Sir John's invitation, I made careful study of the cause of death.'

'And?'

'Well, if it's arsenic, particularly red arsenic, we might well see what the populous would call a miracle. Let me surprise you, Father.'

The physician went and watched the labourers as their spades and picks began to ring hollow as they reached the coffin lid. More earth was dug out. Athelstan peered round the graveyard and shivered. The shadows were growing longer. The birdsong had stilled. Nothing except the grunting of the labourers and the shifting of earth broke the eerie silence.

'Why are these places so quiet?' Athelstan murmured. He strained his ears: he could just hear the sound of chatter and laughter as the traders and tinkers on the other side of the church cleared away their stalls.

'We are ready, Sir John!' the physician called.

'Then pull it out, lads!'

One labourer jumped down into the grave on top of the coffin, ropes were attached and, after a great deal of heaving and cursing, the faded, dirt-covered coffin was hoisted out of the earth. Cranston thanked the labourers and told them to go and rejoin Father Odo. He pulled out his long dagger and began to prise open the coffin lid. Athelstan watched attentively as the clasps were broken. The lid creaked open slowly, almost as if the person inside was pushing it up and threatening to rise. He pushed his hands inside his sleeves, closed his eyes and muttered a prayer.

It's God's justice, Athelstan thought. This is God's work.

The last clasp broke free. Cranston lifted the tattered winding sheet. Athelstan opened his eyes as he heard Cranston's gasp. The physician was kneeling beside the lid of the coffin, carefully examining the inside.

Athelstan drew a deep breath and walked over and looked down in the deep wooden coffin. The friar stared in stupefaction at the corpse's face: fatty, white and waxy as if fashioned out of candle grease. Nevertheless, it was free of any corruption. The dead woman's features were quite pretty, oval-shaped and regular, with a generous mouth and aquiline nose.

'For God's sake!' Athelstan breathed. 'She's been dead three years! Corruption should have set in!'

Chapter 13

The physician touched the face carefully then ran his hand inside the coffin. When he brought it out, Athelstan could see it was covered by fine red dust.

'Nothing remarkable,' the physician observed dryly. 'You see, Brother, arsenic is a subtle deadly poison, particularly red arsenic. Its only weakness is that the corpse, after death, reveals the presence of this deadly substance for corruption is halted.' He tapped the coffin. 'I have seen such cases before. The fine red dust, the lack of putrefaction, indicates this poor woman was fed red arsenic over a considerable period of time.'

'What happens now?' Athelstan asked. He gestured at the corpse. 'There's our evidence.'

'I will take an oath,' the physician replied, 'and so will Sir John and yourself about what we have seen here. That will satisfy any justice.'

'In which case,' Athelstan said, sketching a blessing in the air above the corpse, 'may she rest in peace now that God's justice and that of the King will be done.'

He and Cranston re-sealed the coffin. The labourers re-interred it and, after thanking a sleepy Father Odo as well as Master de Troyes, Cranston and Athelstan walked slowly back down the Ropery into Bridge Street. The cordwainers, ropemakers, the sellers of tents, string, hempen and flax, had put away their stalls. A street musician played bagpipes whilst a drunken whore cavorted in a crazy dance. The beggars, both real and professional, were crawling out of their hideaways, hands extended for alms, whilst a little old woman, a battered canvas bag in her hands, was busy sifting amongst the rubbish heaps.

The taverns were full as traders celebrated a week's work, but after that eerie graveyard and the wickedness he had seen, Athelstan felt tired and depressed. From a casement window above him a baby cried and a young girl began to sing a lullaby, soft and sweet through the warm evening air.

'We are surrounded by sin, Sir John,' Athelstan sombrely remarked. 'As in the blackest forest, everywhere we look we see the eyes of predators.'

Cranston belched, stretched and clapped the friar on the shoulder.

'Aye, Brother, and the evil buggers can see ours. Look, cheer up, murder runs in all our veins, Brother. You said that yourself: the Inghams, the bloody business of the Guildhall, and now the Hobdens. Life, however, is not only that. Listen to the mother singing to her baby. Or friends laughing in a tavern. What you need, Brother, is a cup of claret and a good woman.' Cranston grinned. 'Or perhaps, in your case, a really bad one!'

Athelstan smiled back but then his face became sombre again. 'What shall we do about the Hobdens? We have no proof they killed Sarah.'

'Oh, for God's sake, Brother, you are not thinking straight. I can prove they did. The bitch Eleanor actually admitted, in my presence, that she tended to the sick woman. Who else would approach her? Do you know what I think, my good monk?' Cranston helped himself to another swig from the wineskin. 'Walter Hobden is a man of straw who met and fell in love with the darling Eleanor. They then put their heads together. Walter began feeding his poor wife a few grains of arsenic. She falls ill and dearest Eleanor is brought in to tend to her. The poisoning continues apace.'

'Wouldn't the physician detect it?'

'Not really. Increased stomach cramps, lacklustre appearance. Anyway, the majority of physicians couldn't tell their elbows from their arses!' Cranston scratched his red, balding pate. 'What the great mystery is, Brother, is how the young girl knew? Not only that her mother was poisoned but the actual potion used. Didn't she say her mother told her in a dream?'

Athelstan nodded and shivered at the cold breeze wafting in from the river.

'Do you believe that?' Cranston urged.

'Sir John, every morning I take a piece of bread and, according to faith, turn it into the risen body of Christ. I believe that. A baby is born in Bethlehem who is both man and God, and I believe that. The same boy becomes a man who is crucified but rises in glory from the dead, and I believe that.' Athelstan looked squarely at the Coroner. 'And I am told that the Spirit blows where it will and that God's justice will be done. And so, My Lord Coroner, if I can believe all that, I can believe young Elizabeth's story. The human mind is subtle, Sir John. Perhaps she had her suspicions and so the seed was sown.'

Athelstan blew out his cheeks. 'God knows what happened then. All her life centred on the fact that her mother had been poisoned and so she entered into an alliance with her old nurse. Perhaps the latter knew something of potions. Whatever, they devised their little game to force the weak-willed Walter into confession or at least remorse. Anyway, what shall we do now, Sir John?'

'Oh, I'd let them stew in their juice for a few days. Meanwhile, I'll visit the girl at the Minoresses.'

'Thank you, Sir John, and then?'

'As I said, I'll return home and swear out a warrant for the arrest of Walter and Eleanor Hobden. My constables can serve it, and before they are much older the Hobdens will both stand trial before the King's Justices at Westminster.'

Athelstan thanked him again, assuring the Coroner that he would study all the evidence regarding the murders at the Guildhall, and so they parted, Cranston going up to the Minoresses and Athelstan turning down towards London Bridge.

–

'*Ite, missa est.*' Athelstan extended his hand in blessing at the end of the Sunday Mass. He smiled as those of his congregation who knew a little Latin shouted back '*Dei gratia*'.

Athelstan went down the altar steps, genuflected and followed Crim into the sacristy then back out again to stand on the porch and to shake hands with his parishioners as they left. Watkin and Pike the ditcher stayed behind as he had asked them to before Mass. He said goodbye to Ranulf the rat-catcher, still full of glee at the way he had helped Cranston, Pernell the Fleming, Ursula and her sow, Tab the tinker and Cecily the courtesan, looking resplendent in a corn-coloured dress.

'You have been behaving yourself?' Athelstan asked her.

'Of course, Father.'

So miracles do happen in Southwark, he thought. The last to leave was Jacob Arveld, the German with his pleasant-faced wife and brood of children. An industrious parchment-seller, the German had soon settled down in his pleasant, three-storeyed house and garden just behind The Bishop of Winchester inn, though he was still having difficulty with the language.

'Those were nice words,' Jacob reassured Athelstan now. 'A most precise sermon. I thank you from the heart of my bottom.'

'Don't you mean bottom of your heart?'

'And that, too, Father.'

Athelstan smiled and watched his congregation gather in the alleyway around a small booth where Tab the tinker sold ale and sweetmeats. He walked back up the nave and into the sacristy where Watkin and his formidable wife, and Pike the ditcher and his equally redoubtable spouse, were waiting for him.

Oh, Lord, Athelstan prayed, please make this peaceful. He darted a glance at Pike whom he had secretly met before Mass: the ditcher, who considered himself in the priest's debt, had quickly agreed that his son's betrothal to Watkin's daughter was the best thing possible. He had then attentively listened as Athelstan told him what he must say when they met Watkin.

'Well, we are here, Father.' Watkin shuffled his great dirty boots. 'I know why you want to see us, though it seems we were the last to realize that our daughter is smitten with Pike's son.'

'Young man.' Pike the ditcher's spouse intervened.

'I don't like this at all,' Pike the ditcher spoke up. 'I see no future prospects in their being betrothed. My son should look further afield.'

'What's wrong with my daughter?' Watkin's wife snapped. 'Do you think your son's too good for her?'

Athelstan smiled to himself, stood back and watched Watkin and his wife launch the most vitriolic attack on Pike. After that there was little problem. Pike first reluctantly apologized and then, just as reluctantly, it seemed, agreed that the matter was settled; his son would marry Watkin's daughter on the first Saturday after Easter. After that they crossed to the priest's house to drink a cup of wine in celebration. Watkin swaggered in like some successful lawyer from the Inns of Court. He had extolled his family's name, he had defended his daughter's reputation, he had brought his great rival Pike the ditcher to book and made him accept what he proposed. Athelstan poured the wine, refusing to look Pike in the eye, and whilst they toasted the young couple, quietly prayed that Watkin would never discover how he had been tricked.

After they had left, Athelstan ate a little breakfast and walked back to the deserted church to say his office. He then cleared the table in the kitchen and laid out his writing implements: quill, ink horn, pumice stone and the roll of new parchment Cranston had given him. Once ready, Athelstan sat and wrote everything he and the Coroner had learnt about the Ira Dei: Mountjoy's stabbing, Fitzroy's poisoning and Sturmey's sudden and violent death in Billingsgate. The day wore on. Athelstan paused to eat a little soup, some dried meat and bread. He crossed to the church to say prayers then walked through the graveyard reflecting on what he had written. He drew a fresh diagram of the Guildhall garden, a seating plan of the banquet where Fitzroy had died. Now and again he remembered some other items and made a neat insertion.

By dusk Athelstan believed he had written down everything he and Cranston had learnt and began studying his notes carefully. He smiled as he remembered his mother looking for a thread in an old cloak and, once she did, carefully teasing it out, unravelling the precious wool. However, there was no loose thread here.

'Cold-blooded murder,' Athelstan muttered to himself. 'No crime of passion, no impetuous gesture which would betray the assassin.' He listed no less than eight possible culprits whilst the identity of Ira Dei remained a mystery. Athelstan got up and stretched, lit the candles and built up the fire as Bonaventure slipped through the open window.

'Good evening, my prince of the alleyways.'

The great tom cat stretched in front of the hearth, his little pink tongue darting in and out. He purred with pleasure as Athelstan brought out a pitcher of milk from the buttery and filled his battered, pewter bowl. The friar crouched down and stroked the one-eyed tom cat between the ears.

'I wish you animals could talk,' he muttered. 'I wish I was like the great St Francis of Assisi and had the gift of conversing with God's little creatures. What mysteries do you see, eh, Bonaventure? What wickedness do you glimpse as you hunt amongst the alleyways and runnels?'

Bonaventure kept lapping the milk, his tail twitching with pleasure. Athelstan rose, sipped from his tankard of beer and went back to his problem. Darkness fell, owls hooted from the cemetery and the friar's irritation grew. He went back upstairs and collected the scroll he had taken from Cranston's house about the investigation some fifteen years ago in which Sturmey had been involved. He went downstairs and carefully scrutinized the document, using his ruler so as to study each line.

'Oh, Lord help me!' he whispered. 'Please, just one loose thread!' Athelstan read on and then, in a corner of the margin of the manuscript where the scribe had made a little annotation, he found it. 'Oh, Lord save us!' he whispered. 'Oh, of course!'

The friar extinguished the candle and trudged upstairs, lay down on the cot bed and stared up at the ceiling. On such a beautiful autumn evening, particularly a Sunday, he would usually be at the top of the church tower, scanning the stars and talking to Bonaventure about the theories of Roger Bacon. He had to confess, however, that a study of the human heart was more fascinating as he began to build a logical explanation which might flush out the murderer into God's own light. His mind sifted the possibilities till his eyes grew heavy. He drifted into a troubled sleep and a recurring nightmare of standing under the moonlight in the Guildhall garden.

He was sitting where Mountjoy had been and could see the assassin moving behind the fence paling. He tried to get up but realized he was fastened and unable to move. He knew the assassin was going to strike. Then Athelstan would turn, conscious of someone beside him, and see the greyish faces and red-rimmed eyes of a line of corpses: Mountjoy, Fitzroy and Sarah Hobden, whilst on a spike in the centre of the garden was the decapitated head of Jacques Larue, the French pirate. The corpses pressed against him, mouths gaping. Athelstan wanted to shove them away but was terrified of taking his eyes off the assassin lurking behind the fence.

At last he awoke, sweating and moaning. He swung his legs off the bed, breathing deeply to control his thudding heart. He looked through the window. The sky was already shot with red so he washed, changed and went down to the kitchen for something to eat. Eventually the terrors of the night faded as he sat before the rekindled fire, gently rocking in the chair with Bonaventure curled in his lap. Then he went back to his writing. At first slowly, then with greater vigour and speed as he drew up what he termed his bill of indictment against the assassin.

Outside the birds stirred, swooping and singing; the sun rose higher and stronger. Athelstan put down his pen and went across to the church to celebrate Mass. No one came. Crim, heavy-eyed, burst through the door just as he finished, shouting his apologies. The lad explained how both his family and that of Pike the ditcher had spent the previous evening celebrating the forthcoming betrothal. Athelstan reassured him all was well, took a penny from his pouch and led Crim out on to the porch of the church.

'You know the Lord Coroner, Crim?'

'You mean old Horse Crusher?'

'No, Crim!'

'Yes, Father, I know the Lord Coroner and where he lives.'

'Well, go across and see him. Deliver this message. He is to meet me at The Holy Lamb of God.' Athelstan paused. 'Yes, just as the market opens. Also tell him to ask My Lord of Gaunt and the other nobles to meet us at the Guildhall at noon.' He slipped the penny into the boy's grimy hand and made him repeat his message three times. Crim faithfully did so, eyes closed in concentration, and then was off, running like a hare down the alleyway.

Athelstan went back into the church and crouched at the foot of one of the pillars. He'd be glad to have this business finished. He only hoped he was right. He had some proof but not enough: that would come when they were all assembled in the Guildhall, though he would have to confess that the identity of Ira Dei was a mystery that had eluded him.

Athelstan stared round the church. He really would have to catch up on parish business. Huddle had not finished his painting above the baptismal font, whilst Cecily had not cleaned the church for days. Athelstan closed his eyes. If only he could persuade someone to buy stained glass for one of the windows. Some brilliant picture like those he had seen in the well-patronized London churches. A story from the life of Christ or even that of St Erconwald, portrayed in great detail so he could refer to it when he gave his sermons.

His mind wandered. He hoped Elizabeth Hobden would be safe with the Minoresses, and had Cranston issued the warrants for the arrest of her father and step-mother? Athelstan sighed and got to his feet. Returning to the priest's house he cleared the table, packed the leather bag with his writing implements and went out to saddle a rather surly Philomel.

He rode down to London Bridge, past the one-storeyed tenements of many of his parishioners. He resisted the temptation to ride directly at Ursula's great sow, which was lumbering up the street, its ears flapping, probably heading direct for Athelstan's garden patch. The friar stopped beside a small ale-house where Cecily sat, legs pertly crossed, deep in conversation with Pike the ditcher. Athelstan handed him the keys to the church.

'Cecily,' he pleaded, 'the church needs a good clean and I have paid you to do it.'

The girl's child-like blue eyes filled with tears. 'Oh, Father, I am sorry but...'

'Cecily has been busy,' Pike interrupted. 'With Alberto.'

'Who?'

'A sailor from a Genoese cog berthed at Dowgate.' Pike's grin widened. 'Now he has gone, Cecily is back with us and the church will be clean.'

Athelstan smiled. 'Did you like him, Cecily?'

'Oh, yes, Father. He promised he'd be back within two months.'

Athelstan nodded and urged Philomel forward. Aye, he thought, poor Cecily. Cranston would say: 'Alberto would be back when Ursula's sow takes flight.' He patted Philomel's neck.

'We are the poor, Philomel,' he whispered, 'remember that. And if wishes were horses, beggars would ride.'

'Are you talking to yourself, Father?'

Athelstan looked up. He'd passed the priory of St Mary Overy and was on the broad street leading down to the bridge. People were shoving and pushing around him and he couldn't see the person who had spoken.

'Father, it's me.'

Athelstan stared down to where Burdon, the keeper of the gatehouse, stood almost hidden beneath Philomel's muzzle.

'No, Master Burdon, just praying,' he lied.

The mannikin slipped towards him. 'Where's Sir John? Oh, don't tell me, deep in his cups in some city tavern. What about my heads?'

'What about them?' Athelstan asked. 'Have more gone?'

'No.' The little man squared his shoulders. 'But them that's gone should come back.'

'Well, I'll see Sir John about that.'

'Good! And tell him to stop by soon. My wife is expecting another child.'

Athelstan waved and urged Philomel on. He didn't want Burdon to see the surprised grin on his face, for surely it was one of God's great mysteries how such a little man could be the proud father of enough children to fill a choir stall?

London Bridge was packed with carts and dray horses and Athelstan had to wait patiently, remembering not to look between the gaps at the seething river below. At last he was across, riding up Bridge Street, Lombard Street and then into bustling Cheapside.

Sir John, full of the joys of spring, had received Crim's message and was seated in The Holy Lamb of God busily munching on a dish of eels and newly baked bread. He looked fresh and rested, and almost crushed Athelstan in his embrace.

'I have said it once,' the Coroner boomed, 'and I'll say it again! For a monk, you are not too bad!' He held Athelstan at arm's length. 'Have some claret.'

'No, Sir John.'

'You've discovered the murderer?' Cranston whispered.

'You have sent the message to the Guildhall?'

Cranston nodded.

'Then, Sir John, sit down and I'll tell you what I think.'

Cranston sipped his drink whilst Athelstan developed his explanation. The Coroner asked a few questions then sat cradling his tankard, staring out into Cheapside.

'Are you sure, Brother?'

'Not fully, but it's the only logical conclusion.'

'How do we know the person you name might not be Ira Dei?'

'I doubt that, Sir John, but it's possible.'

'But could someone use a dagger like that? No, no.' Cranston waved a hand. 'On second thought, it could be done. Let me take you to Simon the armourer. Our comrades of the Guildhall are not to meet us until noon, yes?'

Athelstan nodded. Cranston heaved his great bulk up and swaggered out into Cheapside and up Friday Street. The houses crowded together here; shop signs jutting out on poles swung dangerously above people's heads. Cranston stopped under a gaudily painted picture of a steel basinet and a pair of gauntlets.

'Let's have a word with old Simon.'

Despite its narrow frontage, inside the shop was large and cavernous. In the back yard beyond was a small smithy, where sweating apprentices brought pieces of metal from the roaring fires and placed them on anvils to hammer with all their might. A small rubicund man appeared as if from nowhere. He reminded Athelstan of a goblin with his bright, darting eyes, thin hair and long, pointed ears.

'Sir John!' The little man's eyes gleamed at the prospect of profit as he surveyed the portly bulk of the Coroner. 'You have come to buy armour?'

The little man wetted his lips as he calculated the fee for protecting such a wide girth in chain mail and plate armour. For a while Cranston teased him but then clapped the little fellow on the shoulder, almost driving him into the ground.

'Nonsense, Simon, and you know it. My fighting days are over. This is Athelstan, my clerk.' He waved one podgy hand airily. 'And he has a theory. Explain!'

Athelstan did so. Simon heard him out, pulled a face and shrugged. 'Of course.'

He went into the back of the shop, opened a huge chest and became involved in a heated discussion with Cranston over daggers, dirks, Italian stilettos, long bows, crossbows and arbalests. An apprentice was called in to demonstrate the proof of Simon's argument. An hour later Cranston, Athelstan and the little armourer, a leather sack over his shoulder, walked back into Cheapside, heading directly for the Guildhall. Athelstan stopped at a baker's to buy some marzipan and doucettes wrapped in a linen bag. They had also to pause as beadles led a line of malefactors and felons from the Newgate and Fleet prisons to be punished.

There was the usual despondent procession of footpads, felons, and night-walkers, but then came a cart preceded by two musicians playing bagpipes – a jaunty skittish tune. Then a horse and cart, the latter filled with all forms of grisly objects which made the air stink like a sewer and provoked cries of outrage and clamour from the crowd. At the tail of the cart were the two relic-sellers Cranston had arrested the previous day. The men's faces were bloody, their tousled hair covered in all sorts of filth as the crowd pelted them with offal and refuse.

Cranston grinned. Athelstan felt a twinge of compassion, for both men had their hose pulled around their ankles whilst their bare buttocks were sore and bleeding as two beadles lashed them with thick leather belts. Behind the malefactors another official walked with a gaudily painted proclamation describing 'The horrible crimes of these two counterfeit men'.

'What will happen to them?' Athelstan asked.

'Not what they deserve,' Cranston growled. 'The carts full of their so-called relics will be taken down to London Bridge to be burnt by the public hangman. After that our two beauties will be whipped to Aldgate, cut loose and banned from the city, under pain of forfeiture of a limb for the first offence, their lives for the second.' Cranston gazed over the crowd, now yelling abuse as the carts disappeared up the Mercery. 'It's a lesson for the others which by tomorrow they will undoubtedly have forgotten.'

They continued across Cheapside, the little armourer drawing Cranston back into an acrimonious debate over the superiority of certain weapons. At the Guildhall they had to cool their heels for a while before a tipstaff took them up to the council chamber where Gaunt, flanked by Clifford and Hussey, sat with the Guildmasters. The Regent dispensed with ceremony, not even inviting them to sit, whilst he looked disdainfully at the little armourer. Simon was so overcome in the presence of such august personages he couldn't stop bobbing and bowing, until Cranston hissed at him to stay still and stand by the door.

'You have something to report, My Lord Coroner?'

'Yes, Your Grace.'

Gaunt played with the leather tassels on his expensively quilted jacket. Athelstan could see that the Regent had been looking forward to a morning's hunting in the fields and marshes north of Clerkenwell. Hussey was his usual diplomatic self, pleasant-faced but quiet. Clifford rubbed his wounded shoulder thoughtfully, whilst the Guildmasters were like a pack of hunting dogs, Goodman the Mayor tapping his fingers loudly on the table while Sudbury and the rest were arrogant and resentful at being summoned from a morning's trade.

'Well?' Goodman snapped. 'We are busy men, Sir John!'

'As am I, My Lord Mayor.'

'You have come earlier than we thought,' Sudbury snarled. 'Do you have our gold?'

Cranston shook his head.

'Have you arrested Ira Dei?'

'No.'

Gaunt leaned forward and smiled falsely. 'So why in God's name are we here, Sir John?'

'Perhaps to arrest a murderer, Your Grace. All entrances to the Guildhall must be secured.'

Gaunt stared back, a spark of interest in his eyes as he realized this was to be no ordinary meeting. 'You have discovered something, haven't you?' he said softly. 'You and your little friar.'

The atmosphere in the chamber changed dramatically. They'd dismissed us as failures, Athelstan thought to himself. These arrogant hawks thought a fat Coroner and his dusty friar too dim-witted to search out the truth. He breathed deeply to control his anger. Gaunt sat back and spread his hands.

'Sir John, in this matter we are your prisoners.' He glared over his shoulders and bellowed at a captain of the guard standing against the wall behind him: 'Have the Guildhall secured! No one is to leave or enter until I say.' He looked at Cranston. 'What else do you need, My Lord Coroner?'

Athelstan spoke instead. 'I want the banqueting table laid out, as it was the night Fitzroy died.'

Gaunt nodded. 'And what else?'

'I want cushions and bolsters where Sir Gerard Mountjoy the Sheriff was sitting. The garden must be cleared.'

Gaunt smiled. 'And finally?'

'Until I and Sir John have finished, Your Grace, I would be grateful if you would all stay here.'

A hubbub of protest broke out but Gaunt slammed the tabletop for silence, his face flushed.

'A few days ago,' he roared, 'I came to this Guildhall to seal a pact of friendship between myself and the city. The deaths of Fitzroy, Mountjoy and Sturmey put an end

to that. Sirs, you will wait until this business is finished.'
He jabbed a finger at Cranston. 'And, My Lord Coroner,
God help you if you are wasting my time!'

The servants were summoned. Gaunt gave his instructions. Athelstan led Cranston and the trembling armourer
out of the chamber, down the stairs and into the small
pentice which connected the kitchens to the Guildhall. Athelstan tried to curb his excitement as he peered
through the gaps in the paling, watching the servants place
the cushions and bolsters as he had ordered. From where
he stood, he could see through the gaps that they were
piled high on the very spot Sir Gerard had been murdered.
He waited until the servants had gone back to the Guildhall then smiled at the armourer.

'Well, Simon, now's your opportunity to prove our
theory correct.'

The armourer placed his sack on the ground, taking
out an arbalest or crossbow. The gulley where the
bolt would be slipped had been specially widened. He
then took a long dagger, identical to the one found in
Mountjoy's chest. He placed this carefully in the deepened
groove and slowly winched back the powerful cord.

'Very good,' Athelstan murmured. 'Now, Simon, try
and shoot the dagger from the arbalest into the centre of
the top cushion, the green-fringed one.'

Cursing and muttering, Simon lifted the crossbow and
released the dagger. It sped like a stone from a sling, but
the aim was wrong and the dagger struck the wooden

fence, narrowly missing the cushions. Cranston, huffing and puffing, went to fetch it, bringing it back and telling Simon to steady himself or they would all spend the next week in Newgate. Again, he put the crossbow to the ground and winched back the powerful cord. The long dagger was inserted into the groove. He took careful aim and this time the dagger sped well and true, sinking deeply into the cushion, pinning it securely to the wooden fence behind. Cranston crowed in triumph and clapped his hands like a child.

'It works!' he said. 'It works!'

He hurried back into the Guildhall, reappearing a few minutes later with Gaunt and the rest of his companions from the council chamber. Athelstan and the armourer, his crossbow back in the sack, stood by the wicket gate staring at the cushion.

'What's this nonsense?' Goodman shouted.

'You have brought us down here, Cranston, to see a dagger driven into a cushion?'

Gaunt, however, pushed the gate open and walked in, putting his hand on the dagger and prising it gently loose in a small puff of dust and goose feathers.

'You didn't stab it, did you, Cranston?'

'No, Your Grace,' he replied. 'The dagger was shot from a crossbow through the gaps in that fence.'

'Can it be done?' Denny exclaimed.

'Oh, yes it can be done!' Sudbury smiled sweetly at the Mayor. 'Wouldn't you agree, Sir Christopher? You are a member of the Bowyers Guild.'

The Mayor looked pale and rather shaken by Cranston's announcement.

'Well?' Gaunt glared at him.

'Your Grace, it's easily done,' the man mumbled. He waved a hand. 'This dagger is like the one which killed the Sheriff, it has no hilt or cross guard; it can be shot from a crossbow if its groove has been deepened and widened. After all, it's just an elongated bow and thus the dagger becomes an arrow.'

'You see,' Simon the armourer interrupted, but suddenly covered his mouth with his hand as he realized where he was.

'Do it, Simon!' Cranston urged gently. 'Fire the dagger again!' He hurried away. They saw him behind the pentice the cord twanged and again the dagger smacked into the cushions.

'You see,' Cranston extended his hands. 'Imagine, good sirs, Sir Gerard Mountjoy sitting in the afternoon sunshine enjoying his wine and the company of his hounds in his own private garden.' He looked at Denny. 'You saw him there. The Guildhall is quiet, everyone dozing or resting in the afternoon heat, but our assassin slips along the covered way. Beneath his cloak he has a crossbow, an arbalest, or some other type of bow specially bought for one purpose. The gap in the fencing there is wide enough.

The assassin takes aim, Sir Gerard is killed immediately, the dagger piercing his heart – whilst the assassin has not had to enter the garden or pass the dogs. He slips away.'

'I suspect,' Cranston continued, 'the assassin had practiced beforehand and so the murder was carried out in a matter of seconds. The dogs hardly knew what had happened whilst Sir Gerard died almost instantly.' He nodded as Athelstan grasped his sleeve and whispered in his ear.

'And Fitzroy?' Gaunt asked.

Cranston waited until Athelstan had disappeared through the Guildhall door.

'Oh, Fitzroy's murder was much more clever. We must return to the room where he died. However, the assassin who killed Mountjoy used the same method to murder Sturmey. That pathetic locksmith, for reasons I shall explain later, was lured down to the quayside at Billingsgate. He was waiting for someone. He walked up and down, anxiously wondering when the man who had been blackmailing him would arrive. But the murderer was already there, hidden between the stalls or behind one of the warehouses. Again the crossbow was lifted, dagger in place. One minute Sturmey was standing on the quayside, the next a dagger struck deep into his chest and tumbled him into the river. This explains why there were no reports of anyone being seen even within hailing distance of the murdered man.'

Gaunt stared at the Coroner, tapping his fingers on the broad leather hunting belt round his slim waist.

'My Lord Coroner, the banqueting chamber has been prepared. Our clerk, Brother Athelstan, has gone up. I expect he awaits us. You have explained the deaths of Mountjoy and Sturmey.' He was going to speak further but caught Cranston's warning glance so instead turned, dug into his purse and flicked a gold coin at the armourer who had returned to the garden.

'You have earned that, fellow. Stay here until this business is finished. And when you leave, keep a still tongue in your head or I'll see you have no head or tongue to wag!'

Simon the armourer fell to his knees, overcome by a mixture of gratitude and fear, whilst Cranston led the rest back into the Guildhall.

Chapter 14

Athelstan was waiting for them in the banqueting chamber. The steward had laid out the tables as on the night of Fitzroy's murder, a silver trencher at each place. At Athelstan's request, Gaunt, Hussey and the rest took their seats. For a while there was some mumbling and muttering but Cranston's lecture in the garden had made them fearful and apprehensive. Athelstan, who sat where Fitzroy had, smiled at Goodman on his left and Denny on his right. He allowed the murmur of conversation to die as Cranston turned to Lord Clifford standing near the door.

'My Lord, you can take Brother Athelstan's seat.' Cranston looked away. 'On the night Fitzroy died, I know you were absent.'

The young nobleman, toying nervously with the hilt of his dagger, quietly obeyed. Athelstan once more peered round the room; two of the Guildmasters had already fallen into his small trap. Gaunt banged the tabletop, demanding they should continue, and Athelstan got to his feet.

'Your Grace, the night Fitzroy died, we were, I believe, in the middle of a splendid banquet?'

'A perceptive observation,' Gaunt replied tartly.

'No, Your Grace, it is important. Tell me,' Athelstan continued, 'had we finished the banquet?'

Gaunt wriggled in his seat, 'Of course not. The main course had been served and the cooks were preparing dessert when Fitzroy brought matters to a macabre conclusion.'

'Yes,' Athelstan said, 'I had forgotten about that until the other day when I ate a plum.'

'For God's sake!' Denny snarled. 'Don't pose riddles Brother!'

'No, I did,' Athelstan continued softly. 'I ate a sugared plum. I was embarrassed because the sugar and honey syrup stuck to my gums and teeth. I had to prise bits loose from my mouth. So I washed my hands in a bowl of water. I suddenly realized the last time I'd had so much sugar on my fingers was when I examined Fitzroy just after he died. I wondered why the dead Guildmaster had so much sugar in his mouth when dessert had not even been served.' He stared around the quiet room. 'Your Grace, sirs, think back on what we ate that evening. Can any of you remember eating anything coated with thick sugar and syrup?'

'Fitzroy could have eaten something before he came to the banquet.' Hussey spoke defensively.

'No, no,' Athelstan replied. 'We have already established that if Fitzroy had eaten such a poison beforehand, he would have died within the hour.' Athelstan smiled as another of his listeners fell into his trap.

'What do you mean?' Gaunt snapped.

'I mean, Your Grace, that we established that Fitzroy did not take the poison before the meal. We also established that nothing he ate or drank at the banquet was poisoned. Yet,' Athelstan continued, 'Fitzroy was certainly poisoned in this room because he ate something none of us did.'

'What?' Hussey exclaimed, leaning forward. 'Enough riddles, Brother.'

'Fitzroy was poisoned by someone who knew he had a sweet tooth. Indeed, Fitzroy had an appetite for sugar. Some even called him a glutton. What I think happened is this. Someone who knew where Fitzroy was going to sit, placed a sweetmeat, something very sweet, beneath his silver plate before the banquet began. Only the cloying sugar helped hide the fact that this sweetmeat was soaked in poison. It was that sugar which I detected in the dead man's mouth. I suspect this is how Fitzroy was killed.'

'Nonsense!' Goodman exclaimed, his arrogant face now white and pale. 'Wouldn't Fitzroy think it strange?'

'No.' Athelstan replied. 'First, he had come to a banquet. Perhaps he thought a servant had dropped it or left it there as a small treat for him. Second,' Athelstan smiled, 'you have all sat down. Before you on the table is a small trencher. Beside each of these, before you entered, I placed a sweetmeat. How many of you ate that sweetmeat? Popped it absent-mindedly into your mouths?'

Denny, Goodman and Bremmer smiled in embarrassment.

'How do you know it wasn't poisoned?' Cranston barked, enjoying the look of stupefaction on their faces. He lumbered to his feet. 'You did what any person might do, seated at a table waiting for a meal. You found something nice and popped it into your mouth. Fitzroy was no different. Indeed, with his appetite, he could scarcely resist.'

'Yes, but who placed it there?'

The atmosphere chilled as Gaunt's question hung like the sword of Damocles above them. Cranston pointed to Lord Adam Clifford.

'You, sir, are a traitor, a liar and a murderer! I accuse you of maliciously causing the deaths of Sir Fitzroy, Peter Sturmey and Sir Gerard Mountjoy!'

Clifford sprang to his feet, his eyes wide with anger, his face suffused by rage. 'You fat old fool!' he yelled. 'How dare you?'

Gaunt sat back in his chair, looking as if he had been pole-axed, whilst the Guildmasters started unbelievingly at Cranston. Clifford advanced threateningly towards the Coroner, hand on his danger. Sir John drew his own sword but the captain of Gaunt's guard moved swiftly between the two men.

'Lord Adam, I suggest you sit down,' the solider said softly. He looked over his shoulder at his master. Gaunt had now regained his composure and nodded silently, his eyes never leaving his young lieutenant.

'Sit down, Adam,' he said quietly. 'My Lord Coroner, continue. But if his allegation is false, you shall answer for it.'

'I will answer to God,' Cranston retorted. He stared round the assembled men. 'Now let me tell you a story,' he began, 'of a kingdom where the prince is a mere child and all power rests with his uncle, the Regent. In the absence of a strong ruler, factions emerge, jostling for power. At court the nobles become immersed in deadly rivalries; in the city powerful burgesses vie for power. Outside in the countryside the labourers mutter treason, forming secret covens and groups to plot treasonable rebellion.'

'Be careful, Sir John!' Gaunt snapped.

Athelstan closed his eyes and prayed that Cranston would not go too far.

'If I tell a lie,' Sir John answered, 'let someone here contradict me.' Cranston gazed round the Guildmasters but they were silent, as was Clifford who now sat with beads of sweat running down his face.

'A leader emerges,' Cranston continued. 'A mysterious man who calls himself Ira Dei, the Anger of God. He directs the Great Community of the Realm, the secret council of peasant leaders. They do not know who he is, nor does anyone else. He comes and goes, sowing the seeds of dissension. Now things change. His Grace the Regent here decides to form a bond of amity with the leading merchants of London. Ira Dei wishes to frustrate this, so he looks for a traitor close to the Regent. He finds him in My Lord Clifford, a young man who has not forgotten his humble beginnings, or at least those of his family. And Clifford, either for idealism or for personal profit or for both, agrees to be Ira Dei's agent in bringing My Lord of Gaunt's plans to nothing.'

'A lie!' Clifford shouted, though the tremor in his voice did little to convince any of his companions, who gazed stonily back.

'Now My Lord of Clifford's father,' Cranston continued, 'was a captain of archers, a skilled bowman – a skill he passed on to his son Adam. On the afternoon Sir Gerard Mountjoy dies, Clifford brings a hunting bow or converted arbalest and, when everyone is either resting or involved in their own affairs, slips like the shadow of death along the pentice. He shoots the dagger, Mountjoy dies in mysterious circumstances, and we become engrossed in the riddle of how he died rather than considering why or who did it.' Cranston helped himself to a generous swig from his wineskin. 'The following evening, the assassin strikes again.'

'Impossible!' Goodman shouted. 'Don't you remember, Sir John, Lord Clifford was absent from the banquet?'

Cranston pushed the wine stopper back in firmly. 'Yes, he did say he had business elsewhere but not before he left the poisoned sweetmeat beneath Fitzroy's plate.'

'Of course!' Gaunt got to his feet and pointed to his pale-faced lieutenant. 'Adam, you were responsible for deciding who sat where, then you excused yourself, claiming pressing business in the city.' Gaunt's face became mottled with anger. 'You were most insistent. My Lord Coroner is correct: not even I knew where everyone would sit. That was left to you and you told each of the guests.'

The Mayor suddenly sprang to his feet. 'Cranston,' he yelled, 'you're a fool!'

'Sir Christopher,' Athelstan intervened softly, 'explain yourself.'

The Mayor advanced into the centre of the room, his fat face wreathed in a smug smile. 'Can't you see, My Lord,' he addressed Gaunt. 'Mountjoy was murdered. Fitzroy was murdered. Sturmey was murdered. But let's not forget the vicious attack on My Lord Clifford!'

'Oh, no,' Athelstan replied. 'Let's not forget that. Bruises and cuts! Nothing very serious. I am sure Lord Adam knows this.'

Goodman stepped back, gnawing his lip as he realized the stupidity of his outburst. 'You mean?' he began.

'I mean,' Athelstan replied quietly, 'that when Lord Adam is taken into custody and examined, the bruises and so-called wounds will be found to be merely superficial.'

Goodman hurried back to his seat.

'What a marvellous ploy,' Athelstan continued. 'But think of it. If Ira Dei had meant to kill Clifford, he would have done so.'

'The ambush was arranged!' the Coroner roared at Goodman. 'A mere distraction!' He jabbed his finger at Clifford. 'You know that, My Lord. If you disagree, remove your shirt and let's see those terrible wounds.'

Clifford glared back.

'And My Lord of Gaunt is right,' the Coroner continued. 'You knew where each of us would sit that night!'

'I was elsewhere,' Clifford muttered.

'You're a liar!' Cranston barked.

Clifford shook his head but his eyes betrayed him.

'A clever ploy,' Cranston continued. 'So when Fitzroy died, you were elsewhere. But how, My Lord Clifford, could you go wrong? If Fitzroy took another seat, someone else may have eaten the sweetmeat. Don't you see?' Cranston grinned wickedly at the Guildmasters. 'It wasn't necessary for Mountjoy and Fitzroy to die, so long as some of you did, murdered in mysterious circumstances, causing enough chaos and confusion to destroy any schemes devised by His Grace the Regent.'

'And the gold? And Sturmey's death?' Nicholas Hussey spoke up as the Regent leaned forward in his chair and glared at the traitor at the other end of the room.

'Oh, the gold,' Cranston murmured. 'Of course, that really set the seal on matters, didn't it? You see, unfortunately, My Lord Mayor and the late Sheriff chose Peter Sturmey, a famous locksmith, to fashion a new chest which was to be secured by six locks. However, what you, Sir Christopher, had either forgotten or not realized was that our Master Sturmey had a secret life. He was a lover of young boys. Indeed, fifteen years ago, he, like many great ones in this city, was involved in a scandal. Nothing was proved against Sturmey but I am sure he became more secretive, cautious in his secret passions.' Cranston stopped speaking and looked at the King's tutor. 'Sir Nicholas, I believe you were a scholar at St Paul's school at the time?'

Hussey nodded, his eyes hooded, the bottom part of his face hidden behind his hands. 'I remember the scandal,' he murmured, 'but I knew nothing of it. I was a mere boy at the time.'

'Yes,' Sir John murmured, 'you were only a boy, as were you, My Lord Clifford, a page in a powerful London household – Sir Raymond Bragley's, then Sheriff of the city. Bragley, as My Lord Mayor remembers, was investigating the scandal and you, My Lord Clifford, must have been well aware of the important messages you carried hither and thither round the city. I suspect you knew about Sturmey's secret vices and that he continued them. Who knows? He may even have made advances to you, and so you blackmailed him: either he made you duplicate keys or else suffered the supreme penalty for being a sodomist – being burnt alive at Smithfield.'

Clifford stared down at the table, hands spread. He didn't resist as Gaunt nodded to the captain of his guard to pull Clifford's dagger out of its sheath.

'Of course, Sturmey had to die,' Cranston continued. 'So you lured him down to Billingsgate where he waited for you at the quayside. A clear target for you to strike at from some shadowy alleyway.' Cranston shrugged. 'What more can I say?'

Clifford's head shot up. 'You could produce some proof! This is all conjecture, mere hypothesis. You haven't a shred of evidence to convince one of the King's Justices. Anyone could have killed Mountjoy. Anyone could have put the poisoned sweetmeat on Fitzroy's table. And as for Sturmey – yes, I remember the incident, but you saw his secret workshop! Anyone could have forced him to go there and make six keys.'

Cranston drummed his fingers on the tabletop, trying to conceal his panic. He looked under his bushy eyebrows at Athelstan, who still seemed composed.

'Lord Adam is correct,' the Mayor asserted. 'I agree with you, Sir John, but have you proof positive that Clifford shot the dagger and left the sweetmeat?'

'We have,' Athelstan spoke up. 'We have the gold. That number of precious bars cannot be easily transported round the city or sold on the open market.' He looked at the Regent. 'Your Grace, if you send your soldiers to

My Lord Clifford's house, I will wager you'll find the evidence. You have to look for a hunting bow or more likely a specially constructed arbalest. Daggers of the sort used against Mountjoy and Sturmey. And, above all, the six gold bars My Lord Clifford so deftly removed from the chest. The theft went unnoticed. No one would even dream that someone could hold duplicates of six keys so, when the robbery was discovered, poor Sturmey would carry the blame. But the problem with gold is, once you remove it, what do you do with it? You can only hide it somewhere safe.'

Athelstan went to stand over Clifford. 'Why?' he asked.

The young man stared back.

'In logic,' the friar continued, 'and in mathematics, the first principle is to search for the common factor. You see, you were involved in Sturmey's scandal. You had the skill to kill Mountjoy. Only you knew the seating arrangement on the night Fitzroy died.' Athelstan steeled his features for what he knew was sheer bluff.

'Finally, Ira Dei himself has betrayed you.'

Clifford started. 'How?'

Then he groaned as he realized the terrible mistake he had made.

Gaunt clicked his fingers at the captain of the guard. 'Take ten archers, tear Clifford's house apart! Imprison his servants! If necessary, use torture!'

'There's no need.' Clifford, white as a ghost, drew himself up. 'What's the use?' he murmured. 'The game's been played and it's over.' He licked his lips. 'My Lord of Gaunt, you must think I am a traitor, but no more than any other man in this room. A few merchants who squeeze the poor as they would some damp cloth. Good men strutting down the nave on Sundays, but on Mondays they involve themselves in every filthy sin. Whited sepulchres!'

'And what about me?' Gaunt interrupted. 'I trusted you.'

'My Lord Regent, you trust no man. And can't you see the storm coming?' He jabbed a finger at Gaunt. 'Don't go hunting, My Lord. Instead, ride the filthy streets of Southwark or visit the villages of South Essex. The people will watch you ride by, eyes blazing with fury. The storm's coming!' Clifford made a sweeping movement with his hand. 'This house of cards will tumble, burnt from cellar to garret!' He wiped spittle from the corner of his mouth. 'For God's sake!' he shouted at Gaunt. 'Do you think I am the only one? Don't you realize there are men in this room who already plan to trim their sails when the storm comes?' Clifford paused, swallowed up in his own fury.

Athelstan glanced quickly round at the sly, secretive faces of the Guildmasters. Clifford was a murderer, but he was right. Gaunt was a fool to trust any of these men.

'You are a traitor!' Goodman shrieked, getting to his feet. 'A traitor and a felon! A silent assassin!'

'Oh, for God's sake!' Clifford roared, rising to his own feet, shaking off the hand of one of Gaunt's soldiers. 'Mountjoy was a grasping demon. Fitzroy a corrupt glutton. As for Sturmey – you chose him, My Lord Mayor, not I.'

'Take him away!' Gaunt ordered.

Clifford turned and spat in the direction of the Regent.

'"When Adam delved and Eve span,"' he shouted, '"Who was then the gentleman?" Remember that, My Lord, when they burn your palace at the Savoy!'

'Wait!' Goodman, the first to recover his poise, now puffed out his chest in righteous anger. 'My Lord, how do we know this man is not Ira Dei himself?'

Clifford threw back his head and laughed. 'You stupid poltroon!' he hissed hoarsely. 'Are you so dim-witted? I am not Ira Dei. Yet for all you know he could be sitting in this room!'

Gaunt rapped out his order again. Soldiers hurried Clifford out whilst others, at Gaunt's orders, made ready to leave to ransack Clifford's house from top to bottom.

Cranston and Athelstan sat back and watched as the Guildmasters, happy at the prospect of seeing justice done and even happier at the likely return of their gold, now outbid one another in their condemnations of Clifford and affirmations of loyalty to the Regent. John of Gaunt acted the role but Athelstan could see that Clifford's words had struck home; the revelation he had nurtured a traitor so close had hurt him deeply. Gaunt, who barely trusted his own shadow, had become more withdrawn, more suspicious. He sat in his chair, silently receiving the plaudits of the merchant princes. He did not seem to notice as Athelstan and Cranston took their leave and slipped out of the Guildhall.

'Thank God that's over!' Cranston breathed. 'We had very little proof, Brother.' He glanced shrewdly at the sombre-faced friar. 'You trapped him neatly.'

'No, Sir John, he trapped himself. He was the common factor in all those deaths.' Athelstan pulled a face. 'And as for tripping him up – a well-known device, My Lord Coroner, much used by my old teacher, Brother Paul. He claimed to have learnt it from the Inquisition.' Athelstan stretched his limbs. 'It's fact, Sir John, that in a rage a man cannot stop either the racing of his mind or the chattering of his tongue.'

They walked across busy Cheapside, though after the tension of the Guildhall the marketplace seemed quiet and serene, Cranston hardly bothering to carry out his usual hawk-eyed search for what he termed his 'friends from the underworld'.

'Come on, Athelstan. Even God would judge me worthy of a cup of claret and a blackjack of ale for my clerk.'

They entered the welcoming cheer of the taproom of The Holy Lamb of God and for a while just sipped their drinks and reflected on the drama they had witnessed.

'How do we know he wasn't Ira Dei?' Cranston asked.

'Oh, I think Clifford told the truth.' Athelstan shook his head. 'God knows, Sir John, but he's right you know.

There's a storm brewing and, when it breaks, this city will never be the same again!'

—

Three days later, Athelstan left the Tower and, seeing the crowds thronging round Billingsgate and Bridge Street, decided to take a barge from the Wool Quay across the river to Southwark. The sun was setting in a fiery ball, turning the river a glistening red as he threaded through the alleyways down to the quayside. He felt tired, eager to get back to his church, yet slightly alarmed as he was sure he was being followed. Now and again he would peer down the mouth of an alleyway, glimpse the river, hear the faint cries of boatmen whilst resisting the urge to run. As long as he kept walking, the winding, twisting lanes would eventually bring him out to the Wool Quay. At last he saw the steps, the boatmen congregating there, waiting for custom. He was about to quicken his pace when a dark figure suddenly stepped out of a doorway, cowled and masked. Athelstan stopped as he caught the glint of a dagger.

'What do you want?' He fought to keep his voice steady. 'I am a poor priest. I have no money!'

'True, true, Brother Athelstan,' came the disguised, muffled reply. 'Poor in many ways, rich in some. So you found the culprit at the Guildhall? And tomorrow My Lord Clifford dies on Tower Hill.'

Athelstan leaned on the staff he carried. 'And you must be Ira Dei?'

'Or his messenger.'

'No.' Athelstan shook his head. 'I am sure you have come to speak to me yourself.' He peered over the man's shoulder towards the Wood Quay.

'No, don't do that,' the muffled voice quietly ordered. 'Don't cry out for help, Brother. I mean you no harm.'

'So why don't you ask your question?' he retorted.

'Which is?'

'Do I know your identity? And the answer is no. Nor do I want to, nor do I care!'

The hooded figure stepped back a little. 'You are a good priest, Athelstan. You love the poor. You are a shepherd who is interested in his flock, not just their fleeces. Soon the storm will break around us, but as long as you don't interfere you will be safe.'

'I do have a question of my own.'

'Ask it!'

'Clifford was your murderer?'

'Yes.'

'And there are those at court and at the Guildhall who are in your pay?'

'You said you had only one question.'

Athelstan shrugged. 'You have a captive audience.'

'Turn round, Brother.'

Athelstan was about to refuse but could see little point, so did so.

'To answer your question, Brother, treason is like a vine. It has many branches.'

Athelstan stood still, tensing his shoulders. When he did look round, the alleyway was empty.

The friar continued down to Wool Quay, hired a skiff and leaned back in the stern as a grizzled, toothless boatman with arms like steel vigorously rowed him to the far shore. Athelstan paid him and walked through the dusk, back to St Erconwald's. The house and stable were quiet. Someone had filled Philomel's bin and the old war horse was munching away as if it was his first and last meal. Athelstan walked round to the front of the church and noticed with alarm that the door was unlatched. He pushed it open and tiptoed gently inside. He peered through the darkness.

'Who is there?' he called.

His words rang hollow and empty. Athelstan, gripping his staff, walked through the shadowy nave towards the rood screen.

'Who's there?' he called. 'This is God's house!'

'Oh, for God's sake, monk, you gave me a fright!'

Athelstan whirled round and dimly made out the portly figure of Sir John as he sat resting against the base of a pillar, the miraculous wineskin cradled in his hands.

'Sir John, you'll send my hair grey!'

'Then lose it all, Brother, and like me you won't give a damn!' Cranston patted the ground beside him. 'Come on, sit down. Where have you been?'

Athelstan crouched beside his plump friend.

'Do you want some wine?'

'Sir John, this is a church.'

'I've had a word with the good Lord, he won't mind.'

'In which case, Sir John.' Athelstan lifted the wineskin and poured a generous gulp into his mouth. 'True,' he murmured, 'wine does gladden the heart of man.' He handed the wineskin back. 'Sir John, I have been to see Elizabeth Hobden at the Minoresses. She's happy and contented.'

'Her father and stepmother are in the Marshalsea prison,' Cranston muttered. 'God knows what will become of them. However, until such matters are settled, the girl will remain a ward of court. And where else?' he asked.

'I've been to Hell, Sir John. Or, more precisely, the dungeons in the White Tower. Tomorrow Adam Clifford will lose his head at dawn. He asked me to hear his last confession.'

'You!'

'Yes, Sir John. He said he could confess only to me.'

'And what did he say?'

Athelstan shook his head. 'You can't ask me that, Sir John. Not even the Pope can break the seal of confession.'

'But we did arrest the right man?' Cranston demanded anxiously.

'Yes, Sir John, we did.'

'And is he sorry?'

'He is sorry he is going to die, but he saw it as a game very much like a tourney – a matter of luck and skill.'

'And Ira Dei?'

Athelstan breathed in deeply, deciding it would be best if he didn't tell Sir John about his meeting near the Wool Quay.

'Come on, Brother,' Cranston urged. 'You must have asked Clifford that question? Surely it's not covered by the seal of confession?'

'Yes, I did.' Athelstan gripped his friend's fat wrist. 'Sir John,' he whispered, 'before God I will only tell if you swear, give me your word, that you will not reveal it to anyone!'

'You have my word, that's good enough.'

'Well, I did ask Clifford about Ira Dei. He immediately denied any knowledge then said that since his arrest he had reflected on many things. He was not sure about Ira Dei: he was making his final confession and was about to meet God so did not wish to worsen the situation by false allegations, but…'

'Well?'

'On the few occasions Clifford actually met Ira Dei, the man was hooded, cloaked, his voice disguised and muffled. Nevertheless, by the intonation of certain words, the way the man spoke, Clifford believed Ira Dei was no less a person than Sir Nicholas Hussey.'

'Hussey!' Cranston exclaimed.

'Well, Sir John, Clifford only voiced his suspicions. However, he is about to die and there's no personal profit for him, so why should he lie?'

Sir John sat back and whistled under his breath.

'If Hussey's our man,' Cranston answered, 'that means the young King is involved. What game are they playing at? I mean it's one thing to ally yourself with the Regent's enemies, but actually to control them?'

'I thought that, Sir John, but it seems to add up.'

Athelstan ticked the points off on his fingers. 'First, there will be a revolt. Second, the revolt will strike at the seat of power, in other words the Regent. Third, Sir John, if you want to control a wild horse, what do you do? Hang on to its reins or try to stay seated in the saddle?'

Cranston nodded. 'Of course, Hussey is in the saddle. Yes, yes,' he continued excitedly. 'The Regent hasn't caused the problems but, when the revolt comes, Hussey will make sure Gaunt is the one held responsible. Richard, on the other hand, will play the role of the innocent young King, innocent of any crime, unable to control his wicked uncle.'

'Precisely, My Lord Coroner. The revolt will end, Gaunt may go, and rebel leaders disappear. But the Crown will survive.'

Cranston took another swig from his wineskin and laughed sourly. 'From the lies of princes,' he whispered, 'Lord deliver us. I'll tell no one, Brother. But I'll keep a sharp, wary eye on Sir Nicholas Hussey!'

'Well, it's over, Sir John.' Athelstan turned, feeling the cold pillar against his hot cheek.

'It's never over, Brother. Do you remember Rosamund Ingham? Well, she's committed suicide in the Fleet. Somehow or other some of the powder she denied to poor Oliver was smuggled in to help her escape the hangman's noose. And it was all for nothing. I attended the reading of Ingham's will.'

'And?'

'He left every penny to me. A mere pittance for his wife. His house, movables, gold and silver plate, all to poor Jack.' Cranston wiped the tears from his eyes. 'Before God, I'd give it all back just to see Oliver's face once more!'

'And what will you do with the money, Sir John?'

'Well, brighten up this Godforsaken place for one thing.' He nudged Athelstan. 'A nice piece of stained glass, eh? A fitting memorial to old Oliver!'

'Sir John, that would be a splendid gift.'

Cranston staggered to his feet and stretched. 'And you, Brother, what will you do? Mind you,' he blew out his cheeks, 'we've got more murders: a taverner supposedly drowned in a vat of malmsey in a tavern in Carter Lane. A young wife in Shoe Lane, Farringdon found floating in a carp pond. And even worse...'

'Yes, Sir John?'

'My brother-in-law Ralph is about to descend on us next week. Lord, the ticklebrain will chatter like a garrulous squirrel!'

Athelstan smiled. 'In which case, you'll be by yourself, Sir John. My parishioners and I are going on a pilgrimage to the tomb of the Blessed St Swithun at Winchester.'

Cranston scratched his head. 'Brother, you jest?'

'Coroner, I don't!'

Cranston helped Athelstan to his feet. 'Come on, Brother, let's go and toast old Oliver, just once more, and tease that thieving bugger who owns The Piebald.'

Cranston listed rather dangerously so Athelstan slipped his arm through that of the Coroner and walked him slowly down the nave. Cranston stopped suddenly.

'Did I ever tell you, Brother?'

'What, Sir John?'

'I have always had the deepest devotion to St Swithun...'